Star Fish

Nicola May

Pisces: *You fishes are strong believers in fate but you have to lean forward a bit sometimes so that it doesn't miss you. The time is right to go and grab life with both fins.*

And that is how this whole debacle started.

Chapter One

'A dating agency, are you mad?' my friend Brad exclaimed.

'No, just desperate.' I grinned back.

'Why don't you just go online like everybody else? One click of that mouse and you could be meeting someone in California. I'll have a look with you if you like.'

'To be honest I prefer the more personal touch and I think I should be seen in the flesh to be believed.'

'Well there is that, you buxom wench you.' Brad cocked his head to one side and examined me critically from head to toe.

'I guess you look the right side of thirty on a dark night, and you are quite a nice person, I suppose. In fact, if it *were* a dark night and I had a bottle of Chardonnay inside me, I might consider doing you myself!'

He laughed and then carried on hand-washing his black Versace T-shirt. Why is it that gay friends are just so nice, so rude, and so attractive? But then attractive isn't really a good enough word for Brad. The guy is utterly gorgeous and not just in an easy-on-the-eye way. He is a typical Aquarian in the fact that he never states an opinion on either my vices or my virtues. I can also tell him anything without worrying he'll be shocked.

Brad Sampson is the only male I can ring at any time of the day or night to cry or laugh with, and he'll always listen patiently while I spill out all the general trivia that has occurred during the day. The fact that he just happens to look like Orlando Bloom is a bonus. In short, Brad Sampson is the perfect friend.

Here I was, Amy Jane Anderson, thirty-two years old with shoulder-length dark hair, teeth all in order, an extremely large sense of humour and weighing in at a disappointing, albeit firm, size 14. However, I was also very single with a body clock ticking as loudly as Big Ben.

Brad and I had previously been housemates for two years. If it wasn't for the fact that we both needed some sort of sexual gratification, I could have lived with him forever. We had discussed the turkey baster and stirrup theory of conception but that was about as far as it went, mainly because Brad started retching at the mere thought of me with my legs up in stirrups. These days I spend half of my leisure time with Brad and the other half at my house, 21 Layston Gardens in Reading, with Penelope the cat.

My love-life, to date, had been a disaster. If ever a man stood in front of me with the word, bastard, written clearly on his forehead, off I'd go and throw myself into a relationship from hell. If I had to write my own dating ad it would read something like this: Tall, dark, good-looking womanisers with bad tempers, jealous minds and small bank accounts required for gullible, understanding, pretty Piscean.

Well, now I was going to do something about this area of my life that was causing me so much concern. Surely it wouldn't be too traumatic? I would just give somebody my personal details and a photograph, and then I'd look through their files and choose myself a man. Old-fashioned maybe, but I quite liked that.

'A bunch of wankers and weirdo's probably,' Brad said, then realising that I was serious, decided he would back his fishy friend to the gills on her mission to find a soul mate, or perhaps sole mate. Get it?

It was then he turned into Mario Testino overnight, and took it upon himself to ensure that the photo I supplied was a flattering one. At first he thought that a natural pose would be more likely to attract the sort of man I wanted. There were photos of me with a towel tucked around me coming out of the shower, with a bare, shiny face and smear of toothpaste on my chin. He took snaps of me blow-drying my hair with no make-up on, looking like an extra from *The Munsters*. The worst were photos of me on Brad's multi-gym, looking like a beetroot with features.

In fact, not a single one of the photos was in any way, shape or form, flattering. Brad, loyally said I looked gorgeous in all of them, but I assured him that none of them would get me the man of my dreams. In the end we decided on one of me drinking a cocktail in a hotel foyer in Lanzarote in 2008. OK, so I was looking brown, relaxed, and years younger, but from a sales point of view, we had our product.

Chapter Two

Pisces: *You are about to embark on a big adventure. A green door signifies luck for you today.*

Starr & Sun was not quite what I had imagined a dating agency would be like. Firstly, the alleyway I had to walk down to reach it was dead seedy. And talking of dead, you then had to walk through a funeral parlour to get to the actual stairway that led to the agency. It all gave me the creeps. I very nearly swished my fishy tail and went straight back home to the comfort of 21 Layston Gardens and Penelope my cat.

The person responsible for setting me on my mission to find true love was my Aries friend and workmate, Olivia Irving. Olivia – Liv for short – is one of the funniest creatures I have ever met. She is loud, extravagant, and is a complete and utter man-eater. I'm sure I recall her once claiming to have had more men than Victoria Beckham has Jimmy Choos!

Liv's mane of red hair is always pinned up as she never has time to wash it in the week, but she keeps the male population of the Marketing Department in a permanent state of arousal as her wardrobe only consists of skirts that end ten inches above the knee.

To the outsider, Jenkins Software appears to be a

professional outfit. Situated on the prestigious Thames Valley Business Park, the glass and chrome high-tech building over-looks the River Thames. The intelligent software products on offer do manage to sell like hot cakes, which amazes me, as both the Sales and Marketing Departments appear to employ egotistical boffins or deranged alcoholics. Liv and I being the exception to this assumption of course; with the seminars and events we organise being of the highest calibre.

Despite the majority of the two hundred employees being a little odd, all in all the working environment is fun and friendly. The spacious ground floor canteen provides steamy cappuccinos on tap, ensuring that hangovers can be dealt with immediately on arrival.

Once the dating decision had been made, Liv and I began to troll the websites for suitable agencies. My mission, if possible, was to go on a date with twelve respectable men, one from each sign of the Zodiac. Scorpio is supposed to be the ideal sign for me. The fact that I've never been out with a Scorpio is, I am sure, one of the main reasons why I am still single at thirty-two. Due to my interest in astrology, Starr & Sun had jumped off the screen at me as the obvious choice. They were based down the road in Wokingham which made my decision even easier.

I'm not really sure how my interest in this all too frequently dismissed 'ology started. I'd like to think that my obsession of immediately flicking to the star sign pages of any magazine or newspaper and owning three astrology books allows me to profess I'm a guru on the subject. I do know and believe in the basic fundamentals of each sign's main character traits, and am well informed on who should be shagging who in perfect starry-eyed harmony. OK, so maybe not a guru. 'More like a bloody gnu!' Brad had once exclaimed.

I started to read in more detail the home page for Starr & Son and then shrieked. 'Liv, just read this, look.'

Liv peered over my shoulder. 'For all the commotion you're making it better be the fact they show pictures of applicants' willies.'

'Liv, you are disgusting sometimes. No, even more exciting. It's actually an astro-dating agency. People go there and *have* to state their star signs. And just think, Liv, all the men on the books will be into astrology as well. We'll have so much to talk about on our dates.'

'Ames, sometimes your naivety does astound me.'

'Liv, I'm not talking rubbish, it says it here.'

Liv shook her head and then laughed. 'So you don't think the predatory species will be of the opinion that the female clients will be just that little bit more gullible. Imagine all the yarns they could spin around compatibility.' She stood up and started prancing around the office. 'Oh, Amy, you are so definitely a Pisces, what with those beautiful blue eyes and kissy, fishy lips. Me, being a homely Taurean, would just love to take you home and cuddle you all night, yeah right!'

'Oh shut it, Liv, I'm calling them anyway.'

So, with Liv willing me on in the background, the introductory phone call was made.

'Good Morning, Starr & Sun,' said a very posh voice.

It was then that I started to blurt. When I am nervous, blurting is the first thing I do. Taking a deep breath, I launched into a 100-mph monologue.

'Oh, hi there! I would really like to register with you, please. I've never ever done anything like this before and I don't actually know what to do, and I don't know how much you charge and I'm really quite nervous about the whole thing and –'

'Calm down, madam, it really is all quite simple. I just need to ask you a couple of questions and we'll go from there.'

Liv put her thumb up and gave me an encouraging wink.

'Firstly, are you a graduate?' The posh voice enquired.

Oh God, I hadn't read anywhere that thickos need not apply. I'd have to lie. I did have a couple of A-Levels under my belt but would they count? Probably not. My philosophy on getting anywhere in life is that everyone should run out of the school gates and headlong into real life. Maybe I have this opinion because, at eighteen years old, furthering my education was the last thing I fancied doing, even though my father was adamant that I should go away and get a good degree. The result is that I get a bit miffed when everyone bangs on about how great their Uni days were, to the point that even the word Uni gets on my nerves.

'A graduate? Yes, oh yes, of course.' I felt myself slipping into a really cultured accent as well.

'Splendid, now what did you study?'

What did that matter? If I'd studied Geography, would they match me up with a bloody Geography teacher? I suddenly got an awful vision of Mr Robbins, my old Geography teacher who used to smoke so much his grey beard had turned yellow, plus he stunk of BO. I really had the urge to say that I majored in pleasure but managed to stop myself. My heart began to race. I mouthed at Liv: 'What degree did I do?'

'Think lawyers sweetie, it has to be law,' she hissed.

'Oh, I studied Law,' I told Posh Voice. 'Had a fantastic time at Uni, you know.' This wasn't a complete lie as I had studied O-Level Law. Failed it miserably but studied it nonetheless. I had also had a ball in the sixth form.

'Thank you so much, I just need your postcode now.'

I could now hear Posh Voice clattering away at a keyboard. Thank goodness I lived in a part of Berkshire that has a half-decent postcode. I had visions of PV consulting a tick list of areas that were banned. I put my hand over the receiver and whispered to Liv, 'If your town's not down you're not coming in!'

Expecting a question on current wealth and possible inheritances next I quickly began to think up more lies, but Posh Voice merely requested my name, age, and address. Thank heavens, because I don't think that £22.75 in my Winnie the Pooh savings account and an aged aunt in a two-bed semi in Cleethorpes would have got me on the list either!

'Joining instructions and pricing will be in the post to you tonight, madam,' I was promised. 'Thank you for choosing Starr and Sun.'

I rushed downstairs the next morning as soon as I heard the familiar, and always exciting to me, whatever it may be, thud of mail falling on the front doormat. Penelope was sniffing a green envelope embossed with a star and sun type logo.

'Get your paws off that one, Pen. Today your mother is commencing her mission to find a decent man to keep us in both fine wine and Whiskers.'

A lunchtime emergency meeting was called with Liv. We sneaked into a meeting room and began to look through the forms with trepidation. It was the sample profiles that caused immediate concern.

Annalise – Doctor

Loves travelling. Has recently trekked across Nepal. Enjoys opera. Also trying her hand at Capoeira! Favourite book: Ulysses *by James Joyce. Favourite film: anything by Ingmar Bergman. Wants to meet somebody who is truly inspiring.*

'Capo-bloody-eria? Liv, what the duces is that?' I asked dismayed.

'Think it's some kind of martial art. A Brazilian ex-boyfriend of mine used to go to classes.'

'And is Ingmar Bergman any relation to Ingrid? I've never even heard of him! How on earth can I compete with the likes of Doctor Annalise, Liv? No one will be interested in little old me.'

To squeals of mirth from Liv, I began to recite my suggested sample profile out loud: '*Amy* (even my name sounds dull compared to Dr Annalise!). *Event Dogsbody. Loves travelling. Recently trekked across a beach in Lanzarote. Enjoys singing in the shower and talking to her frogs. Trying hard to drink less. Favourite book: Anything with love and romance in the title. Favourite film:* Love Actually. *Wants to meet anyone who'll have her, particularly if they look like Zac Efron.'*

Once Liv had stopped laughing she put her hand on my shoulder. 'I once convinced a priest that sex was good for his soul. If I can do that, then I'm damn well sure I can convince a whole congregation of starry-eyed suitors that Amy Jane Anderson is a real babe.'

With marker pen in hand, Liv headed for the white board. She was in her element. '*Amy Jane Anderson*,' she said as she wrote it on the board. 'Need to put the whole name in there, makes you sound more distinguished. *Event Manager*. No lie there, you do manage events and quite well too.'

She then looked down her nose at me as if she had schoolmarm glasses on.

'Loves to travel. You do when you can afford it. Recently returned from Africa. The Canary Islands are opposite Morocco so that'll do for that. Enjoys water sports. You like the hot tub at the David Lloyd Centre, don't you?' She beamed happily. 'This is a doddle, Amy. They'll be falling over themselves to meet you, don't you worry. Also trying her hand at yoga. No one need know that you left after the first session because of letting off a massive fart while in the dog position. Favourite book: *The Quotations of Oscar Wilde*. You live by, in my opinion the greatest quotation ever. 'I can resist everything apart from temptation.' Favourite film: *One Flew Over the Cuckoo's Nest*. Because you must be mad, wanting to go ahead with this.'

We both laughed out loud.

'Looking to share her future with somebody open-minded?' said Liv.

I nodded.

'With strength of character?'

I nodded again.

'And an extremely large cock?'

'Liv! You can't put that!'

'Well OK, maybe not that bit, but you can raise that issue, so to speak, once you get to see them face to face, you know.' In true game-show-hostess fashion, Liv, now with pointer in hand, continued. 'Put it all together and what have you got? You've got the lot, Amy Jane Anderson, my old minger mate, you've got the flipping lot.'

'Obviously we need to add my star sign as well,' I reminded her.

'OK, let's start again.' Liv cleared her throat. '*Amy Jane Anderson – Event Manager. Star Sign: Pisces. Loves to travel. Recently returned from Africa. Enjoys water sports. Also trying her hand at yoga. Favourite book:* The Quotations of Oscar Wilde. *Favourite film:* One Flew over the Cuckoo's Nest. *Looking to share her future with somebody open-minded, with strength of character and a big personality.* And there we have it.'

'Liv you are not only an old slapper, you are also a genius. Thanks so much.'

So that was it, sample profile completed, form filled out, photo attached. I was on the shaky stairway to man heaven!

The day dawned for me to face my fate. Starr & Sun was about to gain a new recruit. After negotiating the seedy alleyway and hesitantly climbing the stairs to the agency, I took a deep breath and pushed open the dark green door. I was pleasantly surprised to find a bright and cheerily painted yellow reception area. There were several healthy looking plants dotted around and a plush looking leather sofa in the corner. A glass coffee table displayed various astrology publications.

I walked up to the reception desk and suddenly all my fears returned, as here in front of me was what I can only describe as a 1980s reject. I am not normally a bitchy kind of girl but, when one is confronted with the likes of Cordelia Drake, one can only be grateful for what little breeding one has.

Cordelia Drake must have been around forty-five with bleached blonde, dry, wiry hair with about three inches of dark roots coming through. Her denim mini-skirt, stripy tights, and thigh-length boots were worn with tight red T-shirt revealing a cleavage that would have made Jordan's eyes water.

Ms Drake wore purple lipstick and matching nail varnish in a shade of what I could only call Varicose Vein that clashed horribly with her red top. She was tapping away on her keyboard at about 90 mph. The funny thing was when she opened her mouth to greet me she sounded as if she had not only one, but about fifteen ripe plums in her mouth!

'You must be Amy. The pleasure is mine, dear.' She offered me a spindly hand with a gold sovereign on her middle finger.

I did my best to keep a straight face. Maybe she had gone to a really posh school and was fighting against her upper-class upbringing or maybe the Starr

& Sun clientele were just so awful that the tactic was to make them feel superior next to Cordelia Drake, who did not have beauty or style on her side. I finally decided that she had worked on the voice in order to snare new recruits to Starr & Sun over the telephone, banking on the fact that once you were actually there you would be so gobsmacked by her appearance that you would hand over any amount of money to join up and run way!

'My boss, Mr Starr, will be with you in a minute to interview you,' the posh voice piped up.

Oh my God, I thought. What kind of weirdo would have employed the likes of Cordelia Drake?

But Cordelia's employer turned out to be far nicer than I had imagined an owner of a dating agency would be. For some strange reason I had pictured somebody without a life of their own: somebody who wanted to live through other people's fantasies.

This guy was wearing a smart grey suit, which matched his friendly blue-grey eyes. His smile was open and warm and his handshake firm and welcoming. My dad had taught me that a firm handshake is very important. I am glad that I acknowledged his worldly wisdom on this one, as I cannot bear a wishy-washy limp-wristed offering either. I think it reflects gravely on someone. There is no excuse for not putting effort into that important first bodily contact.

'Christopher Starr, Capricorn, the son in Starr and Sun,' he introduced himself.

'Ah, I see. I thought the company name was just a clever idea for an astrological dating agency.'

'Yes, well, that's my mother for you. It's her

business, although she's semi-retired now and has left the running of it in my capable hands.'

'Is it interesting?' I enquired.

'That's one word for it.' He smiled his friendly smile. 'Wouldn't really have been my first career choice but I am beginning to enjoy it, and there is the perk of meeting a lot of single women.' He then caught my eye and looked slightly embarrassed.

'Right, let's get down to the important business of finding you a man then, shall we?'

I instantly felt at ease. Maybe this wasn't going to be quite as dreadful as I had imagined.

'Your photo is flattering,' he said nicely. 'From reading your introduction form you certainly don't look your age, and your sample profile is spot on.' I laughed to myself, wishing Liv was here to listen to all of this. 'There shouldn't be any trouble at all in matching you up,' Christopher promised. 'In fact, I've got somebody in mind already. You Pisces ladies are very adaptable.'

I liked this man; he was friendly and charming. Don't fancy him, don't fancy him, my inner voice insisted. But hey, he didn't actually know me; he'd read my details on a form I'd filled out, he'd said hello and then thought he could match me with someone immediately. Perhaps it was all just a con.

'Right, Amy let's introduce you to the blue file.' He grinned.

Oh my God, I thought. Blue file? What sort of place is this?

But Christopher had anticipated my reaction. 'Blue for boys, pink for girls,' he explained. 'Cordelia's intricate filing system for you!'

I laughed this time.

The blue file was interesting, to say the least. I opened it to see male creatures of all shapes and star signs appear in front of my eyes. Christopher told me he would leave me to peruse the "lucky contenders" at my leisure in the Green Room. Lucky contenders? It sounded more like bloody *Gladiators*.

The Green Room. How strange! I remembered my horoscope from this morning's newspaper: "A green door signifies good luck for you today." Green room, green door. Oh my God, this was just too much of a coincidence! Christopher had also made a point of seeing if I could pick out the person he thought would be most compatible with me. I wondered cautiously just who was playing this dating game?

It was hard to keep a perspective on the whole situation. On turning the pages and seeing all those men smiling out at me I suddenly had awful doubts about what I was doing. The men were sorted into the twelve star signs. I started to flick through them. Under each photo were a few words taken from the corresponding introduction form. Some of them were hysterical, like Reece, a thirty-five-year-old Geminian and account manager whose likes were scuba diving, Leeds United and anchovies. Reece was looking for a blonde with similar tastes. Or there was Greg, a forty-two-year-old Libran and producer whose likes included animals, gladioli and classical guitar music. He was searching for someone to connect with over dog walks and dinners.

Surely Christopher was having a laugh? But then if there were pages of information I personally wouldn't read it all through. When you first see someone you fancy, you don't know what's behind the initial attractiveness until you take the time to speak to them. So Christopher's logic won this time. Brevity and humour – sounded like the state of my love life really.

I started to look just at the pictures, particularly at the eyes and smiles. My friend Harriet had also advised me to look at a man's shoes. I could never quite understand this one, because if somebody looked like George Clooney but was wearing white tasselled loafers, the chance of looking at the ceiling of the ER would win every time.

After careful deliberation I picked out three men who I wouldn't be embarrassed to be seen with in public.

Steve, 27. Aries. Photographer. Looking initially for fun and friendship.

Neil, 29. Taurus. Legal Executive. Looking for someone to wine and dine.

Laurence, 40. Libra. Managing Director of IT company. Glamorous liaisons a must.

Curiously, Steve, Neil, and Laurence were not truly compatible in an astrological sense, but the words fun, dine, and glamour had helped the sale in this bizarre supermarket of lurve. I doubted very much if any of these manly contenders had degrees or if they could even spell capoeria, let alone know what it was. I found this strangely comforting.

As I handed over two weeks' salary to encompass my twelve introductions, I suddenly felt apprehensive. I also felt quite broke; it would probably have been cheaper to just buy a husband over the Internet.

This was for sure the start of something very big, something very big and very embarrassing.

Chapter Three

Aries: *You could be skating on thin ice today if you make a love decision.*

'I am allergic to my wrinkle cream!' I screamed, running down the landing towards Brad. 'The model on that advert is a bitch. How dare she smirk on television with her smooth face, telling the world how gorgeous she is because of this wonderful product.'

'Calm down, Princess,' Brad replied in his usual relaxed manner. 'They film her from a distance with something over the lens, I expect.'

'That's not the bloody point! Just look at my eyes – they've gone all red and swollen.

Brad was now laughing. 'I bet they say not to put it near your eye area.'

'Don't be smart, that's not the bloody point either!' I calmed down as in the grand scheme of things you could hardly notice it. I was just being dramatic as tonight, Friday, I was going on my first date with Aries photographer, Steve Edwards.

'I'm going to snee – Attishoo!'

'Bless you,' Brad said, hastily getting out of range.

I love sneezing – great big powerful sneezes. I also like the ceremonious bless-you that follows. In fact there are three main things that I want from a man:

for him to say, 'Bless you' whenever I sneeze, preferably a bless-you for every single sneeze, even if they come in a whoosh of say three at a time; that he buys me flowers at least once a month; and, most importantly, I want to hear him say, 'Amy Anderson, don't ever change' just once. Then, I would most certainly marry him.

Steve Edwards was funny. His whole appearance made me smile. He was around six-foot-three, his arms and legs were everywhere, and he had a stubbly chin and smiling brown eyes. Steve wasn't particularly handsome, but he was fun. I like fun, therefore I liked Steve. He made me laugh; he made me feel at ease. I had known him precisely twenty-one minutes and we were getting on brilliantly. Maybe this dating game was going to easier than I thought.

The fact that we had to wait ages in the queue to pay to go ice-skating didn't matter. The fact that I had put on a skirt didn't matter. The fact that I was with a man from a dating agency didn't matter until aargh!

Here I was, Amy Jane Anderson, thirty-two-years-old, being dragged around the ice rink like a whirling dervish by a mad photographer. Whee! My exhilaration was taken over by complete terror when I lost my grip on one of his gangly arms and went hurtling towards an advertising board on the edge of the rink.

'Amy? Amy are you OK?'

I felt as though I was in a *Tom & Jerry* cartoon with stars coming out of my head. If only I could have pressed the off button. And I really wished that I had checked beforehand where Steve was taking me on our date so that I could have dressed appropriately. By now, my skirt had risen right up my thighs and my new M&S hold-in knickers were on show to the whole of Ice City. Who in their right mind would wear stockings ice-skating?

There and then I decided that I should take off my Piscean rose-coloured glasses and get ready to expect the unexpected where this dating lark was concerned. My watery smile suddenly turned into gushing tears of humiliation.

'I'm so embarrassed, Steve. I've only ever been skating on a school trip before.'

'It's OK, don't worry; my sense of adventure got the better of me. I thought you'd be able to keep up.'

I was very wobbly when I got back onto my feet. Steve struggled to pull me up and I rearranged my skirt.

The teenagers nearby were still smirking when Steve asked, 'OK now? See you in a min.' He then proceeded to speed-skate around the rink again.

I had had enough. I felt sore and humiliated. There were the beginnings of a blister on my heel and I wanted to go home. Tentatively I made my way to a gap in the hard boards around the edge of the rink. Finding a gap, then a seat was almost as fulfilling as that first sip of cold wine when you've had a bad day at work.

I thought I'd get back into my own boots, go to the loo and repair any damage to my make-up, and then hopefully bond a bit more with daredevil Steve. When I got to the toilets, however, I realised why the teenagers had been smirking. I had the letter 'a' imprinted like a brand right across my face. How could Steve have let me carry on with that on my face?!

And how could he speed off and leave me when I had just had such a terrible fall? There hadn't even been time to do my sneeze test on him.

Aries man was obviously not for me.

Limping slightly, I hobbled out of the ice rink and headed straight for home.

Christopher Starr phoned the next day, concerned that I'd left my date without a word. I did actually feel quite guilty as Steve was lovely, but a bit too boisterous for my liking. Life would certainly never be dull with an Aries man, that was for sure. Maybe I was being too picky; maybe I should give him another chance? But he wasn't my perfect date and I now had the opportunity to meet other men, so the decision was made that I would go out with Neil.

I was to meet Taurean Neil for dinner in Henry's Wine Bar on Cecil Street at 7.30 p.m. next Friday. Christopher informed me that my second date would be waiting at the bar for me.

Chapter Four

Capricorn: *Nobody said your job was easy. Humour is important to get you through the challenges that today will throw at you.*

The fitness instructor, aka Sex God to me or just Guy to his other clients, was due to call at my house at 11.30 a.m. on Saturday morning. He had sounded delicious on the phone. I was annoyed at myself for thinking this. Why did I have to look at every man as a prospective husband? This meeting with Guy wasn't a date; however, it was my last-ditch attempt at gaining the body beautiful. I had this fear that because I had been lucky with the ageing process so far; I would hit forty and everything would suddenly sag, wrinkle and wither.

At the sound of the doorbell I checked my face in the mirror and casually opened the front door.

'Amy?'

'Hi, yes, that's me, you must be Guy. Come in, come in, sit down,' I said frantically, doing my blurting thing.

Oh yes! Guy Jamieson was indeed a sex god! He was around six foot tall, with dark hair, beautiful blue eyes and obviously the fittest body I had seen for quite some time.

In his casual tracksuit bottoms and crisp white polo shirt he looked like something out of an advert from a health and fitness magazine.

I know this isn't a date, but please let him be a Scorpio, I thought wistfully. With my Piscean rose-coloured glasses firmly in place I was off in a world of make believe. I would wake up every day to this gorgeous being. He would feed me Special K and grapes. I would be fit. I would be happy.

My sexy celestial dream suddenly collapsed into cellulite reality by Guy saying.

'Right, let's get down to business then.'

If bloody only! I thought.

Seating himself on the sofa, he opened up the briefcase-type thing he was carrying and pulled out a blood-pressure machine and something that can only be described as callipers. The sight of them induced yet another classic blurt.

'Well, really I thought it quite extravagant to have a personal trainer but I was thinking that I was getting a bit fat and I have no self-discipline and basically I don't care if you get me fit, although don't get me wrong that would be nice but to be honest I just want to look like a babe by my birthday, well in fact I'd like to lose a stone by my birthday... by the way, when's your birthday?'

Guy was smiling. 'Your birthday is when exactly, Amy?'

'It's the thirteenth of March, so around six weeks away.'

'Unlucky for some, eh?' He then realised he really shouldn't have said that and quickly added, 'A Pisces eh? I'm a Capricorn, Christmas Day boy me.'

Oh God, how embarrassing, he knew why I had asked when his birthday was. I was a bit miffed about his unlucky-for-some comment, as the number thirteen is actually my lucky number. I was quite impressed, however, that he knew that I was a Pisces and was just about to ask if he got two sets of different presents when he continued in a business-like fashion. He was obviously aware that there was no time to lose if I wanted to shed a stone in such short a time.

'Do you smoke, Amy?'

'No.' I smirked proudly. 'I gave up three years ago.'

Short of dumping my ex-boyfriend James Crook – of whom more later – it was the most difficult thing I've ever done in my life. It was verging on a miracle that I gave up smoking. In fact, I should have gone round and sold my story as an inspiration to the whole smoking fraternity who wanted to give up. I was such an addict that I actually had cigarettes and a lighter on my bedside table, so that I could wake up, roll over, and light one up as I watched the news on breakfast television. I was an avid twenty a day girl, going on to forty once alcohol had been consumed.

I chose Valentine's Day to give up – and chewed nicotine gum from 8 a.m. that morning. In fact, I chewed anything that I could get my hands on, and soon put on one and a half stone.

The first week of giving up will remain in my memory for ever. It was dreadful.

I gave up on a work day, by lunchtime everyone in my office was under his or her desk trying not to catch my eye or mention anything to do with smoking. My bad mood was heightened by the fact that I had not received a single Valentine's card, not even from Penelope or Brad who always remembered. Why is it that when you know you can't mention something, you always do? My work colleagues excelled at this.

'Amy you're looking a bit puff, I mean rough.' And so it went on.

I put the phone down on my boss on numerous occasions and started crying on the station platform because the train was delayed. Worst of all I told the woman behind the bakery counter to 'shit off' when she commented on the fact that I'd been in three consecutive times for doughnuts and I must be very hungry today.

The hardest thing was that at that time I was working for a tobacco firm. I had to leave, as the weekly free-cigarette quota was too much of a temptation for an addict fish like myself. Brad was actually disappointed as he enjoyed calling me Fag Ash Lil. I still get the odd urge to have a puff when drunk, but know that one puff could lead to disaster. Brad laughs his head off whenever I say this. 'Ooh and don't I know *that* ducky!'

'Right, I need you to fill out a questionnaire about yourself, Amy, so that I can start to get an idea of your lifestyle and at what level I should pitch your sessions,' Guy said. 'Once I have taken your blood pressure and measured your fat proportions we can go through a few basic exercises so I get the whole picture. I can then work out a programme for you.'

Oh God, the calliper thingies were to pinch my fat! How embarrassing. Surprisingly, my blood pressure and pulse were fine, even though I had a vision of the machine exploding because of the intense lust I was feeling. This feeling soon subsided when Guy said chirpily, 'Now let's just gauge your fat percentage.'

I suddenly had that horrible feeling you get when you're in a meeting and somebody says, 'Right, let's go round the room and just say who we are and a bit about ourselves.' Even though you've lived with yourself for so many years and know exactly who you are, you feel your mouth going dry and your mind going blank, and just don't want your turn to come. Guy noticed my expression.

'Amy, please don't be embarrassed, it's just my job and to be honest you are not seriously overweight. This simply helps me to decide on the right training programme for you.'

'Attishoo!'

'Bless you.'

At that moment I fell completely in lust with Mr Fit. A first session was arranged and, before Guy Jamieson had even got down the front path, I was online ordering all the latest fitness gear on the market.

Chapter Five

My friend Harriet Brown, aka H, who had initially been very cautious about my agency exploits, was now completely into it. She said the whole thing reminded her of a soap opera and she couldn't wait for the next episode. She was on constant mobile phone standby for any updates and also for any necessary SOS calls.

Five years younger, blonde with steely blue eyes and a heart of gold, H is indeed a friend that I know I am very lucky to have. We met through work two years ago. To each other we were PR Tart and Event Slut. We struck up an instant rapport, as she too has a passion for the finer things in life. Before she fell in love with Horace, her husband, she managed to pick the lesser specimens of male, just as I did. We have been to Dublin, Lanzarote and Barcelona together, in fact, we spent so much time together at one stage that people thought we were an item.

Our fascination with the male penis, however, put paid to any possibility of a lesbian interlude. In fact, we used to play a game called The Quest, based purely on the male penis and focusing on its length, girth, and performance. (Mainly length and girth though!) It basically involved finding the perfect penis and, ultimately, the perfect man. Fun at the time but how wrong in essence!

As soon as she met Horace, The Quest was never mentioned again. Well, it's probably a blessing not to know the dimension of your best friend's husband's penis. I think he's got a small one or I'm sure she'd have whispered, 'Quested' to me on a drunken night out, even though the rule was to shout it across a crowded bar on meeting up if you had really found what you thought was the perfect one.

I thought I had Quested when I met James Crook. When in fact he was he who went on to cause me the most heartache in my whole life. We broke up about four years ago, which was initially devastating but now I know that I'm better on my own than being within a sniff of him.

Nobody had ever before evoked such passion in me and, on a similar level, such anger, as James Crook. To prove it, my carpet regularly resembled that of a Greek restaurant after we tried to settle our disputes by chucking things at each other.

Anyway, a month after we split up I was in complete and utter turmoil, torn between deciding was it my fault, his fault, the cat's fault or was my Neptune just not rising over my Capricorn at the right time? Then, after an intensive bout of therapy I realised that it was he who was the complete bastard. He was never there when I needed him, like not showing up for the funerals of two grandparents for example.

However, he also turned up at my flat naked in his

convertible and played 'Hello' by Lionel Ritchie at full blast so I would come down and he could say sorry for one of our many arguments. It was he who sent flowers not only to my office, but also to my flat and to my dad's house just to make sure that wherever I was that day he could say sorry for something else.

Finally, it was he who even more magnificently bought me a whole outfit from pants to pashmina that fitted and suited me perfectly. He used to have my sizes written inside his wallet so that wherever he was, he could just buy me something special that would fit me. It was like having my heart at the end of a yo-yo on a daily basis and in the end the string got so weak it just had to snap.

The very sad thing about James and me was that we did truly love each other – so, so passionately – but we hurt each other over and over again. It was a typical can't live together, can't live apart scenario. The making up was amazing but the hurt involved in getting to that stage was too destructive to carry on. I like to think that I was like Elizabeth Taylor, she too a Piscean. I would, however, hate James Crook to think he was in any way like Richard Burton. From what I could gather, Richard Burton had a heart. James Crook just had an exceptionally large penis!

In the end it was for my own sanity that I had to get out of the relationship. Sometimes when I am at home alone with only the cat to talk to, I think I still love him. Maybe I do, but not in any useful or viable sort of way.

I can never go back to him anyway, firstly because my self-respect is a little higher now and secondly my arse would be kicked black and blue by everybody who cares for me. I was lucky that all of my friends, apart from being loyal, fun and drunk most of the time had also taken on the extra duties necessary to support my new sort of quest, for Mr Right.

Harriet's role was to be my dresser prior to dates, while Sam Clark was to be my romantic adviser. Sam was so excited when he thought of calling my quest the search for my solemate, because of the Piscean/fish connection, that he actually fell off a bar stool in our local. This got us all barred for one week as the landlady's poodle was under the stool at the time.

Sam is cool. He is Cancerian. He is not like any other man I have met before, in that he is kind, sensitive, and caring. He also has an amazing mop of curly dark hair, which when not in its usual pony-tail style is so wild and sexy that if it doesn't turn the girls' heads with lust, then it turns them with envy. Sam started working as a web designer at Jenkins Software six months after me. The minute he sat opposite me my heart took a little leap. It was actually quite annoying in a way. I have always been one to turn up at my desk at a minute to nine, dump all my bags and then head down to the toilets to put my make-up on. This is due to the fact that I am always late getting up in the morning. I now had to get up fifteen minutes early to fit in some personal grooming so that I could glow and smile at Sam in full glory from 9.05 a.m.

Once I'd got over the initial shyness and really got to know Sam, I realised that he was far too nice for me. He didn't have a nasty bone in his body. If I were to go out with him, I would lead a life on an even keel. There would be no shouting, he wouldn't come in late from the pub, and there would be no flirting outrageously with other women on a Friday night. Oh so normal – and oh-so boring. I soon started turning up at nine again.

As well as H and Sam, I had my sister Anna, who did her best to stop my dramatic outbursts happening too often. Brad was Brad and my friend Katie Cook, who had moved out to Lanzarote after she fell in love with the ice delivery man in a bar, became my most patient listener.

But back to my date with Neil on the following Friday night. After a bracing shower, and lots of girly applications of perfumes, sprays, and slap, H had squeezed me into black hipster jeans and a black top with *Foxy* emblazoned across my chest.

'Are you sure it's not a bit too tarty for a first date?' I fretted.

'Not at all. You look great, bird, and despite being ancient you do look pretty damn foxy.'

I laughed, slung on my long black coat as it was a cold February evening, and rang for a taxi.

Cecil Street was buzzing. I laughed to myself thinking how funny it would be to meet a man called Cecil on Cecil Street, or indeed a man called Henry in Henry's Bar. I then began to feel the same butterflies I had experienced before when meeting Steve. These dates certainly required nerves of steel.

Two burly, ugly bouncers greeted me at the door of Henry's.

'Evening, madam.'

'Hi there.'

I could feel their eyes on my bum as I started to push my way through the Friday-night drinkers, some still suited and booted, having their after-work drink, others freshly perfumed, like me taking that first luxurious sip of the weekend. I had in my hand a little photo of Neil. Neil was what can only be described as nice. Nice is not an adjective I like to associate with men, as over the years nice creatures have been dismissed on a regular basis. However, on this occasion I was going to make a massive effort to find out more about Nice Neil. I was not going to be shallow. I was going to do what Sam always told me to do and look for the person behind the pecs.

Nice Neil had cropped blond hair, big brown eyes, and thin lips. I've got a thing about thin lips. I don't even know why. Maybe it's because I like big, full-hearted snogs and guess that if somebody hasn't got the right equipment for this then they will peck at me like a hungry sparrow. He also had a soulful expression that reminded me of a dog, rather than a Taurean bull. Let's face it: there was *nothing* about him that I found attractive.

Oh God, a whole evening ahead with somebody I didn't remotely fancy! I began planning an early escape. Then I spotted him. He was dressed smartly in black jeans with a shocking blue shirt on. I did a quick take on his shoes: black boots, quite trendy. H would most certainly approve. I guess in the big scheme of the male rat race he wasn't that bad really. He looked more like a Labrador than a rat so I would give him a chance.

'Hello, you must be Neil.'

'And I'm really hoping you're Amy. You look

very foxy, ha ha ha.'

I gave a feeble laugh. How on earth was I going to get through this one? However with his next words I felt better.

'Fancy a drink before we sit down to eat?' He asked loudly as the music seemed to go up.

'Large dry white wine, please, not Chardonnay though.' It isn't that I dislike Chardonnay, Chardonnay doesn't like me and I'd been turned into a white wine witch on too many occasions.

I sighed inwardly. I had had a really hard day at work and wished I was going out with the gang for a big drinking session. I wasn't in the mood for polite chit-chat. Dating was exciting but also such drudgery. If only you could get over the first embarrassing meeting, quit talking the usual bullshit, and just be bold enough to say, 'Look we both fancy each other, so why don't we go back to mine, do the deed and if it's good, let's see each other again?'

I wondered if anyone at Starr & Sun ever did that. I pictured Cordelia's look of horror at the thought of it, and grinned. I vowed not to get too drunk and disorderly tonight. This man was a stranger and a good impression should be made. Even if he appeared to be a bit nerdy at first I must try really hard not to turn into a gibbering wreck by midnight. I actually wanted to end the date there and then but my inner voice said that if that happened to me, my self-confidence would be dented for ever and I would be found half eaten by Penelope, having never left my house again.

By 10 p.m. Nice Neil had mentioned how wonderful his mother was at least five times. I had hardly got a word in edgeways and suddenly realised that we hadn't yet eaten.

'She is fantastic,' he was enthusing now. 'She still pops round once a week and has a bit of a clean, then washes and irons my shirts, and changes my duvet when required.'

At every mention of Mrs Nice Neil, I decided a bar trip was required. By the time Neil got to, 'In fact, Amy, you remind me of her. You really must meet her,' I could now see two of him. *Please keep your balance and dignity*, my inner voice warned.

I was astounded at Neil's ability to remain so sober after drinking the same amount as me, until I disturbingly noticed that when he bought rounds, he was drinking bottles of low-alcohol lager. He noticed my incredulous expression.

'Mother thought it would be best if I stayed sober on a first meeting,' he explained helpfully. 'You know, so I can get to know the true you. Now let's go to our table, shall we? She also says…' Nice Neil paused suddenly. 'Amy, are you OK? You look a little pale.'

'I'm absholutely fandabidosie, thank you for ashking. Jushed a little hungry, that's all.'

'Good, good. Well Mother also says that home is where the heart is and I do love to keep it immaculate. I also love a girl who likes to eat. Every weekend I do a little bit of DIY – not too much, mind – maybe put up a new shelf, or touch up the paintwork here and there. Then I'll make a cake or, if I'm feeling really daring, I might bake a loaf or two.'

Paintwork, I guessed, was probably all that Nice Neil had touched up in a while. He was so boring I couldn't even be bothered to sneeze. Oh no, I was starting to be unruly! My inner voice was having trouble containing me with five large glasses of wine to fight against it.

'So, Nice Neil, what makes you tick apart from a clean DIY-ed house?' But before he could answer I carried on: 'Have there been any other women in your life apart from your mother?' I then let out a resounding hiccup, laughed, and staggered to the toilet.

When I returned to the spot where we had been standing, there was no sign of him. I began to think in that strange drunken logical way that maybe I had been given Chardonnay by mistake and that I had upset him. However, I couldn't remember saying anything bad.

'Are you OK, darlin'?' Ugly Bouncer Number One was suddenly by my side, looking at my *Foxy* intently.

'Absholutely marvellous, thanks, but I think my friend may have left.'

'Of course I haven't left.' The voice of Nice Neil boomed behind me. Even Ugly Bouncer Number One was a little taken aback.

'Mother says however upset you are by a woman you must never leave her to get home alone. I've just called you a taxi.'

'But what if I want to stay here?'

'You are in no fit state to be in a public place, Amy.'

'But what if I think I am, Nice Neil?' In fact he was right: I was a very drunken fish. I began to slur and flirt at the same time if that is humanly possible.

'You are getting in that taxi when it arrives and that is that.'

'No I'm not, I'm walking,' I said cockily.

'You are going in the taxi and I'm not changing my mind on this one.'

And then I realised that I could never be with a Taurean. I was not particularly tidy – yes, home is my haven but not to the extent of lovingly stroking it once a week – and as for stubbornness! I was too much of a free spirit for somebody not to come round to my way of thinking once in a while.

I leaned out of the taxi window 'Seeya, Nice Neil. Thanks for all the wines, you shwine.' And then I promptly passed out.

H, Sam and I were lounging in Sam's trendy second-floor flat as I started to recite the story of Nice Neil. I love Sam's flat, it's about a ten-minute walk from my place and overlooks the river. I always feel really decadent when I go out on to his balcony.

'Slurred and flirted? H quipped. 'Slurred and farted more like, knowing you.'

'How dare you!' I laughed.

As I finished telling them what had happened, I started to feel a bit guilty and conveyed this. 'He wasn't a bastard, just a wimp.'

'Poor bloke,' Sam piped up. 'I'm beginning to feel quite sorry for him now.'

'I was awful,' I sighed. 'He did have thin lips as well, though.'

'I will ignore that shallow comment but don't put yourself down, Ames. It's just he wasn't the right man for you, that's all,' H told me.

'Fate, fate, it will all be down to fate,' I say.'

Sam lit yet another candle. 'Love candles, Amy, in the feng shui love corner. This one is to make you lucky in love.'

My mobile rang. 'Oh my God, what if it's Christopher? What on earth do I say this time?' I looked at the name flashing on the mobile screen.

'Arggh, it is him!'

'Don't panic, babe,' Sam soothed. 'You need to talk to him to arrange the next date. Now just be calm and honest.'

'Christopher? Hi, how are you?'

'Amy, I'm fine thanks, albeit a little concerned at yet another date you seem to have upset.'

'I really don't know what you mean. Neil and I had a wonderful evening. We discussed his house, his mother, his shelves, his mother, his garden, his mother.'

I could sense that Christopher's bluey-grey eyes would be twinkling and his lips curling up from the corners. I knew he found me very amusing and that he wouldn't be cross with me for long.

'I say you set me up with Laurence,' I told him boldly. 'Third time lucky and all that.'

'OK, Amy, but please give him a chance and don't judge him on first impression.'

I really hoped that from that comment, Laurence wasn't a complete bug. He had looked OK in his photo but I did wonder if the blue file photos had been tampered with slightly. I could just see Cordelia getting busy with Photoshop.

'I'll call you back with rendezvous details.'

'I look forward to it, Mr Starr!'

My phone rang again. I could see H and Sam at the edge of their seats waiting for date details, but it was my sister Anna.

'All right, sis? Are you having a nice day?' I asked. Anna had texted earlier to say she was on the train to London.

'I was till my irritable bowel kicked in: in the Food Hall in Harrods.'

Poor Anna, if it wasn't her irritable bowel it was her irritable boyfriend, Boyd. However traumatic I knew this was for Anna I always laughed. 'Hope you were in the chocolate section,' I said. She was now laughing her head off too. My family have always loved toilet humour. Most people find this hard to understand but it gets us every time.

'At least the facilities have gold taps there, so just sit down and enjoy it, dear!'

'Anyway,' Anna continued. 'That was it, just wanted to share the moment with you, sis. Oh, and Ames spoke to Dad last night, he sends his love. He's in Sydney at the moment, having a fantastic time.'

My Dad, Edward John Anderson, was a man of great character. He had retired from the fire service a month ago, and was now working his way around the world for a year.

'Good on him. Seeya.'

'Seeya.'

My sister and I had an amazing habit of talking about nothing in particular to each other.

'Everything OK?' enquired H.

'Fine, fine. Just Anna shitting everywhere as usual, and my eccentric father climbing the Sydney Harbour Bridge.'

The afternoon continued with cups of herbal tea being made. Sam only buys herbal tea. As much as I complain that he might as well have strained some bog peat into a cup, he is relentless in his mission to make me drink it. I usually have a couple of sips then lose the rest. I do have to say that all of the plants in his flat are very healthy though.

'He's forty years old!' I shrieked as I got off the phone to Christopher.

'Amy, how many times do I have to tell you that age is not an issue?' Sam reproached me. 'Do *you* look *your* age?'

'No, I know that, but forty!'

I had known his age all along but I didn't want my friends thinking that I was getting desperate or anything. 'He's the MD of an IT company, based in Surrey, so he's obviously loaded.'

'You know my opinion on that,' said H.

'Oh, please don't go all sensible on me. I know that money's not everything but for a couple of dates at least I'll hopefully get a decent meal out of him.'

'Well done, Ames. This could be it: you've projected a second date already.'

'Shut up, Sam!' H and I shouted in unison.

Chapter Six

Pisces: *Allow people to appreciate you for the beautiful fish you are inside. Don't run before you can walk today.*

Why is it when I walk around communal changing rooms I always imagine veruccas immediately forming on my feet? I also think that everyone is staring at my arse or, worse still, are thinking, 'What a shame.' To be honest I don't think that I look bad for my age. My bum could do with being higher and my thighs could do with a small liposuction session, but the face is in quite good nick really. Oil of Olay is most definitely worth its weight in ceramides and pro-retinal. In fact, if I ever become famous (another dream of mine) and have to fill out a fact file for *Grazia,* my answer to the question, "To whom would you say you are most grateful in your life?" would have to be the creator of Oil of Olay beauty products and Zovirax cold-sore cream.

It was a chilly Monday morning, 8 a.m. and my first training session at the gym was about to commence. The embarrassment of getting changed, having holes in the toes of my tights and revealing my sad old grey smalls, then having to jump up and down while frantically trying to shoe horn my flesh into

Lycra shorts, was nothing compared to the horrors to come.

I had been on the running machine for a grand total of five minutes, my face resembling a crying beetroot and sweat marks appearing in the most embarrassing places, when I felt my sports vest rising up. Guy was making all of the encouraging noises that personal trainers are supposed to make, when I suddenly felt really uncomfortable.

I looked down and realised that my heart monitor had caught on my vest, and an unattractive bit of my flabby stomach was poking out.

I frantically tried to move the monitor and pull the vest down, which resulted in me losing my footing, careering off the end of the running machine and hurtling into the foreboding cross trainer machine. It wasn't the only cross trainer, I can tell you; Gorgeous Guy was not impressed.

'Amy, I am here to ensure your safety while exercising. If you have a problem with anything then let me know and I'll help you.' He really was quite stroppy. 'You are in the early stages of training so you need to concentrate.'

I felt like telling him to get lost and question whether he wanted my money or not. However I refrained, carried on with the torturous hour, handed over the £45 with a grateful smile, and vowed that from that day on I would never have any more dealings with a personal trainer. I could jog, I could power walk, and I could swim. If I found the man of my dreams I could just have sex every day and burn off the required 1000 calories.

'Next session? I'll call you, Guy. Bit busy at the

moment.'

'But Amy–'

'Seeya, must dash.'

See? I could run when I had to.

Chapter Seven

Libra: *A prickly encounter leaves you feeling cold today. Don't despair, there are plenty more fish in the sea.*

Seven-thirty Saturday, and here I was, Amy Jane Anderson, turned out like a movie star, awaiting yet another contender in the Search for a Soulmate Competition. I'd decided – well, H had decided – on a little black dress and fake diamond earrings for this evening's soirée. All my adult life I've wanted a pair of real diamond earrings. Libras are renowned for their love of luxury, so maybe here at last was the man to load my lobes with carats.

As Laurence was that little bit older, I'd put my hair up in an attempt to look glamorous and sophisticated. I'd also donned a cute pair of black kitten-heeled sandals. I couldn't walk in them but I guessed, as we were going out for dinner, that not much walking would be involved.

One of the rules of the agency was not to let dates pick you up from home. Brad was all up for me getting collected from his house, mainly so he could check out the men before me.

'Princess, Princess, he's here!' Brad shrieked. 'Oh my God, he's driving a Porsche! Go girl, go go go!

Marry him, marry him. This is it, I can see him. I can see him! He looks like George Clooney.'

Brad's excitement was contagious and my heart was beating fast. Although I'd seen a photo, the reality is always different. Laurence knocked on the door and Brad opened it. George Clooney? He looked more like Wayne Rooney!

'A-a-Amy?'

Oh my God, he had a stutter. Brad poked me in the back and I tried not to laugh.

'Yes, hi there, nice to meet you.'

'Let's get on with it, shall we? I mean f-feeling like a fast ride? I mean oh let's g-g-go.'

Laurence's nervousness was slightly endearing but even though his shoes were Gucci, his hair was beautifully coiffeured, and his car was to die for, he had an awful eye tic and he looked like a monkey. Luckily my inner voice went into action and told me to give him a chance and stop being such a cow.

Brad was doing huge thumbs-up signs out of the window at me as we roared away.

'I thought we could g-go to The Holly. I h-hope that's OK?' Laurence stuttered in his plummy accent.

'That sounds absolutely great, thanks, Laurence.'

Oh my God, The Holly; I had wanted to go there for years. I'd tried once to book lunch there and it was fully booked. Even the phone there had a certain ring tone which seemed to say that plebs need not apply. I told myself to act cool. He might look like a monkey, he might stutter, but he obviously had a wallet like George Clooney.

I loved the thrill of a fast car and the thought of who we might see at the well-known celebrity haunt was making me feel quite tingly. I looked at Monkey Man and suddenly found him quite attractive.

'Attishoo!'

'B-bless you, s-sweet girl.'

Ergh, sweet girl? Just bless you would have been quite enough. In the back of my mind I could hear H with her money's-not-everything speech and I realised that I would have to make the best of a bad job. I was determined to enjoy myself, whatever.

As we sped away from Brad's house I realised that I had never been in such a fast car before. My head was being physically pushed back against the headrest and despite my religious disbeliefs I began to pray that my kitten heels had nine lives. Where the hell were speed cameras when you needed them? Relieved to have arrived in one piece, I waited while Laurence miraculously found a parking space then swished into The Holly, doing my best to look a million dollars in my £60 dress.

'Good evening, Mr Smith-Bourchier. Your usual table is ready for you.'

Usual table? I couldn't believe it. Here we were, at The Holly and Laurence Smith-Bourchier had a usual table! I then was completely star struck, as sitting two tables away from us were David and Victoria Beckham.

I was trying to act really cool by putting my menu virtually over my face so that I could just peep over and see what they were ordering. I then saw Laurence smile; he was pleased that I was so impressed.

In principle I agree that it is the person inside that we all should love, not the external beauty or good looks. However, just seeing how stunning David

Beckham is in the flesh was making me the right side of moist, I can tell you.

'Amy, you really are quite b-beautiful, you know,' Laurence professed as we started on our second bottle of Dom Perignon.

'Why, thank you, Laurence,' I smiled sweetly. Oh, if only I could say the same back then I would have been in a total dream. Sitting in a top London restaurant with A-list celebrities and a man who owned a Porsche *and* had his own table at The Holly! I couldn't wait to tell everyone all about this date. It would get awkward though if they wanted to see a picture. Maybe I should engineer a photo of David Beckham & myself, and pretend for a while that Laurence looked just like him.

Realising how shallow I was being, I tried to start an interesting conversation, but all I could come out with was, 'My dad used to be a fireman, you know.'

'Really? Well, his daughter certainly lights my f-fire.'

'Yes, he always drummed into me the perils of drink driving,' I continued, noticing the amount of alcohol Monkey Man was quaffing and suddenly becoming very worried about the drive home.

'Well, darling, I was s-so hoping you'd drop that hint,' Laurence leered, 'because I've already booked a suite at The G-Glitz.'

I felt a tingle go through my body: not one of lust, I can tell you, but one of complete horror. The thought of spending a night next to the monkey was too much to bear. 'Just need to get some air,' I told him. 'I'll only be two mins.'

'OK, I'll order for you.'

I can't bear men who order for me. He couldn't possibly be a Libran; they can barely make a decision for themselves, let alone somebody else. This was the last straw. I teetered out on my kitten heels and immediately phoned Brad.

'Brad? It's me.'

'Why are you whispering, Amy?'

'I'm at The Holly.'

Just saying these two little words sent Brad into complete raptures.

'Oh my God, oh my God, *The Holly.* Princess, who's there? Please say A list.'

I told him about the Beckhams.

'Oh my God, is he as sexy in the flesh? Oh, I lust after that man. Anyone else I should know about?'

'I'll fill you in when you come and pick me up.'

'Pick you up? Emergency situation?'

'Well actually, yes.'

'What level?'

'Just a two but I need to get out of here fast.'

'OK, now go and wait somewhere safe. I should be about forty minutes this time of night.'

Brad as usual arrived exactly when he said he would and ushered me towards his car. 'Princess, I can't believe you've walked out on a man with a Porsche who took you to The Holly,' he tutted. 'Nor can I believe you didn't let me take a sneaky peek in there.'

'Brad, if you had David Beckham and an extra from *Planet of the Apes* in the room, who would you want to sleep with?'

'Amy, that's stupid and hypothetical, it's obvious.'

'Yes, I know, but I just wanted to make the point

that I had been in a room with David Beckham again. Ha!'

'Saying that I think I did sleep with some sort of baboon after I left The Angels Club the other night.'

'Brad, you really are quite unbelievable. I love you though, thanks so much for saving me.'

I gave him a big kiss as we reached my house.

'Anything for you, my love. Stroke that pussy of yours for me before you go to bed.'

I laughed out loud. If anyone ever overheard Brad and me they would be appalled.

Chapter Eight

Pisces: Destinies will merge today. Intense aspects will bring your feelings right up to the surface. Swim to the top and enjoy!

Undeterred by the affluent Mr Smith-Bourchier, another date was arranged.

'Laurence Smith bloody Bourchier!' I exclaimed to Brad after the debacle.

'I'm never being enticed by status and money again. I'd rather plain old Larry Smith picked me up in a rundown banger and took me to a burger van than have to suffer that sort of thing again!'

Christopher was really sympathetic that the date had been such a disaster and laughingly promised that he would not subject me to anymore stuttering monkeys. A date with a Mr Declan O'Shea was arranged for the following week.

Friday night, 7 p.m. Tonight I was wearing a black knee-length skirt, a low-cut turquoise top and the infamous kitten heels. I felt a bit overdressed as I sat in the hotel lobby alone. I had questioned Christopher about why I was to meet a strange man in an airport hotel lobby, but he explained that Declan was a very busy man. He was flying back from Dublin that night and wanted to make the most of his time with me. This in itself sounded slightly ominous but in for a penny, in for a pound!

I was also swayed by the fact that Declan was indeed a looker. Compared to gangly Steve, thin-lipped Neil and ghastly Monkey Man, he was all my favourite male pin-ups rolled into one. If Declan was even half as good-looking as his photo then I was on to a winner here. I had actually forgotten to bring his photo with me, but was so hoping that Declan was going to be Mr Right that I had his smile imprinted on my brain.

Nervously I sat down in the bar area and ordered a gin and tonic. Surely dating agency bods didn't stand each other up. Weren't they all so desperate to find a mate that no opportunity, however small, must be missed?

Just then an assortment of people started walking into the bar. There were a few smart couples in black tie. There was one particularly beautiful couple with hand luggage in tow, and I imagined that they were flying off for a long weekend to somewhere exotic.

In true Piscean fashion I started to daydream of being whisked away somewhere wonderful. Another fifteen minutes passed by and no Declan. I decided that I would have another drink and then, if he hadn't turned up when I'd finished that, I would leave.

I was beginning to feel a bit embarrassed sitting in the hotel lobby alone, all dressed up with nowhere to go. Oh my God, what if people thought I was a prostitute?

'Large rum and coke please,' I mouthed to the waiter. Why did the word large always come out when I was nervous?

Bloody Geminis, never reliable, I thought to myself. James Crook was a Gemini as well. I should have left the twins out of the equation, simply on the strength of my ex-boyfriend's unreliability. However, I realised that I couldn't tar everyone with the same brush, as that would ruin my chance with a whole twelfth of the zodiac signs, and I was sure this would equate to millions of prospective husbands.

I've always had a terrible inability to stick to the same alcoholic beverage. Anna said it was because I had a butterfly mind and that was why I flitted here, there, and everywhere without settling on anything or anyone. I always tried so hard to be consistent, but being consistent at being inconsistent was another forte of mine.

Why, oh, why, did I carry on mixing my drinks, instead of drinking just mixers? Through a haze of gin and rum, I felt somebody approaching. I looked up and oh my God I could almost hear the church bells ringing as he walked over to me.

He was tall, oh yes, and he was dark, plus he had the most amazing piercing blue eyes I had seen for quite some time. I doubted if Cordelia had needed to touch his photo up one bit. He was gorgeous, with a big, fat capital G!

'Hello, and what's a pretty girl like you doing in a bar like this on your own?' The Irish lilt serenaded.

I liked this; I played up to his part. 'Waiting for a gorgeous man like you to join me, obviously.' I laughed flirtatiously. This was more like it. My heart was pounding already. Thank you, Christopher. Thank you, Cordelia. Thank You, Lord. At last I had met a date who I fancied instantly.

It hadn't crossed my mind that he might be Irish but with a name like Declan O'Shea I suppose I should have guessed. Irish accents have always made me quiver with desire. When I visited Dublin with H this got me in all sorts of trouble. People thought I was having some sort of fit every time I walked down Herbert Street.

'What are you drinking?'

'Well, it was rum in here but I actually fancy a whisky and coke now.'

'Large one?'

'Yes, please.' Oh, here I go again.

Large drinks, large blue eyes – fantastic! A pianist started to play, and all I could think of was Humphrey Bogart and Ingrid Bergman in one of my favourite films, *Casablanca*. I thought back to the sample profiles; maybe old Ingmar had directed it and I didn't even know. The godlike creature returned. He was dressed casually and he smelt gorgeous; his shoes passed the test and his face was like that of an angel. I felt no need to sneeze as he could have said, 'Burn in hell,' and I've have still sat there! Desire hit me. I hadn't slept with anyone for over a year and it was fantastic to feel those sensations again.

'It's really awkward meeting someone like this for the first time, isn't it?' I piped up.

'Not when that someone is so beautiful and I feel instantly at ease with her, it isn't,' The Irish accent soothed.

I pinched myself. Surely this couldn't be true? Ouch!, No, I was still here; what's more I was still feeling quite sober.

'Good flight?' I enquired.

'Flight? Oh yeah, grand thanks.'

'This agency lark. I'm so pleased that it isn't just the uglies of this world who apply.' If I were a dog my tongue would have been splashing right around my face by now, and my tail would have flown off!

'Well just listen to you. Flattery will get you everywhere!'

'So, Declan, how long have you been on the shelf, I mean books for?' I laughed and leaned forward, ensuring that as much cleavage as possible was showing without falling out of my push up bra. I was behaving like a harlot and enjoying every single minute of it.

'Actually, you are my first encounter, and wow, what an encounter!' Declan smiled.

When I had gulped back my fourth large spirit and Declan had brushed his hand over my thigh three times, I realised that I would not be returning to 21 Layston Gardens and Penelope the cat tonight.

'Now what did you say your name was again?' Declan teased.

I laughed thinking how funny he was. 'Amy Jane Anderson at your service, sir, and is there anything else at all you might want to find out about me this evening?'

That was it: harlot status confirmed. The rules had flown completely out of the window. Retain a bit of mystery? I might as well have been undressing there and then in the hotel lobby, while licking his face. I was smouldering. I just had to rip this man's clothes off. I didn't however want him to know how drunk I was; it's bad enough being a harlot, but a drunken one is even worse. I tried desperately to maintain my sobriety.

'It would be interesting to see if you like room service as much as I do, Ms Anderson.'

I excused myself and went to the toilet to check out my face: make-up intact, no dribbles down my top, fantastic. In fact, I was positively glowing. Making sure the other cubicles were empty I quickly sussed out the condom machine and strutted back to the bar, baby stoppers in bag! Just in case, I thought to myself, returning to innocence for a nano-second. I could imagine Liv saying, 'What? Just in case his run out?' Thank heaven I had shaved my legs and put on my sexiest G-string.

Declan tasted as good as he looked when he pulled me to him in the lift and confirmed that it wasn't only his eyes that were big. It was the hardest, most passionate kiss I had ever experienced in my life. His tongue found mine and I forgot where I was for a minute, until *ding!* In walked a very sedate middle-aged couple who both frowned intently.

We ran laughing to Room 301. Declan slammed the door shut and pushed me against it. Our breathing was loud and hard and I could already feel the wetness between my legs. I had never experienced the sort of scenario that was happening right now, and I was lost in the moment totally. Even the mere touch of my breast made me moan out loud.

Declan had a broad and muscular back. I love backs and just had to massage him. He had a small shamrock tattoo on his left shoulder and pecs to die for. I sat astride him and massaged his back tenderly at first and then quite hard, making sure my breasts rubbed against him as I went back and forward.

'Amy, I have to have you now,' he whispered.

After what seemed like hours of rising and falling to the beat of Declan's amazing love-making, we lay on the bed sweating, red-faced, and bright-eyed. I reached over to hold Declan's hand.

'Maybe this dating agency lark does work after all, you Irish beast.'

'Maybe it does, Ms Anderson. Now what would you like for dessert?'

I lay back and smiled a huge smile of pure satisfaction and happiness. Whatever, whoever, there was no doubt that Geminis did it for me in the bedroom department. We slept for what seemed like minutes. I woke up and looked across at Declan. He was the best-looking creature I had ever woken up next to.

'I have to see you again – you know that, don't you?' I whispered

'Amy, you know sometimes you can just get too much of a good thing.'

'What's that's supposed to mean?' Please, please don't let him be a complete bastard. I had to see him again; he was too delicious not to.

'I'm winding you up, you beautiful personage. Of course I want to see you again. Let's keep it mysterious though, no numbers exchanged – let's get our person at the agency to set up another date. It will make it all the more sexy.'

I had been looking for this sort of excitement for ages. It was like all my birthdays and Christmases coming at once.

Declan was in a hurry to leave and gave me cash to

pay for the room. Without looking up, the receptionist in robotic fashion asked. 'Name? Room number?'

I replied without thinking. 'Anderson, 301'

The receptionist seemed to wake up then. 'Is your name Amy Anderson?'

'Yes, that's me.'

'I have a message here for you, left late last night. We called out for you in reception but you were nowhere to be seen.'

Declan waved and blew me a kiss as he walked through the revolving door. I laughed and blew one back.

'A message?' I asked.

'Yes, a Mr O'Shea called. He apologised profusely for the fact that his flight was delayed and said he would get Mr Starr to rearrange your appointment as soon as possible.'

Chapter Nine

Pisces: *The letter D spells danger. Single? Hard as it may seem, try to use your head instead of your heart today in a romantic situation.*

I arrived home. My head was spinning. The mystery of the whole event even outweighed the huge hangover I had.

Who an earth had I just slept with?

I thought back to our initial conversation and realised that I had done all the talking and had opened myself up to a complete stranger. This was dangerous. Or was it? The dating game was one of the complete unknown initially anyway. And I did not regret sleeping with this person, whoever he was. We were both consenting adults. I am neither a slut nor a prude, but sometimes you know when the deed has to be done and lawdy Miz Claudy, it just *had* to be done last night! My horoscope had said D for danger – what a load of rubbish. Darling, debonair, dishy, delectable Declan! Dangerous? Never!

'Cordelia, it's Amy Anderson here.'

'Oh, morning, dear. Christopher was just about to call you to apologise for the Declan mishap. He is still very, very keen to meet you.'

'Er, right. OK.'

'Are you all right, Amy? You seem a little

hesitant. It really was a genuine reason he couldn't meet you; his flight was delayed.'

'I'm fine honestly, thanks, Cordelia. Could we maybe leave it until next Friday now, as I'm really quite busy at the moment? Oh and could you resend me a photo of Declan I appear to have lost the other one?'

'Of course. Oh and by the way – Laurence Smith-Bouchier phoned. He'd love to take you for dinner again.'

Good grief. This was all getting slightly out of control. Going from the company of Penelope the cat for a whole year and now to the company of half of southern England and Ireland was quite overwhelming.

'I'll call you back about Laurence. Thanks, Cordelia,' I replied. The man must be completely mad, I thought. I ran out on him and he still wanted to see me. A bloke with no self-respect – how novel.

Even more disturbing was the fact that Cordelia had not annoyed me once throughout the phone conversation. I too must be going slightly deranged. It was then that it hit me: I would probably never see the false Declan O'Shea again. This should have felt like a good thing in a way, as he was obviously a complete charlatan who had used me with no compunction. But my low self-esteem, which rose and fell on a regular basis, suddenly perked up again. He had obviously liked me – a lot. My loins were doing the thinking for me. The false Declan O'Shea was gorgeous and he had made me laugh. He had also made me orgasm in seven different languages. *I had to see him again* – but how?

Chapter Ten

Pisces: *The new moon in Aquarius spells fun today. Take the time to catch up with some old friends.*

'Oh my God, sweetie, I just saw six of the little darlings poking their heads up at me.' Brad shrieked with a white mask over his mouth.

'Where? Where? I thought they were all dead.'

'You've frightened them now.'

Brad and I were in my garden checking out the frogs in my pond, he looking like an extra from *Holby City*. I love my house, especially my garden. It is a two-bedroom Victorian terrace and I have at last decorated every single room. It has a little square courtyard area with an archway of honeysuckle leading to a ten-foot strip of grass with rose borders each side and then further on is the pond.

I had always wanted a pond. I was so excited when I first viewed the house and saw the pond from the upstairs bedroom window that I squealed, jumped up and down, and then kissed the estate agent full on the lips. Which wouldn't have been so bad apart from the fact that the estate agent was a sixty-year-old she, with a moustache.

Every year, the frogs carried out their mating ritual (watched over eagerly by me and Penelope), leaving behind their tiny black dots of babies in the hazy clouds of spawn that decorated the secret green surface of my pond. My ritual every morning after breakfast was to run down the garden to my pond to see the progress of my babies. They were defying all of my childhood knowledge of tadpole development in the fact that they were refusing to grow. I was so concerned that I had been feeding them raw minced steak. This resulted in the pond turning into a stinking shrine to my frog family.

It has also resulted in Penelope sitting on the edge of the pond sneering at me with jealousy for making such a fuss over pondlife. If it hadn't have stunk so much I'm sure that he would have just dived in and eaten them all despite his fear of water. Penelope was a huge part of my life. His connection to James Crook was the only low point, as during one of the few romantic moments in our time together James had bought me Penelope as a birthday present.

Yes, Penelope is actually a tom. I was both delighted and disappointed when I went to the vets to pay the bill for what I thought was tubes being cut and was informed by a very young snooty female vet that, 'Ms Anderson, your pet is actually a male and I have removed his testicles.'

Delighted, because the bill was quite a bit cheaper. Disappointed because I knew that Penelope would be confused for ever as I couldn't change his name; it really suited him. Well, I did consider it momentarily, but couldn't think of a male equivalent of anything that sounded remotely like Penelope.

Living with me, Penelope has heard more swearing, more heart-rending stories, and licked off more tears than anyone else I know. In fact, I'm sure I once heard him squeak, 'Shut up!'

I say squeak because he had a nasty accident as a kitten which destroyed his miaow box. I used to live in a one-bedroom flat that had a hot water system that was put in before they were officially invented, I reckon. I used to be able to make a reasonable cup of tea from the hot tap, it was so boiling. One day I went off to work and Anna, having stayed overnight on my collapsing sofa bed, decided she'd have a nice long bath before she went home. The water came out of the bath taps so slowly that a bath took an hour to run which was actually quite handy because by the time you were ready to get into it, the water had cooled to exactly the right temperature. If you needed to top up you had to make sure your toes were well out of the way and I used my largest rubber duck to swirl the hot water all around.

Penelope, a mere eight weeks old, being a typical inquisitive kitten decided to check out the huge swimming pool in the bathroom. Anna, patiently waiting for the bath to fill, feet up on the sofa bed reading a magazine, suddenly heard what she described later as a child screaming in my bathroom.

Penelope had done the unthinkable: taken a dive into two inches of boiling water. He was immediately rushed to the vet, with scalds on all paws and an affected mew box. I don't know who looked more terrible when I got in, Anna or Penelope. Ruminating sadly on all this, I suddenly heard a familiar slipper-shuffling noise from next door. A quavering voice called out, 'Gloria? Gloria, is that you?'

Smiling, I mouthed a big oh-no to Brad. 'Yes.

Hello, Jed, everything OK?' I shouted.

Jed was my neighbour. He was eighty-two and going deafer by the day. Ever since I had moved in he had called me Gloria. I had tried to correct him on several occasions and he had done his familiar slow nod, which only mildly disturbed the cigarette that was stuck permanently to his bottom lip, as if he had understood. However, the next day he would always say, 'Morning, Gloria,' as I did my pond dash after breakfast.

He also always said, 'Rain today, I reckon.'

And I always replied, 'Let's hope not, Jed.'

That was the basis of our neighbourly relationship. However, today he excelled himself, maybe because it was a Saturday.

'Morning, Gloria. Rain today, I reckon.'

'Let's hope not, Jed.'

I had to hit Brad, as he was hysterical. For some reason Jed's mere presence just cracked him up and then suddenly there was a cough, another shuffle and, amazingly, more words.

'Blimey, Gloria, that pond don't half stink!'

I then was holding back my laughter. 'You're right there, Jed, but Brad has offered to clean it out, so hopefully tomorrow we shall have fresh air again.'

With another shuffle and a snort he disappeared inside number 19.

'Clean your pond out? You'll be lucky.'

'Oh, Brad, please, I'll help you.'

'But it's a boys job,' he whinged.

Eventually deciding that we needed expert advice before we went ahead with the awful mission of cleaning out the pond, we proceeded inside for a bottle of dry white. After a couple of glasses Brad suddenly announced, 'I know! Amy Anderson can't sing, eats like a horse, will strip for a packet of jelly babies! That might get you a few more suitors.' Laughing wildly we carried on along the same theme.

'Brad Sampson, trainspotter, likes cabbage, can fart the national anthem'.

'Amy Anderson, can't cook, closet lesbian, used to be shot-putter from Cardiff'.

'Brad Sampson, face like a smacked arse, likes pressed flowers and puppies in curries! That is so enough! I'm going to wet myself,' I shouted as I rushed upstairs to the loo. Why couldn't I meet someone as funny as Brad, I thought, and then the phone rang.

'Amy?'

'Yes, who's that?'

'It's Carl.'

'Carl? Oh hi there. Sorry, I was miles away. You're my Piscean, I mean you're my date for Saturday. Christopher did mention you were going to call.'

'Yeah cool. Well, I hope you don't mind me phoning, Chris said it would be OK. He's such a dude, don't you think?'

'He's OK, I suppose.' I had given my mobile number to Chris for him to give out to prospective dates as I figured I could screen calls more easily that way.

'I've been invited to a wedding last minute like, and rather than see you in the evening as I had originally thought, I wondered if you'd like to come along with me as my guest for the whole day?'

'That would be really nice, Carl.'

'Cool. See you Saturday then, babe.'

'Wait a sec, where shall we meet?'

'Oh yeah, the wedding's in Windsor, can you make it there? How about we meet in the reception of the Royal Hotel at around 11 a.m.?'

'Fine by me, see you then.'

'Yeah, see you, babe. Looking forward to it.'

I had to let H know. 'H?'

'Hi, hon, what's happening? Any news I should know about?'

'Just spoken to the new contender. Cordelia has sent his photo through. He's Spanish-looking with longish dark hair and surprisingly dark eyes. Pisceans tend to have light eyes, must be the Spanish connection. Anyway, he sounded like he was very laid back so we shall see. He's taking me to a wedding on Saturday.'

'A wedding!' H shrieked. 'Oh my God, how exciting, how romantic! Oh my God, and he's Piscean, that means he will be romantic too, and you know what they say about weddings.'

'H, calm down, love. Impressed you've been reading up on the old star signs though.'

'You know it will evoke all sorts of lustful feelings, you're bound to shag him. Oh, and as for the reading up on stars bit I should know what Pisceans are like. I've been friends with the daftest one in the world for a few years, you know.'

'H!' I was now giggling too.

'Could do with a bit of a clinch with a Spanish stallion myself. I'm really excited for you,' she said.

'Poor Horace, what he has to put up with. I'd best

go and sort an outfit. Will you be free to dress me on Saturday?'

'Sure I will. Talk soon.'

'Seeya.'

'I don't know why you don't stick that phone to your bloody ear, sweetie,' said Brad.

'Shut it. You'll have to go; I'm going to The Oracle Centre to find an outfit for this wedding.'

'Shopping, sweetie? Count me in. Let's go.'

'See you later, Pen.'

'I'm sure your cat just said, "shit off, bitch".

'Brad! Come *on*!'

The phone rang. 'Amy, it's Christopher here. Just wanted to check that Carl had called you?'

'Yes, he sounds nice actually. Well, apart from the fact he called me babe.'

'He's the one I mentioned on our first meeting, I thought you'd get along with him really well, so go for it, girl.'

I was never sure if Christopher was genuinely concerned or whether he got some sort of bonus if a date actually went well.

'Oh, and Declan is still keen to meet up with you next Friday,' he added.

'OK, Friday it is for Declan and Saturday for Carl. Better to squeeze Declan in before Carl, I guess, as if you think Carl's the man for me, it might be my last fling.'

Joking aside, this whole dating business was becoming quite exhausting. I did want to meet up with the real Declan, but I knew somehow that he wouldn't live up to my experience in the hotel, so something in me was putting it off. I kept having rose-tinted daydreams that I would bump into the false Declan and we'd make mad passionate love again and he'd realise that I was the woman of his dreams.

'Princess! Wakey, wakey. The shops won't stay open all day, you know'

'I'm coming!'

Chapter Eleven

Pisces: *A marriage of minds will lead to a fulfilling experience today.*

It had been a bloody expensive lunch hour. Suffering from an extreme hangover, I suddenly felt sorry for all the homeless people I came across in Reading town centre and gave them money. Then I got back to my car and found I had a parking ticket. This distressed me greatly, as one of my New Year's resolutions had been *not* to get parking tickets.

I usually got at least six a year. However I had already paid out £160 since January and it was only the beginning of March. I had left my standard note for the attendant explaining I had no change but would pay on return, but the bastard had completely ignored it. Well I'm writing to the council, so there. No one will know that I had no intention of paying on my return.

'Parking ticket?' Sam asked when he saw the look on my face as I returned to my office.

'Shit off!' I tried really hard to look annoyed but had to burst out laughing.

'Maybe you should have a herbal tea, love, it might calm you.'

I stood up dramatically, swished my hair back over

my shoulders, and stormed towards the kitchen. 'I'm getting a black coffee, after which I shall attempt to source a circus tent, so please leave me alone to get on with some work.'

I really enjoyed my job as the Event Manager in Marketing. My job involved arranging anything from small seminars for twenty people right up to the huge event I was working on at the moment for a thousand delegates, which was to be hosted in a big top on the banks of the Thames. It was certainly going to be a challenge.

My boss Mr Parkinson was really good to work for. He always gave me pay rises at the right time, praised me at the right time, and even bought me flowers on my birthday. Too good to be true, one may think. To be honest I think he fancies me a bit. I have never had even a slight reciprocal flutter in the nether regions, which is a blessing as I'm not really in to short balding men with nasal hair and 2 inch thick spectacle lenses. Mr Parkinson is married to Pru in Accounts. She too has nasal hair and thick spectacles, so heaven help them if they were ever to breed as I think they may actually produce a mole.

Before I set about the task of looking for a big top supplier, I thought I'd take a quick look for pond websites to get some hints and tips on cleaning out my pond without killing the tadpoles. Amazingly, there were loads of them. I started to have a bout of hysteria when I came across not only Frank's Pond Page but also Bert's Pond Life, both outlining in great detail, with pictures, how these poor sad blokes had built their ponds step by step.

I was relieved from my mirth by a familiar number

flashing up on my phone monitor.

'Event Slut helpline!' I trilled.

'Whatcha doing later, minger?' Liv asked. She only sat about ten feet from my desk but we always rang each other to save shouting our business across the office.

'Well, amazingly, my friend, I'm not out on a date so do you fancy doing something?'

'Well…' Olivia hesitated.

'What's up?'

'Well…'

'Spit it out, Liv.'

'You don't have to if you don't want to.'

'Don't have to what?'

'I've roped myself in to going on one of those dinner-date things. Everyone is single and you basically have dinner and then mingle with the guests. If you get on, then fine, if you don't, well same as with you and your astrology dates, you don't have to see them ever again.'

'Fab, so do I take it there is a space then?'

'Yeah. The woman who runs it has just called to say there has been a dropout and did I know any nice eligible young ladies to come along instead? I said, sadly no, but I knew you.'

'Ha bloody ha. Just let me know where I have to be and when, my love. What a laugh!'

'Oh, and Ames, don't forget I'm cooking you a sumptuous feast for your birthday next week.'

'Forget that? It would be like forgetting Christmas!'

The changing of the guard at Windsor Castle always

gives me a little bit of a tingle, don't know why really. It's not even anything to do with all those uniforms. Maybe it's just the noise and extravaganza.

I was sitting in the reception of the Royal Hotel waiting for Carl. It was hectic there, I can tell you. The hubbub of excited tourists with all their different spatterings of language could be heard above the bang, bang of the soldiers' drums. The Saturday morning shoppers were rushing around wishing the tourists would get out of their way and here I was, Amy Jane Anderson, slightly nervous, looking resplendent in bright blue (my favourite colour) on yet another date.

'Amy Anderson?'

'That's me.'

'How ya doing, chick? Like the funky dress.'

'Thanks. I was worried you might not see me amongst this lot.' I pointed to a busload of Chinese tourists who had just congregated in the reception area.

'In that dress?' Carl laughed.

He wasn't bad looking. He was a true likeness to his photo; Cordelia hadn't had to touch him up much. His shoulder-length dark hair suited him and his brown eyes could have been transplanted straight from a deer. He was, however, wearing a cringeworthy red shirt with big white flowers on that clashed dreadfully with my dress. He was also wearing baggy jeans, to a wedding. Only his shoes redeemed him in the fact that they were black Doc Martens. I had a thing for men in Doc Martens, a teenage fetish kind of thing. What did put me off, however, were his sideburns, which were long and trimmed to a sharp point, almost down to his mouth.

Carl was a trendy young dude in my books. A toy boy at twenty-nine as well, which was nice. I've always liked younger men, which I feel has possibly been to my detriment in the settling-down stakes. I once spent a fantastic night with a lad eight years my junior whom I met in Lanzarote. I was visiting my mate Katie and her Ice Man (he delivered ice to bars in his special refrigerated truck) and we decided to hit the town. Me being the ultimate party animal, we always had to go to what I called the red-light district of Puerto del Carmen. It's basically one of those awful holiday bar areas, with the even more awful PRs who drag you in off the street for your free glass of camel pee.

Anyway, it got to around 3 a.m. and Ice Man decided we should go to Charlie's Bar to meet up with some staff from a Scottish bar that had just closed for the night. I staggered along and was immediately thrilled as firstly a live band was playing and secondly sitting in the crowd that Ice Man was moving towards was a vision of loveliness.

Tom was cute; he had a wide smile with beautiful teeth. I *love* perfect teeth. He had blond hair with a floppy fringe and a fit, brown body, emphasised by the tight white T-shirt he was wearing. He had a silver dolphin earring in his left ear and when he threw his head back to laugh, I spotted a stud in his tongue. I found this instantly erotic. The seven rum and cokes I had had in the sea-front cocktail bar had made me very brave. Without any introduction I was over to Tom like a shot.

'Hi, there. I'm Amy and I'm staying with my mate

Katie for a long weekend.'

'Hi there, great to meet you, your tan's coming along well.' He smiled his big white smile and then with no warning took my hand and kissed it. I could actually feel a tingle run right through my body. Not just because of his touch, but the soft Scottish accent had nearly the same effect on me as an Irish one.

'So I take it you work out here then?' I asked rather hoarsely.

'Yeah, I work in the Scots Bar. Been here with a couple of my mates since we left university.

'Lucky you. I could do with waking up every day and being able to walk to that beautiful beach.'

'I don't go down to the beach that much, actually. In fact, I've only been down there about five times. I rarely get to bed before dawn so I get up late afternoon, eat, maybe lie on my balcony for an hour, then it's back to work, party hard and off to bed again.'

'So why do it?'

'I love the buzz of it all and I do get a day off a week. If you do want to slow the pace you can go into the mountains and it beats being in the rain at home.' He then smiled and looked at me with his piercing green eyes. 'I also get the chance to meet pretty girls like you.'

'Tequila slammers for all!' Katie was off and running. I had a feeling this would be a long night.

Three slammers later, I was so full of alcohol I felt like I was actually drinking myself sober. My lustometer was almost off the scale. There is something about the sun and sea that makes me feel very horny, and all I wanted to do was grab Tom right

76

here in this crowded bar and snog his face off. Instead I came out meekly at first with, 'If you don't mind me asking, Tom, how old are you?'

'I was twenty-two on May the twenty-fourth. How about you?'

I screwed my face up. 'I'm thirty, actually.'

'Fantastic! So we're both at our peaks, I reckon. Where did you say you were staying tonight?'

He was a Gemini, hallelujah; we could sleep on the beach for all I cared! We decided to move on to Dreams nightclub after Charlie's Bar. Katie and Ice Man had to leave, well, were asked to leave as Katie thought she was dancing on a table but she was actually dancing on a bouncer who had bent down to look for a missing handbag. Katie shouting across the dance floor, 'Go for your life, Ames!' did not deter Tom. In fact, it inspired him to grab me firmly and press his lips to mine.

Oh my God, what a kisser. I thought I was going to melt against his lips, so moist and warm, and then I suddenly felt something hard and cold! I was just about to scream when I realised that it was his tongue stud. Once I got the hang of it being there, I can honestly say I have never kissed anyone so sexy in my whole life. It was like some sort of tongue challenge; all I wanted to do was sort of suck it and kiss at the same time. He probably thought he was kissing a fish but I didn't care.

We practically ran back to Katie's apartment. I pulled out the sofa bed in the lounge and started to rip my clothes off. Tom's body was amazing. His muscles were really defined, accentuated by his golden tan. His skin was smooth and taut. I was quite scared that I might come just kissing him, so instead I started to kiss him from his toes upwards. He had a Questful penis, to be sure. He was standing proud and I just had to have him inside me. I teased him slightly by blowing on him until he pulled me towards me.

'Amy, you are completely gorgeous. I want you so badly.'

I felt so, so good. I was brown, I was wearing my best white lacy G-string and I had remembered to spray John Paul Gaultier in all the right places. I have to say my head was swimming slightly with all the tequila, but it was also feeling fuzzy with desire. I could hear the sound of the waves on the beach in the background. This was just *so* fantastic.

'Shit – condom,' Tom murmured.

For some strange reason Katie had left a condom on the kitchen worktop. I had spotted it earlier and thought it must be fate that this was all so organised.

'Quick, give it here. I have to have you right now.' He tore open the gold wrapper and then started laughing heartily.

'What's up?' I was quivering with desire now and in no mood for laughing.

'Don't think this will have quite the desired effect.' He giggled as he held up a mosquito repellent tablet.

'Shit, shit, how embarrassing. Sorry.'

'It's OK, we'll just have to be careful.'

'Let me just check in the bathroom first.'

'Hurry up then.'

I had a quick wee and rifled through Katie's bathroom cabinet. Fate again: I found an in-date Durex and ran back into the lounge.

'Drum roll, please. Tom and Amy can have it off right now!'

No response.

'Tom?'

Tom was lying on his back snoring. I kissed his beautiful lips and then put my fingers under the covers so I could touch myself. I was so aroused and just had to come. I fantasised about Tom pushing hard into me against a rock on the beach and fell asleep feeling completely satisfied.

'Amy, are you OK?'

'Sorry, Carl. I blinked and came back to the present. So where's this wedding then?'

'Upstairs, actually. They are having a civil ceremony and the evening do here as well.'

'Great, so what are we waiting for?'

'I say that we have a cheeky glass of champagne and then go for a walk by the river as the wedding doesn't start until three.'

'Three!' H and I had really rushed to make me look magnificent and I could have had an extra few hours to do so.

Carl, the ever-sensitive Piscean, saw the look on my face. 'Sorry if this isn't OK with you, Amy. I just thought that it's so cool by the river here and it would give us a chance to chat and get to know each other better.'

'That is just so sweet. Of course I'm fine, champagne it is.'

The fact it was early March and there was a biting wind did not deter Carl. For reasons of vanity I hadn't put on my thick winter coat; instead I had just madly thrown a woollen pashmina over my shoulders.

Luckily the two glasses of champagne we had just swigged in the bar were giving me some slight alcoholic warmth.

'Babe, sorry, I didn't think. You must be freezing. Put my coat on.'

'No, it's my fault for being so vain. I'll be fine, we just need to walk faster, that's all.'

'I tell you what, Amy. We've seen some swans, we've had some fresh air, why don't we give up on this river bit and find a nice warm pub to sit in?'

I think he must have heard my huge sigh of relief.

Two gin and tonics, a rum and Coke, and a cheeseburger later I was beginning to feel fantastic.

'Amy, you really are such a beautiful fish I can't believe that no one has caught you yet.'

'You're making me blush,' I told him ' and you're not so bad yourself. Now tell me, if you were really a fish, would you be a shark or a minnow?'

Carl was undeterred by this strange question. 'A minnow, I reckon. I'm too nice to be a shark.'

Good job Liv wasn't here, as she would be raising her eyebrows. This was my favourite getting to know someone game. Once I started, that was it, I could go on for hours. The other player always seemed to respond with gusto so I guessed it couldn't be too boring.

'Black or white?' I continued.

'It has to be black.'

Fab, Carl was obviously on my wavelength.

'Sweet or sour?'

'Oh sweet, definitely. You?'

'Yes, sweet as well.'

This made me think of a birthday treat that my

mum and dad took me on when I was about twelve-years-old. We went to a really lovely restaurant, which was renowned for its puddings. The sweet trolley came round and Dad had said, 'It's her birthday, you know. Give her a bit of everything.'

I had eleven different puddings on one plate: cheesecake, pavlova, lemon meringue pie, chocolate brownies, the full works. This was the first and only time I have ever been sick in a public place, all over the next table. Needless to say, we never went back there. Anna still finds great joy in ribbing me over this.

'Now, Ms Anderson, I don't think you can always be the question master. Brandy or vodka?' Carl teased.

'Ergh, I don't like either, but if it was the only alcohol left in the world I would say brandy.'

'Roses or carnations?'

Bless Carl, only a Piscean would be so sweet.

'Oh, roses for sure and they have to be yellow.'

'Yellow roses? That's a new one on me.'

'OK, Mr Peters, how about a hug or a kiss?'

'Kiss, definitely.'

His beautiful brown deer eyes bore straight into mine. Oh my God, and I so wanted to kiss him. You could almost drown in his eyes. Not only that, he had long sweeping lashes, ones I'd always dreamed of having myself. I spent a fortune on mascara just trying to make mine curl slightly up on the ends.

'You can't beat a good old snog now and then, can you, Ms Anderson?' And he reached right over the table there and then and gave me a mind blowing frenchie. I felt slightly giddy when we eventually pulled apart.

'Wow, us fish know how to snog, that's for sure!' I sighed.

'We also know how to make an entrance to a wedding. Quick, we've got five minutes to get back to the hotel.'

Carl held my hand throughout the ceremony. The bride looked beautiful. The two bridesmaids were very cute and the mothers both cried on cue. I managed to remain calm as I had no association with Carl's cousin whatsoever. However, when it came to the kiss-the-bride bit and Carl squeezed my hand I was off then. The butterfly mind was flying over as many buddleia bushes as it could manage.

That was me standing there. I was in that white organza dress, hair tied up in uniform bride style. I was looking thin and radiant. My husband-to-be was waiting at the end of the aisle, looking at me with complete love and adoration. I could hear the church bells ringing and my friends singing. The sun was shining brightly outside and the honeymoon was booked to St Lucia.

It was at times like these that I was really glad to be a Piscean, seeing life through my rose-coloured spectacles. If I had had a logical, earthbound mind, in truth Brad would be in the white organza, my cute little bridesmaids would be in the guise of Anna, Katie, Liv, and H, all jostling for position in the photographs. My groom would have his fingers crossed hoping I wasn't staggering down the aisle and the honeymoon would probably be in Katie's apartment, as I would have spent all the wedding money on food.

'Amy, we're on this table, come on.'

A colourful character addressed Carl. 'All right, geezer?' He was about six-foot-four with a shock of red hair, pulled forward into a quiff. He was accompanied by his girlfriend who was about four-foot-four, with jet-black hair cut into a severe bob with an earring in the shape of some sort of animal in her nose. She looked quite scary but was in fact a real laugh.

'Carl, geezer, how's it going, man? Haven't seen you for ages.'

Ginger Geezer Man had gone to university with Carl. His sense of humour was as amusing as his looks. The other two people on our table were Auntie Marge and Uncle Doug from Scunthorpe. The pair of them must have been nearing eighty.

'Hi there, I'm Amy.' I held out my hand to Uncle Doug.

'You're lame, duck? Why? What on earth have you done?'

Auntie Marge intervened. 'It's OK, Sammy duck, he's a little deaf.'

By this time the other three on the table were in hysterics.

'Oh, how annoying. I missed the joke, Doug,' Auntie Marge continued.

'Missed what, duck?' Uncle Doug replied, while letting off an almighty fart.

This is going to be fun, I thought. The wine was flowing. We were all getting on really well, despite the fog of Uncle Doug's obvious bowel complaint. I really wished that Anna had been here, she would have relished this toilet humour.

'Nice beaver,' I commented to Severe Bob.

'What?' She looked at me as if I was either a closet lesbian or completely mad.

'I said nice beaver, nice beaver nose ring.'

Ginger Geezer, Severe Bob, and Carl were laughing so much I thought they would fall off their chairs.

'It's a rabbit!'

'Oh sorry, how embarrassing.'

'Who's had it?' piped up Uncle Doug and then promptly farted again.

As the wine continued to flow I felt more and more at ease with Carl. I could still almost feel our kiss from earlier and actually couldn't wait to be alone with him. I knew he felt the same way as I could feel his hand occasionally brushing my thigh. The speeches had started. The father of the bride stood up.

'Firstly I would like to say that I am so, so proud of my beautiful daughter. She surpassed herself at college, got her degree, and continued to maintain her healthy twelve-year relationship with my new son-in-law, without even a single row. She is a constant support to me and I love her dearly.'

How wonderful, I thought weepily, and then started imagining my wedding again. I pictured my father standing up to speak.

'Firstly I would like to say that despite a turbulent thirty-two years, I am proud of young Amy. Neither the fact that she was chucked out of college for having an affair with her music teacher, nor the fact that she brought more inappropriate men home than her cat brought in mice, nor even the fact that she has actually *paid* her husband to marry her allows me to not still love her dearly.'

I was brought abruptly out of my thoughts by a hand slowly creeping up my leg and under my dress. Carl's hand felt rougher than I had imagined. I smiled and began to squirm slightly. I looked to the side to give Carl a sultry look and nearly fainted as I found myself looking straight into the bloodshot eyes of Uncle Doug.

By ten o'clock I was feeling the effects of copious amounts of Pinot Grigio.

'Do you want to dance, Amy?'

'Do you know, I'd love to, Carl.'

Carl smelt divine; I do love a man who wears strong, musky aftershave. As we smooched our way through 'Three Times a Lady' and 'Angels' Carl leant down and gave me another mind-blowing frenchie.

'I've booked a room, Amy. Totally up to you, of course, but I would really love you to spend the night with me. We can just hug all night.'

Bless Carl, he was so sweet. Maybe Christopher was right in his matchmaking; perhaps at last I had met a soulmate, a gentle man with whom I could bond.

'I would really like that.'

The room that Carl had booked in the hotel was amazing. I don't know what it is with me and hotel rooms but I get really excited every time I stay somewhere. I always have to run around the room checking everything out. Most importantly, I have to check out the bathroom and even more bizarrely, despite my religious disbeliefs, if there isn't a Bible in the bedside cupboard I feel quite put out.

This particular room caused more of a furore than

usual as, not only did it have a balcony that looked out over Windsor Castle, but also an exquisite bathroom. It was huge and all white. There was a huge white Jacuzzi in the corner and even more excitingly, huge snuggly His and Hers white bathrobes hanging on the back of the door. Carl seemed amused at my whoops of delight.

Just seeing the Jacuzzi made me feel quite horny; I'd always wanted to have sex in a whirlpool and here I was with an extremely sexy Piscean, feeling fuzzy-headed and relaxed. The night was our oyster and I was ready for anything. I put the comment about hugging all night to the back of my mind and started to initiate the Anderson School of Seduction technique. Oh God, I was about to have one of those moments that would cause me to wake up in the morning and physically cringe at my exuberant behaviour, but once Amy Jane Anderson was on a mission there was no stopping this gal!

'Tonight, Carl Peters,' I slurred and held my arm in the air dramatically. 'I am going to be... Shirley Bassey!'

I shimmied into the bathroom and quickly undressed down to my underwear.

Thank goodness I'd bought new for the occasion. Waltzing out in my grey smalls would have not created the right image at all, oh no siree. I also was glad that I was drunk and that my inhibitions were at zero level. I no longer cared about any excess flesh that was oozing out of the corners of my shocking pink, super cleavage lifter with matching G-string and suspender belt. Dramatically emerging from the bathroom, the singing, or should I say wailing, commenced.

'The minute you waltzed in the joint, der dum!' I gyrated my hips and pointed my arm seductively at Carl. He was now lying on the bed, looking bemused, rather than amused. 'I could tell you were a man of decision.' More gyrating. 'Hey Big Suspenders!'

I ripped my suspenders undone, then started to try and peel off my stockings erotically. Unfortunately, in my drunken state I lost my balance and started hopping around like I was on a pogo stick for the first time. I then fell headlong through the open French windows onto the balcony.

I was just about to start crying as I could feel blood dripping down my knee when suddenly there was an almighty round of applause and whoops from across the street. Not only had Carl had to witness this whole sorry performance firsthand, but so had Regiment 151 whose living quarters at Windsor Castle were obviously right opposite the hotel.

Carl didn't seem too amused now. He came outside, threw a robe around me and ushered me inside, he then shut the doors and curtains as quickly as he could to the resounding cries of, 'Heh, Shirley Bassey, show us your assy one more time, baby!'

He gave me a look reserved purely for a parent to a naughty child and said quite firmly, 'Amy, although very honoured to receive such a performance, I really do think it's time for bed.'

Chapter Twelve

Gemini: *An unexpected encounter leaves you feeling hurt and embarrassed today.*

'Hugged all bloody night? Princess, I can't believe you haven't had a shag yet! I know you can't hit the coconut every time, but it's about time you had a shot at the target!' Brad exclaimed.

'Obviously Shirley Bassey isn't his cup of tea!' I laughed.

I hadn't told Brad about my passionate night with Declan; in fact the only living creature I had confided in was Penelope. I felt a bit mean about this, but thought if I told my friends, they were bound to try and talk me out of the dating lark, and I was beginning to quite enjoy myself.

'Well, I'm off to this dinner-date evening with Liv tonight, and you know what she's like. She will probably talk me into going off with the waiter if none of the dinner dates are worth pursuing.'

Christopher had left me a message yearning to know how my date with Carl had gone. I was feeling extremely hungover after the wedding experience so couldn't be bothered to talk to him. I sent him a text message instead.

'SUCCESS! SECOND ROUND REQUIRED! PS:

IS THIS EXTRA?'

He replied immediately. Hadn't he got a life of his own? 'GREAT.OK NO.' How bloody dull. I liked a text message with at least a bit of humour. Maybe he was being short with me for cancelling my date with Declan.

I almost felt like I was betraying Carl by going on this dinner-date thing. I don't know why, really. We had hugged and kissed and I felt completely at ease with him, but a girl had to keep her options open and a night out with Liv would certainly allow me to do that.

'All right, minger, let's party.' Liv had arrived. She was carrying a bottle of pink champagne and a packet of dry-roasted peanuts. 'I thought we could have a little aperitif and snackette before we leave.'

'So, are you going to put some clothes on before we leave as well?' I enquired.

Liv made one of her screwed-up faces that looked so funny even the Mona Lisa would have let out an enormous belly laugh. Actually, she looked fabulous; only she could get away with the very short black mini-dress that she was wearing. Her breasts were heaving out of it and her mane of red hair was piled on top with seductive little ringlets hanging down the sides.

'Underwear?'

'Obviously not!'

'So no dropping your napkin then, sweetie.'

Penelope sauntered in, sniffed Liv's leg, gave one of his glares to both of us, then sauntered off again.

Feeling tipsy after the pink champagne we arrived at the venue of the dinner party: a beautiful old cottage, in a village about ten miles outside of Reading. Rosalind, the hostess with the mostess, greeted us. Her voice was low and husky; she was wearing a high-necked, straight black dress that touched the floor, and burgundy lipstick. Her nails were like eagle's talons. She could easily have passed as Cordelia's sister.

'Hi there, girls, you must be Liv and Amy. We've been waiting for you.'

I felt like I was on the set of some sort of horror movie.

We were ushered into the dining room. The ceiling was low and just two single candles in the middle of a huge bench table gave the room an eerie glow. There were three people standing chatting in the corner, drinking champagne. One girl and two boys, each beautifully dressed in their black tie ensembles.

'Liv!' I jabbed her in the back. 'You didn't say it was black tie, you cow.'

'I didn't know,' she whispered back.

Liv was all right in her black creation. I did have a dress on but it was a gold-halter neck number that I had had made for me for H's wedding. I suddenly felt very un-chic and really out of place. I also was slightly perturbed that there were more girls than boys.

'Dinner is served,' Rosalind huskily announced.

'For those of you who haven't been before, remember it's boy, girl, boy, girl. I'll sound the gong, you chat for twenty minutes then I'll sound the gong again and you all move round.'

I grimaced at Liv. She smirked back. I knew she would be in her element.

'By the way, ladies, there is another man for you on his way. He's in a taxi as we speak. The spare lady will have to listen in until he arrives.'

Dong! Rosalind bashed the worn golden gong in the corner of the room. I glanced at Liv again; she could sense my apprehension. What sort of night was this going to be? Liv, of course, was loving it; she gave me one of her faces and then promptly proceeded to home in on the louder of the two contenders.

Sam had this theory that all people resembled animals or birds of some sort. He had labelled me as a Jack Russell. 'Nothing at all to do with you being a dog, Ames, 'cos you know you're not. It's just you tear around making lots of noise, you have a nasty bite sometimes but everyone still loves you.'

Throughout my life I had come across nearly the whole deckful of Noah's Ark. I had worked for a shark and a fox and had been out with more magpies than I care to remember. Tonight was certainly like feeding time at the zoo. Liv made straight for a bloke I immediately named Lion Man. He had a mane of long, blond wavy hair and was tanned in an orange sort of way. A gold medallion clung to his excessively hairy chest. He obviously wanted to be the centre of attention. Leo was written all over his face. Next to Lion Man was Scorpion Woman. Her features were pointy and she had the most piercing green eyes I had ever seen. Her hair was black and cropped short, and every time she laughed, or should I say cackled, she threw her head right back as if she had just stepped out of the asylum. Scorpion Woman was actually quite frightening. She also had inch-long talons painted purple. What was it with these women and their nails? I have never had nails. I can't even remember when I started biting them. It bothers other people that I have stubby-looking hands but I don't actually care. I reckon that nail biting is not as dangerous a habit as smoking so I shall continue to do it. In fact, me with nails is actually quite dangerous. I did try the false nail thing once, got drunk, stuck my finger in my ear to scratch it and ended up in casualty with a damaged eardrum.

Lion Man, aka Evan, was enjoying himself hugely. With Liv one side of him and Scorpion Woman the other, he was in his element. The girls had taken it on themselves to share the twenty minutes with Lion Man. I heard Liv's opener and realised why I loved her: 'So, Evan, do you feel that sex on a first date is appropriate?'

As Stranger Man had not turned up yet, I was on the other side of the bench next to Slug Man. Slug Man because I find slugs particularly dull. Looks-wise he wasn't really ugly, he just had what I would call an insignificant face. He had straight mousy hair, in no particular style, and murky hazel eyes. His face never seemed to change expression and he had a thin upper lip, so an instant no-no there. His voice was monotone and without taking any sort of breath he spurted the following

'Hello, you look lovely in gold. Your eyes are a pretty colour. Your lipstick suits you.'

Ergh,, vile man. I knew that I would have to ask him some questions but really felt like saying, 'Look, you have no dress sense, your eyes are the colour of a slug, and your lips need a Botox injection.'

Suddenly I sneezed, three times in a row.

'Bless you, bless you, bless you. Hey, you look amazing when you sneeze.'

Now why couldn't the ones I fancied come out with something like that? When I regained my composure and managed to find out that Slug Man, aka Crispin (I guess even his mother wasn't too keen on him) was an accountant who lived in Hertfordshire. He was thirty-nine and had only ever had one girlfriend. His favourite hobby was stamp collecting. Even with Lion Man being the only other choice I was quite pleased when the gong sounded for a change around. I did actually feel quite sorry for Crispin though, knowing that Liv and Scorpion Woman would make mincemeat of him. Just as the gong sounded for the second time, the dining-room door flew open and in walked Stranger Man.

My mouth began to open and shut like that of a startled goldfish in disbelief.

Chapter Thirteen

Pisces: *The cosmic whistle is calling full time on a past encounter. Dry those eyes, hold your head up high, and face the future with pride*

Once I had managed to control my mouth I felt tears stinging my eyes. For there, right in front of me in the candle-lit dining room, was the one and only James Crook. Fate had played her part in my life before, but this was incredible.

'Boy, girl, boy on this side of the bench,' I managed to spit out. My heart wasn't racing. Instead, a dull thud had gone through it with the awful prospect of having to spend an evening with an ex-boyfriend.

'Liv, let me introduce you to James Crook,' I whispered.

Liv sat bolt upright. 'Oh, hi there, James, pleased to meet you.'

Bless Liv, she had never met James before but knew the trauma that he had caused me and she was being polite, sensing immediately how shocked I must be feeling.

'Excuse me one moment,' she said. 'I must powder my nose. Amy, can I borrow that compact of yours?'

I took this as my cue for a toilet break. I muttered,

'Back in a minute,' to James and dutifully followed Liv out of the dimly-lit room into the cramped, pot-pourri scented loo.

'Oh my God!' Liv shrieked. 'This is so unreal! What do you want to do, Amy? Do you want to leave?'

'Do you know, Liv, I feel quite calm. This is an ideal time to have a chat, as he can't flare up if there are other people here and it was years ago; we can surely talk as adults now. This is my final chance for closure. I've always felt we left things slightly unresolved.'

'OK, but if I see you distressed in any way we're out of here!'

'Thanks, mate. And can I just say one thing?'

'Sure, Ames, what?'

'I'd rather you slept with Lion Man to my left, than Slug Man to your right.'

'Ha bloody ha! I'd rather sleep with Rosalind.'

I caught James's eye as I sat down. He had amazing brown eyes that you could drown in. Memories starting flooding back, like when I'd told him I was pregnant.

'Pregnant? You can't be! I thought you were on the pill?'

'I was, but I told you I was having a break and we must be careful.'

And as if he hadn't even been there during our passionate encounters he asked, 'So were we careful?'

'Yes, as far as I know but I guess withdrawal is not very reliable.'

'Amy, Amy, I can't believe this!'

'James, we are twenty-eight-years-old, we are adults. I will get maternity pay.'

'I don't want this baby, Amy.'

I suddenly saw red. 'How can you say that? It's like saying you don't want part of me.'

'Well maybe that *is* what I am saying, you've trapped me.'

James Crook was a prize wanker in the wanker stakes and thankfully I did realise that now. In those days, my low self-esteem had kept me glued to him, but this was too much to bear. Huge teardrops started to fall slowly down my face.

'That's right, feel sorry for yourself, you stupid cow. Well, you had better deal with it, hadn't you?'

'Yes I better had, like I've had to deal with everything throughout this pitiful relationship,' I screamed.

'I doubt if you can be sure it's mine anyway!'

'How fucking dare you. You are despicable! In a way I wish it fucking wasn't. Imagine another one of you gracing this earth!'

James lurched towards me; I had been stupid to give him this news when he had just got back from the pub. I could feel his lager breath on my face.

'I don't want you and I don't want your baby.'

'Our baby, James, *our* baby.' I ran sobbing to the bedroom.

'That's right, stick your head up your arse under the sheets and the problem might go away.'

I was shaking with fear and sobbing. A drunken irrational man is very frightening and, even at only seven weeks' pregnant, I felt a sudden urge to protect my unborn child. When I heard James slam the door and go out, obviously back to the pub as it was still only 10 p.m., I got up and went down to the kitchen to get myself a glass of water. It was then I felt the first pain. It was just like a normal period pain to start with. I calmed myself; my stomach was hurting because I'd got myself in such a state, that was all. It was then I felt wetness in my knickers. I ran to the toilet. I was bleeding. In fact, blood was pouring out of me. I had to phone Anna. I got to the phone and doubled up in agony. The pain in my stomach was intense, flowing through me in great big waves. I thought I was going to pass out. I also fleetingly thought this must be just a fraction of the pain you get when you give birth.

'Anna, you've got to get round here, I'm losing my baby.'

I woke up in hospital, my sister at my bedside. Anna told me that I had been heavily sedated and yes, I had had a miscarriage. She said I should have told her before but I explained that I had wanted to tell James first.

'I'm sorry Ames,' Anna went on compassionately. 'But I had to tell dad. You've got to have an operation to check there is nothing left inside of you and I knew he'd want to be here for you.'

I cried all the way down to the operating theatre and then cried for an hour when I came round. I had just about cried myself to sleep when I heard a familiar voice.

'Amy, I am so, so sorry. You do know how much I love you really. I was just shocked last night.'

'James, we are finished. I'm due home tomorrow. I want you to be gone when I get there.'

'You're just being irrational; your hormones are obviously still all over the place.'

'No, James, *you* are all over the place and this is it. I've finally seen the light and I want you out of my life for ever.'

He moved out and the next day, just as I was about to go to bed early, the phone rang.

'Amy, it's me, James. Life won't be the same without you. I've cashed in a savings plan. I will take you anywhere in the world you want to go. I promise that I will change. I promise that I'll stop drinking.'

From that moment on I promised myself I would never, ever have anything to do with him again. My love for him died, as did part of me when I lost our child.

'So how's it going, Amy?' James said breezily. 'Can't say I'm surprised that you're still a singleton. Ha ha.'

I saw red. 'Do you know what, James Crook? I would rather be a singleton for the rest of my life than end up with a complete wanker like you.'

And then I tipped a whole bottle of red wine over his head. Closure!

'Liv, get your coat. We're going.'

And in true best-friend style, even though she was now making eyes at Slug Man, Liv headed towards the door. Rosalind started flapping like a hen in the hallway.

'Was there something wrong with the food, girls?'

'No, no, Rosalind, just a nasty creature in the red wine.'

Chapter Fourteen

Pisces: *If it's your birthday this week you're in for a big surprise. The number two signifies bad luck today.*

'Slut Helpline?'

'Happy Birthday, minger! And can I just say you're looking older, I didn't realise crows had feet that big!'

'If anyone asks, I'm thirty-one, OK.'

Sam as usual salvaged the situation 'Happy Birthday, Ames. You will always look twenty-one to me, so take no notice of Liv. Your present is on your desk, by the way.'

'Bless you, Sam. They look very phallic, now let me guess?' I laughed because I just knew it would be two red candles. Sam had bought me candles for the past two birthdays.

'For your love corner, Ames.'

'Thanks. I'm afraid I will have to kiss you in public for these.'

'Don't slip your tongue in or Mr P might fire me!' Sam joked.

Liv's extension flashed up again.

'Birthday Slut Helpline?'

'I beg your pardon, Amy?'

'Shit, I mean sorry, Mr Parkinson.' I hadn't seen him come out of his office and sit at Liv's desk.

'I just popped out to say Reception has just called and there is a package downstairs for you.'

He was smiling. I knew he had wanted to know what caused such hilarity when Liv or I answered our phones and now he knew. I also knew that the package in Reception would be flowers from Mr P as usual. He really was very sweet.

I took the lift down just the one floor as I was rebelling against fitness again this week, and made my way to Reception. In front of me was the largest bunch of yellow roses I had ever seen in my life. Yellow roses, my favourite; they beat pink or red any time. I was very surprised as Mr P usually got me a general, mongrel bunch. I then got a lurching feeling in my stomach. The only person who knew I liked yellow roses was James Crook. Oh, and Carl now, of course.

My heart then started to pound even harder as I suddenly remembered fleetingly mentioning to the false Declan that I really liked the hotel reception flowers, yellow roses, but no: it couldn't be. I ripped open the envelope faster than I had ripped off his shirt in Room 301.

Yellow roses for a beautiful fish. Happy Birthday. Love Carl.

I was disappointed. I had received a huge bunch of yellow roses from the lovely Carl and I was disappointed? No wonder I was single. By 3 p.m. the receptionist hated me. She would just ring my extension and bark, 'More.' I loved the buzz of receiving flowers at work and on every date I must have slipped that little fact in.

There were lilies from Laurence Smith-Bourchier: *Happy Birthday, Amy. Let's meet again soon.*

There were freesias from my father: *Happy Birthday, Daughter Number Two. Love, Dad xx.*

Christopher and Cordelia even sent a card from Starr & Sun, and of course the obligatory bunch arrived from Mr P with the usual note: *Good work, Happy Birthday from all in Marketing.* I have to say I was completely overwhelmed.

'Helpline for sluts who have never received any flowers ever at work on their birthday!' I trilled when the phone rang the next time.

'If you weren't so old you might be funny,' Liv retorted. 'Just checking if you want eggs with your chips tonight, sweetness? I'm off now to prepare your sumptuous feast.'

'Yes please. I shall bring a bottle and a sick bag! See you at eight,' I replied chirpily and added, 'I'm really excited, is Brad bringing his new man?'

'Think so. Laters, Ames.'

'Yeah, laters.'

It was refreshing to know that I was meeting up with all my dearest friends tonight and not having to feel the jitters of a first date. At home, I bathed and then slung on my comfiest black trousers and, because it was my birthday, a black silky halter-neck top.

Liv cooking was so out of character, bless her. I pulled together a bouquet for her from the beautiful flowers I had received and rang for a taxi to take me the short distance to Marlborough Avenue. As I went to ring the bell at Liv's flat, Sam flung open the door.

He nodded towards his car that was parked right outside. 'Change of plan, Birthday Girl.'

'I knew Miss Party Pants wouldn't be cooking. Where are we going?' I was really excited as I love surprises. I dumped the flowers inside and got into Sam's car.

As we pulled up outside my favourite restaurant I actually felt a little tearful. Liv might be a raunchy old bag but she was always thoughtful. Here we were at The Curry Castle, where I always got greeted by name and they served the best chicken korma I have ever tasted. Liv came running out to meet us, dressed in a leopard-skin top with her breasts oozing over the top as usual.

'Come with me, my cherub,' she shouted as she dragged me to the back of the restaurant. It was then that I did actually shed a tear because sitting right there was my dear old mucker, Katie Cook.

'I nearly did a video diary saying sorry I couldn't be with you this evening as I was filming in Lanzarote, but thought I'd much rather be here in the legendary Curry Castle with you!'

'Katie, you are a gem, it's so good to see you. You look fab, so brown and you've lost loads of weight.'

'Where's Ice Man?'

'I've left him.'

'Oh God no.'

'I'm fine, Ames. In fact, I'm looking for somewhere to crash for a few weeks.'

'I've always told you Layston Gardens is open to any of my friends. I will obviously need to check whether Penelope will be happy to give up his bed to a Canarian refugee, but I'm sure we can persuade him!'

Anna, Sam, Liv and H all then proceeded to sing 'Happy Birthday' at the top of their voices and it was only 8.30 p.m. I could see this evening turning into a debaucherous affair. How wonderful! I then suddenly realised that somebody was missing.

'Where's Brad?' I asked. He was usually so punctual.

'He's bringing the new boyfriend, so I expect he's preening in front of the mirror as we speak,' giggled Liv.

'Trust him to be accompanied the only night we are all unaccompanied,' Anna put in.

We were well on to our third bottle of wine and poppadums when my mobile bleeped.

It was a text from Brad.

SORRY SO LATE, ON WAY. IF YOU LIKE HIM SAY CHUTNEY, IF YOU DON'T SAY RAITA!

God, that boy was so funny.

'Ready to order, Miss Amy?'

'Yes please. I'll have chicken korma with pilau rice and onion...' But all of a sudden I couldn't concentrate on thoughts of food.

'Ames, are you OK?' Sam looked at me, concerned.

No, I wasn't OK at all, as out of the corner of my eye I had noticed Brad walking through the restaurant door accompanied by none other than the false Declan!

'Hi, sweeties, sorry I'm late. This is Sean. Sean, let me introduce you to the motley crew, starting obviously with the beautiful Birthday Girl herself, aka my good friend Amy Jane Anderson.'

Brad kissed me on the cheek. I didn't know whether to laugh or cry. My heart was beating as fast as that of a frightened bird and that is exactly what I was: a frightened bird. I had not only slept with a gay man; I had slept with Brad's boyfriend. This was dreadful! There was no logic in my thinking. Surely somebody who was gay could not possibly have been so aroused and passionate with me? Why would someone take on a totally different name and seduce me in such a way? He must be one sick person.

'I believe we've already met,' I managed to whisper. 'Never forget a face, me.' I then let out a nervous laugh. Everyone looked at me oddly, as they knew this laugh was reserved purely for flirtation or panic and neither fitted on this occasion.

Sean looked at me as if I was completely mad. Then in his gorgeous Irish lilt he said, 'Amy, Happy Birthday, but you are definitely mistaken about us meeting before. I've been living in America for the past four years and met Brad at a club last week, the day after I flew in.'

I couldn't believe how convincing he was. How dare he be so dismissive! We had made love, God dammit! This was the situation from hell and it needed to be handled carefully. How could he be living such a blatant lie? Poor Brad, I had to let him know what he was dealing with. As the wine flowed I did begin to doubt myself. It was him, it had to be him – same eyes, same hair, same height, same voice – unless he had a double.

'Chutney or raita, sweetie?' Brad asked me.

'Neither, thanks.'

'Oh come on, Amy. You always have either *chutney* or *raita*,' he stressed, thinking I had forgotten his game.

I just couldn't answer: I was lost for words. I vowed to really try and keep my usually quick temper under control and carry on with the evening as normal for Brad's sake. However, the more I drank, the braver I became.

'America? Which part? Disneyland, I expect,' I taunted.

'I live in Sarasota. It has beautiful beaches and plenty of golf courses. I give golf lessons for a living.'

'Amy!' Brad exclaimed, hurt by my attitude. 'Poor Sean, stop interrogating him!'

Every time I fired a question at Sean I'm not sure what I expected back, but I kept looking into his eyes hoping to just maybe get a flicker of recognition. But there was nothing there for me. No feeling whatsoever. How dare he? By the time we had all eaten our dinner I was bursting to confront Sean. Loyal to Brad, I couldn't say anything outright and then I had a cunning plan.

'Let's carry on, chaps,' I said expansively. 'The night is young and Pinks will still be open.'

'You have to be young and nubile or mutton dressed as lamb to get in there,' winged Anna.

'Exactly,' smiled Liv. 'Let's go!'

I was drunk and fuming in the taxi. Luckily H, Liv, and Katie insisted we go in one cab and the boys go in the other. Anna, bless her, had already sicked up her chicken tikka in the alleyway next to the curry house and had decided to walk home as she only lived up the road.

'What is it with you tonight, Ames?' slurred H. 'Brad's boyfriend is drop dead gorge and seems like a really nice guy and you seem to be slating him.'

'Nothing's up, just a bit pissed. Reckon that first bottle must have been Chardonnay.' That explanation was enough to shut everyone up as they had all been on the wrong end of one of my Chardonnay-induced mad moments on one occasion or another.

The two bouncers looked us up and down as we arrived at the neon-fronted club. Liv managed to sidetrack them both by virtually pushing her breasts into their faces, so that Sam, wearing strictly forbidden trainers sneaked through the big black double doors.

'A request for Birthday Girl is obviously required. What do you fancy, my sweet?' asked Sam, who had been momentarily sidetracked by the two semi-naked dancers writhing in a cage next to the D.J.

'It has to be 'Staying Alive' I reckon!' I replied. This was my chance!

'Sean, Sean!' I shouted. He was chatting to Brad intently at the bar. I had to be sure it was the false Declan before I caused any sort of scene. I had to dance with him alone. 'Sean, let's dance, baby!' I dragged him away from Brad and proceeded to the dance floor.

I drunkenly bawled the lyrics over the din while seductively pushing myself against the impostor. I began to undo the top button of his shirt. Brad was quite amused at this performance and the impostor was playing along. Liv, H, Sam, and Katie were beginning to get worried. When I was a party animal,

I was most definitely a tiger! The impostor smelt gorgeous. Just being so close to him brought back memories of writhing around in Room 301. I pushed his shirt back off his shoulders and continued to gyrate against his groin. I continued to shriek the song. I then circled around to his back, pulled his shirt down further, and looked at his left shoulder.

For one small minute I felt sick and sober at the same time. It was bare; there was no shamrock! The music changed swiftly to a dance number and Sean and I were ushered by the girls to a side bar for fear of what I might do next. We luckily all managed to get a seat.

'You can dance, I'll give you that. Not bad at all for a girl,' laughed the impostor.

'So did I ask you what brings you over to sunny England, Sean?'

'Amazingly you didn't,' he said nicely. 'My twin brother is getting married next Saturday and I'm to be his best man.'

'Yes, and I'm going to the evening do,' Brad said proudly.

Sean had now hit the Jameson's in a big way and slurred, 'You must all come to the evening party! An Irish wedding is one not to be missed, to be sure.'

'To be sure,' I hiccuped and then promptly fell backwards off my barstool in shock.

Chapter Fifteen

Pisces: A *familiar face in the crowd? Don't be fooled by that old devil called love.*

The next morning I woke up to my mobile ringing right next to my head. I had a terrible hangover but when I saw it was Christopher I thought I'd better talk to him, as I hadn't been on a date for ages.

'Morning!' he greeted me.

'You're cheerful,' I said resentfully.

'Well, when you're playing cupid to three hundred people you have to try,' he said. 'Now, Ms Anderson. Declan is keen to meet up with you and I thought you would see him before Carl and then you cancelled that and–'

'Slow down, Mr Starr. Right, let's get my love life in some sort of order. Firstly, I would love to meet up with Declan. Secondly, I would like you to turn down Laurence for me. Categorically. His birthday flowers were lovely but I don't think I could ever fancy him or even like him, unfortunately. Oh, and of course there's the lovely Carl.'

'Carl? I spoke to him yesterday and he said he was going to be in touch with you.'

'Oh well, I'm sure he'll call. So all you have to do is set up a date with Declan. Money for old rope, I say. Think I may have to set up my own dating agency before long.'

'You are most definitely a one, Amy Anderson. I'll get back to you as soon as I've got hold of Declan.'

'OK, bye then.'

'I need drugs!' Katie shouted from the spare bedroom.

'Drugs?' I hoped Katie had not got mixed up in the drug scene in Lanzarote.

'You know headache tablets or anything to stop this woodpecker drilling in my head.' I heard her yawn. 'It's nice to be back, Ames. Like the pad, it has a certain karma about it.'

Karma? Being near the volcanic mountains and the sea must have turned the usual matter-of-fact Katie a bit spiritual. How bizarre.

'You ain't seen nothing yet, Ms Cook. I have to introduce you to my frogs!'

'Morning, Gloria.'

'Morning, Jed'

'Rain today, I reckon.'

'Let's hope not, Jed.'

Luckily he had never mentioned the stench of the pond again. With luck he was losing his sense of smell as well as his hearing! Katie looked at me with a quizzical expression.

'Don't even ask,' I warned her.

'I won't,' she smirked. Luckily my friends took my eccentricities in their stride.

'Just look at my little bubbas, bless them, sticking their little heads out of the water to get air.'

'Amy, I think you've lost the plot. I'm also sure it's the wrong time of year for frogs. Perhaps the stench keeps them warm.' In fact, I don't even think they are alive; they are just suspended dead in the sludge.'

Penelope came down the garden to investigate. Stuck his nose in the air, squeaked, and went and pooped in a flowerbed.

'Sure you still want to move in?' I asked.

'Yes, but only temporarily. Don't reckon I can stick with this cold weather for long.'

'Get away with you, it will start warming up in April.'

'We'll see,' Katie replied throwing back her long mane of blonde, wavy hair. 'I shall pop round my mum's this afternoon and pick up my stuff. Oh, and Amy, your behaviour last night was very strange. Do you need to talk to me about anything?'

'I do actually.' I grimaced. 'I think we should have a conference round Sam's later.'

'OK, I'll see you there. Call you in a bit.'

My mobile was flashing up the voice message sign when we went back inside. It was Christopher again. 'Good news. Declan wants to take you racing, he's been invited to a meeting at Ascot, in a private box!'

The real Declan, at last! He had looked gorgeous in his picture and a day at the races would be such fun. I suddenly felt really excited. I felt both hungover and apprehensive as I walked along the river path to Sam's flat. I guessed the gang would probably be annoyed that I hadn't confessed about false Declan in the first place.

Sam opened the door. I went through to the lounge and immediately flopped down on to one of his comfy red sofas. 'Jesus, there must be at least thirty candles alight in here!' I squealed.

'Well, I felt that we needed a calm environment for you to tell us about the trauma that was so obviously affecting your mood last night.'

H, Katie, and Liv were sitting opposite me in a row on beanbags. They looked like a jury. Anna was still so hungover she apparently hadn't made it out of bed. Bless Anna, she suffered as greatly with her hangovers as she did with her bowels. Thank goodness Brad wasn't here. He was spending the day with Sean in Brighton.

'Rosehip or raspberry, girls?'

'Now if you were saying red or white, that would be more appropriate as it's the weekend,' Liv piped up. 'After last night, I feel that hair of the dog is most definitely required.'

'No, we need to have a clear head so that we can make a correct analysis of Ms Anderson's case,' he reproached her.

'I'm not sure I want to tell you,' I muttered guiltily.

Two glasses of red later (Sam was easy to bully) and I was feeling far more relaxed. I had managed to keep off the subject of Declan by discussing my birthday presents and how Katie wanted to redecorate my perfectly nice spare bedroom and paint it red.

'It's a grounding colour, Amy, please don't question me,' she interrupted.

'I thought I'd slept with Sean,' I suddenly announced.

'You what?' The gang shouted in unison.

'What do you mean, you thought you had?' said Liv.

'How can you not know? I know you can be reckless sometimes, Ames, but you have to explain this one,' H scoffed.

I sat and told them the whole story of the hotel and me thinking I was with the real Declan. I apologised for not having confided in them before, but explained that I thought they would be worried about me. Throughout my confession there were gasps and the odd comment from Liv that I was a lucky cow. I was quite worn out by the time I had blurted it all out but felt relieved that I had no secrets from them now.

'What do I say to Brad?' I finished up.

'You have to tell him,' Sam advised. 'So that he can keep an eye on you at the wedding.'

'You still think I should go then, knowing that his twin brother, who I shagged two weeks ago, is the one getting married?'

'There is no doubt that you must go, Ames.' put in the usually rational H. 'False Declan has to see you. Imagine his face! There are too many rats who get away with murder in this world.'

'The only thing is,' I continued, 'since it happened I can't get him out of my mind.'

'You'll be fine,' H soothed. 'We will all be there to hold your hand. You have to realise what a bastard he is, then you can get on with your search for Mr Right.'

'I actually agree,' Sam said strongly. 'And afterwards, you have to promise me you'll see Carl again. He sounds lovely.'

'I promise.' Confession was definitely good for the soul. I felt so much happier.

'How about you take Carl?' Sam went on

thoughtfully. 'You know he's already good at weddings and it will help to boost your morale.'

'Fab idea! Sam, you are not just a pretty face,' Liv said.

'I don't think I was even as nervous as this when I left to take my driving test,' I wailed to H.

'It'll be fine, hon. We'll all look after you.'

'Yeah,' promised Katie. 'It's going to be a real laugh, all of us at a posh hotel getting pissed at your ex-lover's expense.'

'Katie, that's terrible. Don't let Brad or especially Sean hear you speaking like that.'

It was still light as I walked the short distance home from Sam's flat. I felt exhausted after my late night, but decided Brad needed enlightening on the whole sorry situation as soon as possible. I called him on his mobile and asked him to pop round that evening.

The never judgmental Brad took my confession well, although he thought it best not to tell Sean yet as they were in the early stages of their relationship and in his words,

'I don't want to put him off, thinking my best friend is a slapper!'

'Not that his brother is a complete charlatan?' I questioned.

Penelope actually excelled himself at this moment because he lifted his tail right in front of Brad and promptly let out one of his silent but deadly farts.

'Well done, darling,' I crooned and stroked him. 'Your timing is perfect.'

'You're a bitch and your cat is a bastard, I'm going home,' Brad snapped and stormed off, but then a few minutes later my phone beeped through a text message.

LUV YOU REALLY. WILL LOOK OUT 4 U ON SAT Bx

SHIT OFF, I replied, just to show my appreciation and the fact that Amy and Brad were back to normal. H, Katie, Liv, Sam, and myself got off the train at Paddington and headed to join the taxi queue outside the station. It was a chilly March evening and it had just started to rain. I wasn't sure if I was shivering with cold or with fear, as I was within minutes of seeing false Declan again.

We swaggered into The Langdon Hotel and were impressed by its grandeur. Brad had been there the whole day. The rest of us strutted in our finery towards the Music Room where the reception was taking place. Sadly, Anna had declined as her irritable bowel had kicked in while she was in the garden centre earlier and she was feeling too bloated to travel, bless her.

Carl was arriving at 9 p.m. as he said he had a meeting to attend first. I couldn't think what sort of meeting he would go to on a Saturday night but didn't question him, as I was so glad he was coming.

H had had terrible trouble dressing me for this forbidding encounter. I must have pulled every single item of clothing out of my wardrobe. She wouldn't let me buy anything new as she said it would be wasting money on bad rubbish. I eventually settled on the black dress, fake diamonds, and kitten heels that I had graced The Holly in.

'I feel sick. I should have had a drink before I arrived,' I moaned, knowing full well that everyone had abstained on my behalf, because a drunk Amy Anderson on a mission was actually quite terrifying. 'What do I say? What do I do when I see him?' I was panicking now.

'Sam, can you deal with her please,' begged Katie.

Everyone sighed with relief, as they knew that the calm and sensitive Sam would soon put me at ease.

First, he told me to stick out my tongue and put some Bach Flower Remedy on it.

'Yum, that tastes like brandy,' I ran my tongue around my gums. He then made me shut my eyes and massaged my temples with his forefingers. He finished this fine healing performance by brushing my lips with his and that was it.

'Sam Clark, you will make someone a wonderful husband one day, you know,' I said dreamily.

'Yeah, yeah, now get in there and behave, we're late.' I think he was actually blushing.

We entered the Music Room and there must have been at least a hundred and fifty people in there. It was smoky, it was noisy, and there was an Irish band strumming out a ditty in the corner. People were dancing, yahooing, drinking and having fun. Sean was right: the Irish sure knew how to party. Brad saw me and came hurrying over.

'Princess, you look beautiful, and just look at Sean. Isn't he just *the* most gorgeous creature?'

Of course I thought he was gorgeous, he was the spitting image of the brother I had slept with. However I just sweetly replied, 'Yes, Brad, he's gorgeous.'

'On a serious note, Princess, are you ready for this?'

'As I'll ever be.'

I didn't want to look out for the false Declan; I couldn't face it just yet. Liv was at the bar beckoning me over.

'I've got you a Jameson's, a large one, obviously!'

After two of the same I felt fine. I had kept facing into the bar and had met an assortment of people. An Irish uncle took great delight in telling me that he'd always had a thing for the fuller-figured English girl and I found this quite amusing until I heard the aunt he was with seethe that if he looked at my breasts again she would feckin give him a fuller face. None of my clan had taken their eyes off me for one minute, for fear of an emotional eruption.

When Grandpa Ferret – well, that's what it sounded like – asked if I fancied being swung round by the oldest swinger in town how could I possibly resist? The band was having a break and 'The Birdie Song' was blaring out from the disco. H, Liv, Katie, and Sam all held their breath as I squirmed my way through the crowd to the dance floor. Brad was too busy with his staged dance routine to care. Grandpa Ferret was actually quite agile for an eighty-year-old.

'I'm so proud of my handsome Kieran,' he panted, twirling me around. We've been trying to marry the little eejit off for years.'

He then started to spin me round by both hands. The effects of the whiskey, combined with dizziness from one twirl after another, caused me to topple right off one of my kitten heels. The pain in my ankle was intense. I shut my eyes for what seemed like seconds and opened them to lots of worried faces looking down at me.

'Oh my God, she's passed out.'

'Princess, Princess, oh my God, call an ambulance. Is there a doctor in the house?'

Brad shrieked dramatically.

And then the voice that I had wanted to hear for weeks soothed, 'It's OK, I'll carry her to our room; she can recover there. Sinead, darling, I'll just be a minute.'

'OK my love, see you soon.'

Thank heaven for friends like Brad, H, Katie, Liv, and Sam. They didn't run after this man taking me to his room, his bridal suite no less. They just left me to settle the score that had to be settled. With his strong arms around me I felt very safe. He had the same aftershave on he had worn in Room 301. I thought the name Kieran suited him better than Declan, gave him more of a boyish charm. I looked up at him from the huge queensize bed. He was very calm.

'Amy, this is a shock. Sean said he had invited some friends of his new partner, but if I had known it was you I would have told him to take back his invite.' He saw the hurt look on my face. 'Oh, I'm sorry, babe, that just came out so wrong. What I meant to say was what I did was wrong and wouldn't want you to have to see me with Sinead.'

My emotions were running high. Here I was in an amazing bridal suite with one of the sexiest men I had ever met and he had just married somebody else. I remembered reading an article in a magazine once stating that however badly a man had treated you, you should retain your pride and dignity. I also remembered Liv reciting, 'Revenge is a dish best served cold.'

So what did I do? I proceeded to slap the beautiful Kieran Docherty around the face as hard as I could and howl like a baby. He carried on as if I had just stroked his face with a feather.

'Oh, beautiful sweet Amy, don't cry.'

I was still lying on the bed as my ankle was very painful and looked up at him. Despite everything a surge of pure lust went through my body.

'I'm fine, I'm fine, in fact my boyfriend will be here in a minute.' I suddenly thought of Carl and wondered where the hell he was.

'Boyfriend? That makes me feel so much better.'

'So much better? You never cease to amaze me, Kieran, you really do. I didn't meet him until after what happened, hard to believe but I do have some morals,' I slurred. 'Right, I want to get out of here. I want to go home. You've had your fun.'

I attempted to struggle to my feet. All six-foot-four of Kieran looked down at me. His eyes found mine and he gently stroked a tear from my cheek. He was so beautiful I could hardly bear to look at him for fear of pulling him down to kiss me with those full, passionate lips. How could I be doing this? That poor girl downstairs had just married him and I wanted to feel him inside me of me again with an intensity that I had never ever experienced before.

His arms were resting on my shoulders now. It was as if some strange force had taken over my body. There was no reason within me. My morals had flown away. I felt no remorse. In fact, at that precise moment there was nobody else in the world apart from Kieran and me.

I whispered, 'I want you right here, right now.'

Kieran just nodded and pushed me back on to the bed. 'We have to be quick,' he murmured.

It was my turn to nod. He lifted my dress up to reveal my black lacy stocking tops, pushed my black lacy G-string aside, and slowly began to rub himself against me. I gasped with pleasure and then his lips met mine. I thought I was going to explode. He entered me very gently and then started to thrust his gorgeous being into me. I grabbed his arse and pulled him harder against me. I was so, so wet and he so hard. We came together within minutes. I was whimpering like a dog. I had never experienced an orgasm of such intensity ever before.

'Oh, Amy, I am so bad,' he whispered, as he pulled himself away from me.

'I have to see you again,' I replied, still not believing what was happening or what I was saying.

'That is going to be difficult.'

'Obviously,' I said indignantly.

'Amy, listen to me for one second. It's going to be difficult because I'm emigrating to America. I miss Sean. My wife and I have both got work over there. We want a fresh start.'

I think it was the word wife that did it. I ran to the bathroom and promptly threw up.

Chapter Sixteen

Pisces: *A surprise revelation helps you see the light today. Don't hide your feelings to save somebody else's.*

I woke up in my own bed with a very sore ankle and a very sore head. Katie heard me stirring from the next room.

'Ames, are you OK, sweetness?'

'How can I possibly be OK?' I said sulkily, feeling extremely sorry for myself.

'I've met the man of my dreams who is married and on a plane as we speak. I've acted like a complete whore and do you know what the worst thing is? The worst thing is that I think I love him.'

'Don't be so bloody ridiculous,' Katie retorted.

'How do you know what I'm feeling?'

'Oh Amy, we've been here before. You have to get out of this pattern. Kieran Docherty is one of life's bastards. He will continually shag his way through his life and not care about the destruction he causes. You were just sex to him, pure a 100 per cent unadulterated lust. Can you imagine being his poor wife? Can you imagine just how she would feel if she found out about last night?'

'Thanks, Kate, thanks a bloody lot. You're

supposed to be making me feel better.'

'I just want you to see sense, to put this whole episode behind you. You are so lovely and you deserve so much better than somebody like him.'

My mobile beeped with a text message. I looked at the screen, wistfully hopefully it was from Kieran, even though he didn't even have my number. It was from Carl. In the entire goings on I had completely forgotten about Carl meeting me last night.

BABE, SO SORRY RE LAST NIGHT, MEETING RAN OVER. CALL YOU LATER.

'See? Even the nice ones of this world blow me out. That's it! From now on I'm being strong and I'm going to play hard to get with any man,' I said in true drama queen fashion.

'What, you mean you're going to let the mobile ring twice before answering?'

Katie sniggered.

'You are a tosser, Katie Cook, and I'm going back to sleep to try and forget any of this has happened.'

Right on cue, Penelope appeared in the doorway. He could sense my mood. He jumped up on the bed and began purring, settled down on my stomach and sweetly put his paw on my cheek.

'There you go, Ames, at least sex-change cat loves you!' Katie said putting her head around the door.

I had to smile. 'Your new landlady is in dire need of a bacon sarnie. So stop your cheek and get down to that kitchen.'

The day continued with me eating my bodyweight in carbohydrates, plus several dozes on the sofa. Just as I was in the middle of a lovely dream about me and Kieran getting married my mobile rang.

'Heh, babe.' I really wasn't in the mood for talking to anyone and sighed out loud. 'Look, I am really sorry about last night. Let me come over later and make it up to you.'

'I'm not sure. I'm feeling really tired,' I said rather snottily and yawned. 'Last night was really heavy and I could do with a night in.'

Carl, however, was not deterred. 'I tell you what, Ms Bass-ey,' he said cosily.

'I let you down last night and feel so bad. How about I bring some ingredients round to yours and cook you a nice dinner? We can just chill and watch telly if you like.'

That sounded quite a good plan. I softened somewhat. Carl was so sweet. I would give him a chance. After all, I had really enjoyed myself with him at his cousin's wedding.

'The show commences at seven,' I told him.

He laughed. 'Will Katie need feeding as well?

'Oh, bless you. No, she's staying with a friend of hers in Winchester tonight.'

'Cool. OK. See you then, babe.'

I continued to doze on and off on the sofa until Carl arrived. As I went to the door to let him in I took a peek in the mirror. God, I looked like a bag of fleas. My hair was sticking up all over the place, my eye make-up had smudged and my clothes were all creased.

'Go in and grab yourself a drink. I need to have a quick wash and brush up,' I shouted as I ran up the stairs to the bathroom. Penelope smirked at me as I passed him stretched out on the bed. 'I know, Pen, he's not the one or I would have made more of an effort,' I whispered.

When I eventually came downstairs twenty minutes later, there were amazing cooking smells wafting from the kitchen. Carl had found his way round my house with ease. He had even laid the dining-room table, complete with flower (yellow rose, of course) and a candle. I suddenly started to feel all mushy towards him. How many other men would make such an effort? He was indeed worthy of his Piscean badge.

'Dinner is served, ma chérie!'

Within one hour or thereabouts, Carl had conjured up the most amazing chicken curry with all the works, fantastic fluffy rice and my favourite Peshwari nan. It was just what I needed to feed the hangover that was still lingering from the night before like smog in my head.

'You are such an angel. Thanks so much, Carl.' I looked straight into his big brown eyes and suddenly thought of false Declan again. Tonight had confirmed my harlot status. There I was, shagging last night, not just any man but a groom hot from the altar. And now here I was, already thinking about shagging yet another man. I was a serial shagger!

'Amy?' Carl said softly. 'About last night.'

A feeling of panic went through me. Maybe Carl had been there after all, watching in the wings. Maybe he had followed us up to the Bridal Suite and realised what I had been doing.

'I'm really sorry that I let you down. I go to these meetings quite regularly, you see, and we were all chatting at the end and time just ran away.'

I interrupted. 'Carl, it really wasn't a problem. It

wasn't as if I was alone, was it? Anyway, what sort of meeting was it?'

'It was a church meeting actually.'

'Oh,' I replied, almost choking on my chutney. Religion isn't really my bag. In fact, the mere sight of a Christian fish on the back of anyone's car evokes hysterical laughter in me and Anna. The main reason for this is that a girl I used to work with stole one from the church and gave it to her mother as a gift! What a Christian act! One day we saw a particularly shiny one on a Robin Reliant.

'I wonder if they ever have a crash with all that godly protection?' Anna piped up just as the old boy driving the Robin Reliant swerved violently and took off our front bumper. Despite the impact, we were laughing so much that Anna actually did wet herself. From that day forward we agreed to keep a wide berth from Christian fish adorned vehicles.

'I attend church once a week plus weekly meetings,' Carl went on.

'Oh right,' I slurped another glass of wine down in one. He must have noticed my expression.

'Do you have a problem with that, Amy?'

'Problem? God, no, it takes all sorts and if you are a churchgoer then that's fine by me,' I lied. I was now feeling a bit drunk and began to see the funny side. 'Nun or none?' I shrieked hysterically. 'Pope or poke?'

But Carl wasn't laughing. We finished our curry in silence. He let out a long yawn. Trying to lighten the situation, I moved round the table and gave him a big hug and kiss on the cheek.

'Thanks so much for cooking for me, it really was

the most delicious curry,' I murmured.

'I'm really tired, Amy, I'd better go. Work tomorrow and all that.'

My serial shagger status resumed as I began to urge Carl to stay. 'I promise not to snore. Come on, come up to bed with me.'

'Amy, I have something else to tell you.'

I put on my best Irish accent. 'Forgive me, Father, for I have sinned.'

'Amy, that really isn't funny. Just listen for a second. What I have to tell you is that I don't believe in sex before marriage. Do you think you could cope with that?'

I didn't even have to think about it. 'To be honest, Carl, I don't actually think I could.'

Carl looked quite disappointed as he got up from the table. Instead of feeling let down my humour got the better of me.

'I suppose a blow job before you go is out of the question then?'

I pulled back the front curtain and watched my real-life Christian fish walk down the path. I started to laugh out loud. I had been dumped for a few things in my time but never before for God.

Chapter Seventeen

Pisces: *No more rain! The solar set-up is offering you a glimpse of something interesting, which is closer to hand than you think. Keep your feet on the ground. Money doesn't always bring happiness.*

I awoke to the rain beating against my window on this particular Saturday morning. I hadn't had a very good night as Penelope had jumped onto my bed at 1 a.m. He was soaking wet and had decided to sit on my face to warm himself. I had also heard a lot of noise coming from Jed's at 2 a.m., which was very rare. Normally, every night on the dot after the ten o'clock news I heard the familiar sound of his slow walk to bed on his creaky stairs.

Maybe he had been taken ill in the night or, worse still, what if burglars had got in? It was weird that although we barely conversed I felt strangely close to him. I suddenly felt guilty about the smell of the pond. Jed was a good, unassuming neighbour and all I had to do to make him happy was clean out the pond, and yet I could never be bothered.

I went downstairs to make myself a cup of tea and give Penelope his breakfast to shut up his squeaking. I looked out at the soaking wet garden and thought I'd make a quick pond-dash to check on frog progress and stench levels. The sight of me might encourage Jed to come out and do his, 'Morning Gloria,' sequence so I could check if he was OK.

Good, the rain had subsided. Looking particularly gorgeous in pink fluffy dressing gown, trainers, and a pair of grey knickers holding my hair up, I sped down to the pond.

'Morning, Gloria!'

Jed wasn't sounding as gruff as usual. I didn't glance up, as the ritual didn't actually involve this.

'Morning, Jed.'

Laughing to myself firstly as I was strangely thankful that he was OK and secondly that he couldn't say, 'Looks like rain,' as it was now pissing it down again, I was amazed when Jed continued.

'Gloria, sorry to catch you unawares in your garden.'

It wasn't Jed's voice I was hearing. Standing rigid with shock, I listened while the youthful voice continued.

'I'm afraid that my grandfather was taken ill and passed away last night and I thought you should know.'

I looked up. Over the fence was a vision of complete six-foot loveliness. He had cropped brown hair and beautiful blue eyes, with to-die-for lashes. Water was now dripping off the lovely lashes down onto his nose and then to his friendly, kissable mouth. I was suddenly overcome with emotion. I didn't know if this was due to the sadness of losing the lovely Jed, the presence of the heart-stopping sex god in front of me or the severe embarrassment of standing in front of said sex god in dressing-gown and pant headdress.

I burst into tears.

'Oh, Gloria, please don't cry,' Grandson Jed said softly. 'He was an old man and he just died peacefully in his sleep.'

I then managed to come out with one of my usual nervous blurts. 'My name's Amy, not Gloria. I'm very sorry about your grandad. I'm very sorry about the pond as well and I really must go inside because I'm soaking wet and I'm semi-naked. The pond smells and not one frog poked his head up to say hello.'

'Amy, calm down, it's OK,' Grandson Jed soothed.

I managed to compose myself as much as a girl could wearing a pair of grey knickers on her head.

'Will you let me know when the funeral is?'

'Of course I will. I'll be staying here for a couple of weeks to sort everything out. Oh, and Amy?' He stopped and smiled. 'Grey suits you, by the way!'

I walked back inside and started to cry again. Without realising it Jed had been a really important part of my life at Layston Gardens and I would genuinely miss him.

'Wonder what it is Grandson Jed wants to talk to you about?' Brad enquired in the car on the way back from the funeral a week later. Despite his rudeness about my poor old neighbour, Brad had also become attached to him in a funny sort of way.

'No idea. Maybe he realises that he's met the woman of his dreams,' I joked.

For some reason, because of Jed's unkempt appearance I had imagined his house to be messy and dirty. When Grandson Jed opened the door I was amazed. As with my house, the front door opened straight on to the sitting room. It was full of beautiful antiques, including a magnificent grandfather clock in the corner. Everything was spotless and there were loads of framed photographs adorning every possible surface.

'Come in, come in.'

I could smell fresh coffee and could hear clattering coming from the kitchen.

'It was a really lovely service. Are you feeling OK?' I enquired.

Grandson Jed chose to lighten things up. 'I didn't recognise you with your clothes on,' he teased gently.

I went bright red. He was obviously feeling all right.

'Coffee, Amy?' A female voice piped up from the kitchen.

'Sit down and make yourself comfortable,' said my host. 'I'll just give Jackie a hand.'

There was a side table next to me and on it was a wedding photo in a silver frame. The groom was an instantly recognisable Jed, with large pointed nose, thick eyebrows, and a mop of black curly hair. I had always known my neighbour with his unruly mop of white hair and miserable face, so it made me smile to see him looking so dashing and happy. I then looked at his wife and my eyes widened. She looked amazingly like me: same hair, same nose, even the same smile. It was spooky. I picked up the photo to have a closer look, when Jackie walked into the room. Grandson Jed followed, carrying a tray with coffee and biscuits.

Jackie's long blonde hair was accompanied by blue eyes and she had a figure to die for. Her smart black dress accentuated every curve.

'Ah, the infamous Amy,' she greeted me. 'How good to meet you at last. From how Grandpa used to describe you I thought you'd be taller, slimmer somehow.'

Not only did I detest her from that moment on, I was also intrigued that Grandpa Jed had even brought me up in conversation at all.

'I guess you take sugar?' she said unkindly.

'Sweet enough, thanks,' I replied through gritted teeth.

'Jon, hadn't you better just get on with the job in hand so that Amy can go home? Maybe she can even consider cleaning out that stinking pond of hers. Poor Grandpa, that vile pond of yours used to annoy him so terribly.'

I wondered what an earth this awful creature was on about. I looked at Jon questioning. 'Oh, so you do have a name?' I smiled at him. 'I've been referring to you as Grandson Jed since our first meeting.'

Jon smiled back. He almost seemed flirty, or was I imagining it? Probably imagining it. I guessed any company other than Bitch from Hell was light relief.

'Yes, sorry, Jonathan McDonald, that's me, but everyone calls me Jon. I see you were looking at Grandpa's wedding photo,' he went on. From what my mum tells me, he used to be a bit of a lad in his youth. He never really got over my gran dying, to be honest. She died of a heart attack at sixty-four and it knocked him for six. From what I remember of her she was full of life and always very kind.' He added quietly as if it was almost a secret, 'Her name was Gloria, you know.'

His beautiful blue eyes suddenly filled with tears and I had an urge to give him a big hug.

'Yes, yes, now get on with it, Jon,' Bitch from Hell nagged. 'Show her what the silly old bugger wrote.'

Jon looked at Bitch from Hell then looked at me, in fact, he stared at me.

'Grandpa was right,' he said. 'It *is* uncanny. You look very much like my gran when she was young. This explains so much, why he called you Gloria and also the contents of this letter.' He handed me a yellowed, crumpled bit of paper. 'Here, read this. We found it yesterday when we were clearing out Grandpa's things.'

The piece of paper was entitled, When My Time Has Come. It was written in a shaky hand and the contents left me speechless.

I have always believed in fate and I always believed in my beautiful Gloria and knew one day I would meet her again. Her silky brown hair and sparkly blue eyes, her fun-loving nature and loud uncontrollable laugh, her ability to make me smile with just the jaunty way she said good morning. Yes, Gloria has come back to me and is living next door!

I read on, completely bemused.

To this end, for making me so happy in my last days at Layston Gardens, in giving me the will to live when at times I was a very sad old man, I bequeath the money I have saved in the blue and white teapot under the kitchen sink to this beautiful being. The beautiful being who I was blessed enough to have met and spoken to almost every day since she moved into number 21. I never wanted to trouble her free, young spirit, therefore please ensure she gets this letter and this gift with all of my thanks. Maybe she can put it towards cleaning out that bloody pond of hers!

I didn't know how to react. Jed had said nicer things in this letter than any man had said to me in the whole of my whole life. I was deeply touched. He thought that I was his beloved Gloria. I was also completely touched by the honesty of the lovely Jon. He didn't have to show me this letter. He could have just thrown it away and I would never have known. From the tone of Blonde Bombshell I could imagine that this would have been her suggestion.

Jon handed me a brown sealed envelope. 'This is for you. I've checked with the solicitor and it's OK for you to have it now.'

I had a massive urge to rip open the envelope there and then but didn't want to look greedy. 'I am completely overwhelmed,' I told him sincerely. 'I had no idea. Jon, I feel like a fraud. I never constructively set out to make your grandfather happy.'

'Don't be so silly. If you made Grandpa happy in his last years just by being there, then that's enough for me. We live in Scotland so have never spent enough time with him. I'm glad you made such an impact on him.' He smiled again. 'Just enjoy his gift, Amy.'

Just then the grandfather clock chimed six.

'I'm sorry to rush off but I must go home and get ready,' I announced.

'Going somewhere nice?' enquired Jon.

I blushed again. The mere presence of this man made me wobbly. I didn't want to answer his question as I didn't want him to know I had a date, even though he was obviously with this awful woman, Jackie, and it would make no difference whatsoever.

'Oh just out for a drink.'

But Jon wouldn't let up. 'With someone nice, I hope?'

'He's OK,' I said shyly, not wanting him to think that I had had to resort to a dating agency in my search for Mr Right.

'Have fun then, and don't do anything I wouldn't do.' He winked.

Bombshell grimaced and I hot-footed it back next door to spill the news in Penelope's furry ears.

I couldn't wait to open the envelope, which in shaky scrawl on the front just read: For Gloria and her cat, No 21. It had obviously been opened and resealed. I bet Jackie just had to know how much I was getting. It certainly didn't feel like it was bulging with cash. It probably contained a £20 note to buy a pump for the pond and some cat food for Penelope I thought. At that moment, my cat was seated at the far side of the room, assuming the playing-the-cello position as he surreptitiously washed his bits. I was now getting that wonderful feeling I always get when opening my birthday cards. Suddenly, the doorbell rang, jerking me back into reality. A folded cheque fell to the floor.

'Prinny, only me.'

I heard the dulcet tones of Brad and let him in, in a complete state of excitement.

'Oh my God, oh my God, Brad. You will never guess what has just happened!' I hurriedly explained the whole story to Brad, including how Jon was drop dead gorgeous but sadly lived in Scotland and had a bitch for a girlfriend.

'So how much did he leave you then?'

In my excitement to get the story out I had forgotten all about the cheque. By now, Penelope was sitting on it, finishing off his ablutions. Brad moved him aside with his toe and knelt down to pick it up. He flicked off a cat hair or two and then turned to me.

'Ames, sit down, sweetie. I've got a shock for you. Cinderella, you *shall* go to the ball. Your darling deceased neighbour has only gone and left you £10,000!'

I looked at the cheque, screeched, picked up a bemused Penelope, squeezed him tight, and whirled him round the room. I then grabbed Brad and began to dance with him. Then started squealing and running up and down on the spot.

'If you'd cleaned the bloody pond out he might have left you a million,' Brad said.

I started to laugh uncontrollably. 'I just can't believe it. What on earth shall I spend it on?'

'The least you could do is buy me a drink for being your bestest friend.'

'I tell you what – let's open the birthday champagne you bought me,' I said excitedly.

After consuming two heady glasses each, while discussing what I would spend my windfall on, I then screeched again. 'Shit, oh no! I'm supposed to be at Waterloo Station right now meeting a new date! Oh God, I feel so terrible letting him down'

'Prinny, we can have some fun with your new mon,' Brad sang.

'But, Brad, he's a new contender, a Virgo.'

'Prinny, if he was a Scorpio I might have let you go but I am gagging for some more champagne. My darling Sean has gone back to Sarasota and I just want to forget my pain and dance the night away with my rich friend. Ring Christopher, tell him Penelope has cut his paw or something.'

'I am so destined to be single at this rate,' I wailed.

'Single but almost rich. Now pass the poo, sweetie, and get on that phone!'

By midnight Brad and I were still bopping round the room to 'Dancing Queen'. I had put some yellow wool over Penelope's ears so he made the perfect Agnetha. The kitchen mop passed as Benny. Abba was in my front room. The world seemed perfect and then Brad started to cry. Not just a few tears down his face, but great racking sobs.

'Darling, what on earth is the matter?'

'It's Sean,' he choked. 'I think I love him and he's had to go back to Florida to carry on teaching his golf and I don't know what I'm going to do without him.' He started sobbing again.

'Brad Sampson, you are not going to be without him for one single minute longer. I am ringing the airport and you are getting on a plane first thing tomorrow. In fact, I'm coming with you.'

Brad was so excited. 'Amy Anderson is rich, crazy woman who treats her friends like gods. She's an angel and I love her.' He then promptly threw up into my yukka plant and passed out on the floor.

Chapter Eighteen

Pisces: *Race cards at the ready! Pisceans are picking their way through the social accumulator.*

I was knee-deep in work at the office when my phone rang. It was Christopher, and he was cross with me for standing up Mr Virgo.

'Now Amy,' he began, but I stopped him right in his tracks.

'Christopher, please don't give me a lecture. I know it was very naughty of me and I am genuinely sorry,' I paused slightly. 'However, I've thought about it and am actually not that bothered about dating a Virgo. I've got a feeling that they'll be far too particular for me, so please don't bother to rearrange.'

Christopher's voice lightened slightly. 'OK, Ames, if you're sure.'

I continued breezily. 'I promise that I will definitely meet Declan. I've written everything down and my day off is booked. April twenty-ninth at 1 p.m., outside Barclays Bank in Ascot High Street. Although,It's probably going to be busy so I'm a bit worried about recognising him. I know he's good-looking but I can't remember his face now.'

'Cordelia will be sending you your photograph as

usual.'

'God, it's so long since I've been on a date I've forgotten the procedure. Thanks, I'll let you know how I get on. Bye, Christopher, and thanks.'

'Bye, Amy, and please try to enjoy yourself.'

A box at Ascot Racecourse, how grand! I was extremely excited by this, as I love the thrill of horse racing and the excitement of backing a winner. I put the phone down and looked triumphantly across the office at a smirking Liv. She made one of her gurning faces and said haughtily, 'Mail me, minger. I'm too busy and important to talk to you right now.'

Dear Liv,

Meeting real Declan next week. Box at Ascot racecourse no less. Let's hope he looks like the false one. Quite excited actually.

Dear minger,
Bitch, dead jealous. Hope he shags like him, more like!

Dear Liv,
You really are the crudest tart that I have ever met. Put your tits away and get on with some work.

Dear minger,
Shit off and source your big top or Mr Parkinson won't be giving you a frenchie at this year's Xmas do.

This last mail sprung me into action. Not because I wanted to snog Mr Parkinson under the mistletoe but the dating lark had actually been affecting my work of late and despite the fact that I now had a few thousand in my bank account it wasn't quite enough to retire on.

I still wasn't sure what to do with my money. I had paid for Brad to go out to the States and see Sean. His boss at the graphic design firm he worked for was extremely flexible, and agreed for Brad to take some immediate time off. Luckily daylight, sobriety, and a huge hangover curbed my impulse to go with him. It would be too hurtful to risk bumping into the very married Kieran. Although my heart and loins were totally against my decision, my head had won on this occasion.

Brad returned bronzed and starry-eyed. Sean was coming over to see him again in a couple of months. I had tentatively enquired about Kieran and got the information that I didn't want to hear: he had settled into married life well and was enjoying living in America.

'Did he mention me at all?' I enquired, only to get a downturned expression and a hug from Brad. Then I knew that I just had to get on with my search for a new man and forget all about the lovely, but dangerous Kieran Docherty.

I treated the gang to a couple of raucous meals. I also went on a shopping trip with Liv to Harvey Nichols, where we ended up being ejected from the premises. We had decided a drink was necessary to prepare us for the mammoth task ahead. Two bottles of champagne later we left the fifth-floor bar and sang 'Jerusalem' at the top of our voices all the way down to the ground floor in the lift. This didn't cause our ejection. It was the fact that we then proceeded to do very loud impressions of Patsi and Eddie from *Absolutely Fabulous,* with Liv finally knocking over the whole Lancôme display and saying in a very posh voice, 'Oh how churlish of me. I *do* apologise!'

I did want to go on a big holiday this year but had to get my summer launch event out of the way first. Luckily I had sourced my big top for the launch. In fact, I had been working with a fantastic agency called Live Events who had helped me enormously, sorting the rigging of sound equipment and producing a fab stage set and pre-show entertainers without much effort on my part. Mr Parkinson was happy that we were all set for the big day. Life was ticking along; I hadn't had a date for weeks and was actually feeling quite calm about life in general.

April 29th dawned: the day to meet the real Declan. I had bought myself a fantastic outfit with my newfound wealth, including a huge pink hat covered in feathers to match my pink and white flowery dress. Declan had called me on my mobile that morning to check I was still OK to meet outside the bank.

'What are you going to be wearing?' he enquired.

'Just think flamingo and you won't miss me,' I laughed.

It was a warm Spring day. I had taken the train to Ascot and cheerily made my way up Station Hill towards Barclays bank. Recognising Declan immediately, I walked towards him smiling.

He had short brown hair, twinkly green eyes and beautiful teeth. The only thing that let him down was a hairy neck. I cannot bear it if a man has even one stray hair at the back of his collar. It has to be clean cut. There was no sign of an Irish accent, in fact he spoke in a clear, calm voice that made me feel instantly at ease. He had greeted me with, 'All right, bird?'

'Bird?' I exclaimed.

'Flamingo and all that? Never mind.'

I laughed, thankful that, as well as being quite lovely in the flesh, he also had a sense of humour.

'You look sensational,' he continued.

'Thanks.'

I looked down, suddenly feeling shy for a minute. He grabbed my arm affectionately.

'Come on, follow me. I shall give you a quick brief on the day as we walk to the box.'

I felt fantastic as I was whisked across past the bandstand and up to the lifts that would take us up to our dedicated box. Declan informed me that he worked for a printing company and had been invited by a customer with whom he did business. He told me that he had only met a couple of the people who would be there and that he would be by my side all the way. What a sweetheart!

It was a shame it wasn't the Royal meeting, but Victoria Cup Day was evidently a good racing day. I could feel a sort of electricity in the atmosphere, the abundance of hope, expectation, and of placing that winning bet. I was shaky inside at the prospect of meeting Declan's acquaintances, but knowing that I was looking the part helped my confidence.

I was introduced to Crystal Barrett, who had invited Declan. She was the Marketing Director of De Lagers diamond factory. In her early fifties, she was wearing an amazing mandarin-coloured Chanel suit.

Her make-up was immaculate and her auburn hair cut in a trendy, cropped style. I really hoped that I could look as good as her when I reached her age. Again, however, I was fooled by looks.

'Flamingo pink? How last year, dear. Never mind, don't let it affect your day.'

She then swanned off leaving me with my mouth open. Declan had heard every word. He handed me a full glass of champagne, brushed my lips with his, and smiled.

'You look fantastic, Amy. Just ignore her, she's renowned for being a complete bitch. I expect she's jealous of your youth and vitality.'

I felt like I was in the ring, not in a box at Ascot, as the next contender I had to deal with was Barry Croft, a work colleague of Declan's. By now I was on my second glass of champagne, I had not yet eaten and was beginning to feel a bit woozy. Declan was chatting to Mandarin Minger.

'Amy, isn't it?' Barry leered. 'Declan said he was bringing along a filly, but I didn't realise you'd be from such fine stock. Ha, ha!'

He pinched my bum really hard and walked off. Surely there was somebody here who was worth talking to? I decided then that I would concentrate on the runners and riders.

'Five pounds to win on Dancing Penelope please,' I said to the red-suited tote lady. Declan looked at me.

'Amy, Dancing Penelope is 50 to 1. Maybe you should have an each-way bet.'

'On the nose or nothing for me!' I exclaimed, in true punter style.

'They're under starter's orders and they're off!'

I was excited now. I loved the buzz of racing.

'Yes, yes, come on Dancing Penelope, she's going to do it, she's nearly there, yes, get over that line!' I hollered.

Despite the roaring crowd, all of a sudden you could have heard a pin drop in our box. Everyone stared at me as if I'd murdered someone. My eyes darted around and then to the floor.

'Declan?' I whispered.

He was trying not to laugh. 'Don't worry, Amy, but there's another circuit to go. They'll get over it.'

To make matters worse Dancing Penelope eventually hobbled over the line last. I was completely mortified. They did get over it, apart from Mandarin Minger who had a field day sniping at me. I wondered just how Liv would get out of this one. Drink all the free champagne she could lay her hands on, I guessed.

'Declan, babe, fill my glass please.'

I found out on the short taxi ride from the racecourse, that Declan rented a one-bedroom flat in Sunninghill, overlooking the High Street. Thankfully, by the time we got back to his place I had sobered up slightly. The winning-line incident didn't seem half as bad, looking back at it. I felt no remorse that I was staying the night with this gorgeous creature. By now I fancied the pants off him, he made me laugh, and I almost felt safe in his company. He had said, 'Bless you,' on demand and walked on the outside of the pavement beside me, so all in all he was worthy of a stopover.

'You haven't got a spare toothbrush by any chance, have you?' I called out from the bathroom.

'Sure, top right, bathroom cabinet,' Declan shouted through from the bedroom. He then added in a French accent. ''Urry up, my leetle flamingo, I have something to show you!'

I laughed. He was great. Maybe at long last I had found not just a date, but a real boyfriend. Just as I was holding this thought, I pulled open the door to the bathroom and there facing me was a pack of tampons and a flowery make-up bag. My heart started pounding. Two years of living alone? Don't think so, matey! I started to cry with frustration and anger. Scrabbling in the make-up bag I found the darkest lipstick I could find and proceeded to write that he was a cheating bastard across the bathroom mirror.

'Are you OK in there?' the cheater shouted.

I grabbed the tampons, stormed into the bedroom, and threw them at him while shouting in a voice that didn't actually sound like my own: 'Stick them up your arse, you cheating bastard!'

'Amy, hey now, slow down, I can explain!' His voice was wavering and I thought he was going to cry.

'Quit the waterworks, mister. I'm out of here!'

I stormed out, grabbing my pink feathered hat as I went, and rang Brad from my mobile phone claiming a level-one emergency.

Chapter Nineteen

Pisces: *The stars are out in the garden today. Take time to plan some time out.*

The sun was out over Layston Gardens. Katie had gone shopping. Brad and I were having a lovely lazy Sunday afternoon with a couple of bottles of wine.

'Ms Anderson, astrologically I would like a summary of your dating extravaganza, please. I'm finding it hard to believe that you have been given countless men on a plate,' he stopped mid sentence and raised his eyebrow. 'Ooh, Prinny, just imagine.'

'Brad, I really do think you need castrating sometimes.'

'I'm also finding it hard to believe that not one of them is rising in Uranus.'

'God, you're disgusting.' I tried hard to keep my stern face on this one but then burst out laughing. Then, in true Eurovision style, I began to recount my past male encounters. 'Steve Edwards, Aries, 5 points. First date so nothing to compare with. Friendly but no spark. Too boisterous for my liking.'

'Mrs Amy Edwards makes you sound like a farmer's wife,' Brad said.

'Neil Foster, Taurus. One point. Boring, dull. Incestuous relationship with mother.'

'No further comment required,' Brad piped up, taking a massive slurp of wine.

'Kieran Docherty.' I paused. 'Oh my God, I don't even know what star sign he is! I've always thought he was a Gemini because that is what the real Declan is. I'm mortified. When is Sean's birthday?'

'Prinny, the last thing on my mind was Sean's birthday, I can tell you.'

'I have to know. What if he's a Scorpio?'

'He will still be a lying, cheating bastard, that's what he'll be. Now please continue. You are actually interesting me for once this afternoon.'

After more peals of laughter I continued with Kieran's profile.

'Kieran Docherty, sign unknown, eight points. Complete sex god. Can't believe the effect he had on my loins. However, lying, cheating bastard!'

'Prinny, how can you possibly give him eight points? He treated you like poo. On the other hand, I have actually shagged him in essence as his brother looks the same, so let's give him a ten!'

I laughed. 'I feel like a right slapper, reeling them off like this.'

'Keep feeling it, baby!' Brad chuckled. After I'd hit him playfully round the face I continued.

'Carl Peters, Piscean oh yes! Six points. Sexy, loving, romantic. No sex before marriage, however. In love with God. Although, Sam did recently enlighten me that it would be against Carl's religion to believe in Astrology. How funny that he had obviously fallen off the path to righteousness way before meeting me anyway.

Brad ignoring my revelation carried on, 'Amy

Peters, wasn't she a shot putter from years ago?' This boy had an amazing ability to reduce me to tears of laughter.

'I think you must be thinking of Mary Peters. She did the pentathlon. Mind you, goodness knows how you remember her. That was eons ago.' I then went off on a tangent, feeling guilty and shallow about the lovely Carl. 'Oh bless Carl, he was gorgeous. I am an unreasonable cow sometimes.'

'Prinny, my philosophy is if they are not banging your front door down to see you again, then let them go, and, sweetie, face it: Carl won't be banging anything up or down for quite some time!'

Penelope sauntered out of the back door. He gazed coldly at the pair of us laughing, brushed against Brad, leaving hair on his black trousers, lifted his tail, shook it slightly, and then skulked away. Brad started to choke and fan the air.

'That cat is a demon, he has always hated me. He is jealous that I love his mummy.'

'Brad, please leave my pussy alone.'

'Touch your pussy? I'd rather clean out the pond!'

We both then squealed again with laughter.

'Now, Miss Anderson, pretty Piscean, please recommence your list of slapperness.'

I took a slurp of wine and continued. 'Laurence Smith-Bourchier, Libra, 4 points. Nice car, nice restaurant, fat wallet, but ugly, off-puttingly randy and bossy, plus has the sex appeal of a dead dog.'

'Prinny, anyone who dines in the same establishment as Posh 'n' Becks should have been seen again, but hey, it's your call.' He threw his hand back in a camp fashion and took yet another large glug of wine.

'And finally, the real Declan O'Shea, Gemini. Would have been seven points if I hadn't found out in time that he also was a lying, cheating bastard.'

'You really liked him, didn't you, Prin?' Brad was serious for a moment.

'Yes, Brad, I did. And do you know what? I am actually sick and tired of this entire dating lark now. It's time to change the scenery for a while. Fancy a holiday with your ol' mucker Amy A?'

'Is the Pope Catholic?'

And with a chink of glasses the holiday talks commenced.

Chapter Twenty

Pisces: *An eventful day. Love is in the air. All you need to do is stop floating in the dark shallows of gloom. Swim fast to the surface in case you miss this chance.*

Real Declans, false Declans, they could all jump off the edge of the planet for all I cared. From now on, that was it, I was going to ring Christopher and stop this dating lark. I would live a life of single contentment with Pen, the frogs, and my friends. I would have to satisfy myself in the bedroom department and, if I got the urge to breed, Brad would just have to shut his eyes while administering the contents of the turkey baster. At least today was the day of the big top event, so my new life as a celibate career girl could commence in grand style. I had provided everyone with a staff uniform of black trousers and a crisp white shirt with the Jenkins logo on it. Liv was assisting me in registering delegates.

'Liv!' I exclaimed as she teetered into the registration tent. 'What the hell do you think you're wearing?'

'Darling, darling, calm down, you know I don't do trousers at work, especially when there's a male delegate list one thousand strong.'

'You'd have covered more with a handkerchief,' I laughed. Liv always got away with everything. Shortly afterwards the delegates started arriving.

'Your badge, sir, tea and coffee are being served in the red marquee, seminar to commence at ten,' Liv oozed, time and time again.

Live Events, the agency working on project, had done a very good job. Their director, Deirdre, was an amazing character. She smoked forty fags an hour and swore like a trooper at her team. She had bleached-blonde permed hair and wore 1980s power suits even though we were in a field. She would turn round and eff and blind at one of her team, then I would appear and her client voice would be engaged.

'Anything you need, Amy darling, anything, just ask.'

The event team had walkie-talkies to make sure everything was running smoothly.

'Liv to minger, come in please!' I smiled and then cringed, realising that everyone was listening to this and I knew Liv would not hold back. 'Minger, please can you make an announcement and ask if Mike Hunt has come yet?'

At this stage I broke down in hysterics, as did the rest of the team. 'Amy to Olivia, if Mike Hunt had come then I would not be talking to you; I would be dancing on the big top stage. Over and out.'

Luckily Mr Parkinson did not have a walkie-talkie or I think a P45, rather than flowers, would have been on the menu for my next birthday. The day ran smoothly. Clowns were running round handing out drinks at break times, and stilt walkers were chasing suits across the grass. Mr Parkinson was grinning from ear to ear, aided by the constant flirting of Deirdre who was already touting for more business.

The last seminar session had commenced and Liv was obviously getting bored. 'Liv to minger, do you read? Over and out!' She was loving this.

'Event organiser extraordinaire here, reading loud and clear. What's up, Registration Girl?' I chuckled to myself, as I knew this would really wind her up.

'There is a gentleman at the registration desk to see you.' She then whispered, 'Call me on my mobile pronto.'

I quickly called her.

'Is it Mike Hunt?' I chortled.

Liv whispered again, 'Ames, he's bloody gorgeous.'

'Well, who is it? What's his name?'

'He just said it was really important he saw you and that you would know who he was.'

'How very strange. I'm on my way.' I quickly darted into the portaloos that Deirdre had provided to check on the state of my face. Unfortunately, because it was peak season I think the loos had been driven here directly from Glastonbury. The smell made me gag and the mirror was cracked. Hopefully, Mr P had not had to take a pee yet.

I sauntered over to the registration area and could see Liv flirting wildly with the dark-haired stranger. My heart skipped a beat and anger surged through me as I realised exactly who it was.

Chapter Twenty-one

Pisces: *Take off your rose-coloured glasses today or your fishy intuition may fail you.*

'Amy, please give me a chance to explain.'

'How did you know I was here?' I demanded looking around to check nobody from work was near her.

The dark-haired stranger held up a beautiful bunch of yellow roses. 'I wanted to deliver them personally to you in the office but the receptionist told me where your event was so I tracked you down.'

Liv let out a quiet whistle and walked away. I was actually quite chuffed at this open display of affection and his remembrance of my love of yellow roses just from one mention. However, I kept up my calm exterior.

'Declan, you said you were single. I can appreciate maybe a lodger leaving tampons in a cupboard but a woman without her make-up? No way.'

Declan held out his soft hand to me. 'Let's go for a walk, I want to explain.'

The big top was by the side of the Thames. I agreed to hear Declan out, so we walked along the riverbank until we came to a bench. It was a warm May day. A family of ducks swam past, quacking.

'In memory of Cuthbert Camel, oh how he loved to fish here,' I read aloud and laughed, forgetting for one minute the seriousness of the pending conversation.

Declan smiled. 'Amy Anderson, you really are beautiful you know.'

I felt a flutter in my stomach.

'Now hear me out, it won't take long.'

'OK,' I whispered.

'The tampons and make-up bag belonged to my wife.' He took a massive deep breath and I'm sure he was holding back tears. 'Her name was Sally.'

I started to shuffle on the bench.

'They thought they'd caught it early enough.' He faltered. 'The cancer, that is. She died two years ago. I'd actually just started to go through her things and throw them away, but it's a very difficult thing to do. I know it probably sounds silly to you, but it's almost like if you still have something of hers, she may come back and collect it one day. I still imagine her walking through the front door and calling my name. I loved her so much.'

I started to well up.

'Oh, Dec, that's so sad. I do understand totally and I am so, so sorry. What a stupid cow I've been.'

'You weren't to know, Ames. I guess you've been hurt in the past, so you jumped to conclusions. Don't cry, it's OK.'

'Declan, it's not OK at all. I'm mortified that I could have been so childish. I'm surprised you've even bothered to come and find me.'

Declan took my face in his, he had tears in his eyes. 'I came to find you, Amy, because for the first time in two years I feel alive again.' He then kissed me so tenderly it made me cry again.

'Dinner tonight?' he whispered.

I nodded.

Several dinners, a weekend in Paris and a Gucci handbag later, I realised that I actually had a boyfriend. Declan certainly knew how to woo me. Nothing seemed too much trouble where I was concerned. He was always kind and caring and would get his credit card out at every instance. In fact, it almost seemed too good to be true. I disappointed Brad by selfishly putting our holiday plans on hold, but for once I felt as if I belonged in the big grown-up world of dating. Christopher professed himself seriously glad that I'd found a partner but he also seemed curiously sad that I was no longer entertaining him with my comic stories.

'I'll put you in the holding bay for now,' he said.

'You've still got a few more dates in the bag, so just ring if things don't work out.'

'Thanks for the confidence,' I had replied.

The day of the Charity Cancer Ball at Eltan Hall arrived. This was a very important day for Declan as he had instigated the whole event.

'I hope you don't feel awkward with this, Ames,' he had said a month into our relationship. 'I want to do this in remembrance of Sally. It's almost like I can finally let her go, while helping a lot of other people at the same time.'

My Piscean nature had always been drawn towards charities of any kind. In fact, as well as giving to the homeless, I couldn't let anyone stand in the cold without putting some money in their tin regardless of which charity it was. Despite my event-organising skills, Declan didn't want me to get involved in any shape or form.

'I just want you there on the day, looking ravishing, that's all. I do need to ask you a big favour though.'

'Sure, what?'

'I feel really bad asking you,' he faltered.

'Just come out with it, Dec. You've done enough for me in the last month.'

'Basically, I need to pay for the venue up front. The ticket costs will cover the caterers and band but Eltan Hall is such a popular venue that they won't waiver the deposit. I was rather hoping that you might be able to lend me this amount out of your windfall.'

'Is that all? Of course I can, babe. How much do you need?'

'Six grand would be great if you've got it. I'll be able to pay you back virtually straight away.'

'That's spooky: that's exactly how much I've got left.'

'Oh really? Wow, that's great. What I'll do is write you a cheque out of my account now, post-dated for the Monday before the ball. The tickets will all have been sold by then so you can just pay it straight into your account. As it's so close to the event the venue want cash, is that OK?'

'No worries. If I give the bank a call now, I'm sure I'll be able to go in this afternoon and pick it up.'

Declan handed me his cheque. He called me the night before the big event. 'Ames, no time to see you later, sorry. Got to make sure everything is ready. This is just so exciting.'

'Are you sure you don't want any help?'

'No, no, I'll be fine. See you tomorrow: Eltan Hall, 7 p.m. prompt. Oh, and don't forget one important thing.'

'What's that?' I quizzed.

'That I love you,' he said softly, and hung up.

I hadn't heard these three little words strung together for quite some time and they sent me into complete raptures. I rang the gang one by one just shrieking the words. 'He loves me, he loves me. Oh my God, he loves me!'

At 6.30 p.m. the gang and I, beautifully attired in our sparkly evening wear, this included Brad's waistcoat, walked up the impressive drive to Eltan Hall. We were met on the door by a smart-looking porter.

'We're here for the Charity Cancer Ball. My boyfriend,' I paused and turned round to the gang and stated, 'who loves me, by the way.' I turned back to the porter. 'Sorry, my boyfriend is organiser, so we don't have official tickets. He just said to ask for him when we arrived.'

'Cancer Ball?' The porter screwed up his face. 'Sorry, love, it's the Annual Pigeon Fanciers Awards Dinner here this evening.'

'We must have come to the wrong entrance then,' I continued. 'Sorry to have troubled you.'

'This is the only entrance, love. You must have got your dates wrong.' The porter shrugged.

'Ames, please don't tell me you've had a dippy minger moment because you're in *lurrve*,' Liv teased, stressing the love word.

'This is so odd!' I exclaimed. 'I'll call Dec.'

His mobile was off so I tried his home number. The answerphone didn't click in as usual which was strange.

'He phoned me last night to say don't be late, something must be wrong. Bless him, maybe he's terribly upset. Or maybe I've stupidly got the wrong venue.'

Sam took control. 'Let's go round to his flat, something does seem odd here.'

Sam and I got a cab on to Dec's and the others said they'd hop in another one and told us to join them in the nearby Carpenters Arms later.

As the taxi pulled up to Declan's flat, I began to feel afraid. Maybe something terrible had happened to him. This was so unlike him. I pressed the entry buzzer, no answer.

'I'll try one last time.' I said worriedly.

'You won't get an answer from him, duck.'

We looked up. Declan's neighbour was leaning out of her bedroom window, headscarf and rollers abundant. 'He's gone. Surprised you're here, actually Thought he'd be meeting you at the airport.'

'Airport, what are you on about? What do you mean?'

'He went this morning. Gave me his key, said the new tenants were moving in on Sunday. Travelling the world, he said. Lots to see and do.'

Sam held my hand. I put it to my heart, as if somebody had just shot me in it. Then I said calmly. 'Sam, let's get to the pub.'

I didn't cry. I didn't really even discuss anything

with the gang. They let me sit quietly and fed me rum and cokes on a regular basis until I nearly passed out.

Monday morning, however, was a totally different story. Fuelled by a white-hot anger I was on a mission. I headed straight to my bank.

'Can you check a cheque for me, please?' I said abruptly to the spotty clerk.

'Check a cheque?'

'Yes, check a cheque,' I repeated, now wanting to drag the little toe-rag out of his glass cage.

Then, realising I wasn't talking any sense at all to the spotty one, I softened. 'Look, I'm really sorry. I'm in a bad mood and I'm taking it out on you and it's not your fault at all.'

'Are you really, madam? I didn't notice. Now let's start again, shall we?' He smiled a smile that would have melted a thousand hearts. My God, this kid must have had some customer service training.

'Right, OK,' I continued.

'I just need to see if a cheque that I paid into my account for £6,000 last Monday has cleared yet.'

The spotty one tapped away at his screen. He bit his lip.

'Well?'

He scratched his forehead.

'Well?' I repeated impatiently.

He looked very pained. 'I really don't know how to tell you this, Ms Anderson, but I'm afraid there is an alert on the computer to send you a letter today.'

'A letter?'

'Yes. There were not enough funds in Mr O'Shea's account to credit yours.'

I went white. 'So basically the cheque has

bounced?'

'In non-technical terms, yes, I'm afraid it has.'

I started to cry. Mr Declan O'Shea, liar, petty crook, bastard, and excuse for a boyfriend, was now obviously on a flight to Australia with my £6,000. I wasn't crying because of the loss of all the money. I wasn't crying either for the fact that I now was single again. I was crying for poor Jed. Poor old Jed who had saved his hard-earned cash for me and now a complete charlatan had stolen it. I was also crying for the fact that somebody yet again could take me in so easily and treat me so badly. D spelling danger again. Why did I preach to everyone about his or her horoscopes and take no heed of my own? Why did I never learn that to me, Geminians spelled trouble? I vowed to myself that that was the last time I would ever get involved with a twin.

Chapter Twenty-two

Pisces: *The number 19 features heavily today. Fellow water signs are causing disharmony in your pond.*

It took me a while to get over the whole Declan situation. The gang thought that I should try and track him down and get him arrested as he had in effect stolen my money. My argument was that I had handed the cheque over to him so it was my own stupid fault.

I felt very torn as to what to do, but in the end I made the very difficult decision to let it go as one big bad lesson for the future.

Penelope and I had settled into our singleton life quite well actually. Katie had gone out to Lanzarote on a cheap break with Sam. 'I'm not rekindling it with Ice Man,' she stated adamantly. 'Sam and I want to chill, that's all.'

I had been asked if I wanted to go but wasn't really feeling up to a holiday at the moment. Aware of my plight, Christopher gave me a weekly call to assure me that there were a lot of really nice new applicants on his books and I should recommence dating. We would end up on the phone for ages chatting and laughing. His main concern was that I would turn into a mad old woman, housing ten stray cats and talking to my frogs every day. I think he was actually only nine stray cats away from the mark on this one.

A For Sale sign had gone up next door but there didn't seem to be any activity. I really missed Jed. It's funny how you get used to things in your life without even realising it. You take them for granted and, when they are taken away from you, you really do notice. I called the estate agent under a pseudonym to see how much the house was going for and was pleasantly surprised.

'Must be because of the well-kept road and wonderful neighbours,' I exclaimed to the estate agent, whose voice I recognised as belonging to the hairy-lipped woman I'd kissed in my back bedroom.

'Are you interested in a viewing?' Hairy Lip asked. I suddenly thought it would be good fun to have a nose around as I had only really seen the living room on the day of the cheque presentation.

'Yes, OK.'

'What's your position?'

I felt like telling her it was up shit creek without a paddle, but managed to control myself and replied, 'Oh, I'm renting at the moment, could be in within six weeks. I'm free any evening this week.'

'Oh, that's great news. Mr McDonald is down this week so he can show you round. Let's say tomorrow at seven.'

'That's fine, thanks.' I quickly hung up so as not to give any of my details to the agent and breathed a sigh of relief that it wouldn't be her showing me around.

How exciting that Jon McDonald was back in town. To be honest I hadn't actually thought that much about him since our first meeting as I had been so caught up with Declan. He was also attached to 'the bitch' so it was probably a good thing that I hadn't been thinking about him. However, I still planned to get home from work early and spruce up before I surprised him tomorrow. Now that I was living a singleton's existence, I again made the decision that I would throw myself into my work. A career girl I would become.

Mr Parkinson had been so pleased with the success of the big top event that he bought me a large box of chocolates and gave me a £1000 pay rise. This was very much appreciated, especially now my savings were at zero again.

Liv was currently in the throes of a relationship. She had met her new man at another dinner date evening, run by somebody else, as Rosalind had banned us for life after the red wine incident. His name was Alec; he was fifty-five and owned half of Suffolk.

'Liv, please tell me you love him for his personality,' I said one night over a glass of wine.

'Well, of course I do. He has got rather a big one!'

'Olivia Irving, you are unbelievable,' I laughed.

'The fact that he is also extremely generous and has given me my very own credit card has nothing to do with the way I feel about him.'

'I'm glad you're happy, Liv, but just the thought of waking up next to a wrinkly makes me cringe. I don't think I could do it.'

'Sweetie, surely waking up next to anything with a pulse would be good for you right now? Especially considering how long it is since you've had a shag.'

'Liv! You are disgusting.'

'Yes, but oh-so honest, my dear Ames.'

Brad was still pining after Sean. His phone bills were extortionate. I thought he would be fine, especially as Sean was making the effort to visit in September, so I wasn't expecting the bombshell when it fell.

'Ames, I can't live like this any more!' Brad dramatically exclaimed as he bounded through my pink front door. 'I need too much love to be in a long-distance relationship. Sean and I had a big chat last night and I'm going to stay with him for three months initially.'

'OK,' I said thoughtfully. 'What about money?' I tried not to let the panic rise in my voice at the thought of my best friend moving away.

'My God, when has Miss I-don't-ever-worry-about-money-until-I-have-only-a-penny-left Fish suddenly become so worried about cashflow?'

'Just care about you, that's all.'

'Well, worry not, my pretty princess. I've saved a bit, enough to last me three months, plus enough to pay you back for the flight you kindly donated out of your windfall. My boss is holding my job open for three months as well, said he will get a contractor in to cover me, so that's cool.'

'You don't have to pay me back, you know. You'll need every cent for your new jet-set lifestyle.'

'Actually, Amy, I do have to pay you back. You are a true, lovely friend whom I would trust with my life and you deserve to be treated well and not always to be so giving; it worries me sometimes. You will take the money and buy yourself something nice, not something nice for somebody else, something nice for *you*, oh, and that vile cat of yours if you feel you have to.'

'When are you going?'

Brad faltered. 'A week Saturday.'

I sat down almost in tears. 'You really are a wanker leaving me like this.' I tried to smile. 'Don't get me wrong though, babe. I am really pleased for you. Despite his brother, I do like Sean very much. Your happiness is paramount and if you're happy, I'm happy. I do love you, you know.'

'And I love you too, sweetpea. You can come out and visit any time.'

'Hold that thought,' I said and smiled weakly.

'Right, must go, people to see, Louis Vuittons to pack. Thought we could all go out and get pissed next Thursday to see me off.'

'Good plan,' I nodded. 'Now get out of my sight and get packing, and if you need help with anything at all, just shout.'

'Oh, and Amy, one more thing: he *is* a Scorpio, by the way! Seeya!'

A bloody Scorpio? Trust Kieran Docherty to be my perfect star match. My butterfly mind went into overdrive. Of course he was a Scorpio. There was just so much passion there. Our bodies were in tune if nothing else. I reconsulted my astrology bookshelf and pulled out my favourite tome that was well into the compatibility of signs.

Scorpio, here we go. I read out loud: 'Scorpians are passionate and intense beings, filled with desire. They are secretive and complex. Don't try and get too much out of them or they'll become suspicious and leave. They are particularly resourceful characters.'

Pen sauntered into the dining room.

'Pen, don't I just know that about him, eh?'

He brushed against my knees as if to say, 'Don't worry'. I carried on reading out loud. 'Compatibility with Pisceans, here we go. Listen to this: Pisces is Scorpio's most compatible astrological mate. Their passion can last a lifetime. The Scorpio benefits from the active imagination of the Pisces, who reacts lovingly to the sensitive and passionate nature of the Scorpio.'

I suddenly began to relive the feelings of intense passion I had felt for Kieran. Part of me wanted to get on that flight with Brad, knock on Kieran's door, and make him admit it was me he wanted to be with. Kieran Docherty was an addiction, a pack of cigarettes to a reformed smoker. I knew he was bad for me but I just wanted to keep going back there to get that short, sharp, wonderful fix.

'Amy! What a wonderful surprise!' Jon exclaimed as he opened the door of number 19. He was looking extremely sexy. He'd had his hair trimmed really short and was wearing cut-offs, a tight black T-shirt, and flip-flops. He had even had his neck shaved. 'I can't chat for long now as I've got someone coming to view the house any minute. It's the last one tonight, so I can pop round for a catch up after, if you're free, that is?'

'Oh God, I feel really bad now,' I stuttered. 'That person you have been waiting for is me.'

'To view the house?' He screwed up his lovely little nose.

'Yeah, well, I wanted to be nosy as I'd only seen the downstairs and I always like to get new ideas for mine, you know. I didn't realise you'd be here,' I lied.

'I wondered why the agent had been so crap in not getting your name or anything. I was half expecting whoever it was not to show and here you are, it's so great to see you.'

'How's Jackie?' I said through gritted teeth.

'Oh, back home in Scotland with the kids, so she's happy to leave the house sale to me.'

'Kids! You never said?'

'Yeah, my beautiful little niece Jasmine and nephew, Robert.'

I laughed out loud.

'What's funny, Amy?'

'Well, it isn't really funny, I just thought that Jackie was your girlfriend and–' I stopped. My God, it was like I'd taken a truth drug.

'Carry on. And what?'

I started to blurt. Jon wasn't deterred by this at all, having already experienced a blurt on that very sad, pants-on-head morning.

'Do you know what, Jon, I am really pleased that Jackie is your sister as I think you are really nice. Actually I thought you were really nice when I met you before and I didn't want to even let you know I was going out with someone that night. And in the end I didn't go out with someone else as I was so overcome with the money that your grandfather had left me that I got completely drunk with Brad.'

At this point, Jon then did take over, worried that if I carried on any longer without taking a breath I might keel over.

'Yes, your rendition of 'Dancing Queen' was amazing!'

I went bright red but with breath back in my lungs I continued. 'Maybe we should go out next week and see how we do on 'Knowing Me, Knowing You'?'

'Not sure about the 'Knowing Me, Knowing You' bit, but let's go out anyway. It will be a laugh.'

Jon then proceeded to show me around Jed's house, chuckling at my *oohs* and *aahs* to all the differences and similarities.

Chapter Twenty-three

Sagittarius: *A chance encounter with an old flame causes you to rethink a current relationship.*

The Thursday of Brad's leaving drinks arrived. The gang was set to meet at eight in Harry's Bar. Sam and Katie were back from Lanzarote. They looked brown and relaxed.

'Almost glowing!' Brad exclaimed.

Liv had been drinking since six but was holding it together as usual. Poor Anna had had a toilet episode earlier and said that her stomach was so bloated that she looked like a stuffed pig and couldn't possibly come out.

'I hope the bitch calls me tomorrow,' Brad said camply. 'Now let's get on with the merriment of seeing me off into the arms of my lover, shall we?'

H arrived with Horace; they too had a glow about them.

'What's with all this glowing?' Brad wanted to know.

'I don't know what you're on about, Brad. Hurry up and get the drinks in,' H retorted.

'No, no, no,' Sam intervened. 'The drinks are on me. Two bottles of champagne, please!'

'Ooh, sweetie, champagne! You must really love

171

me and be sorry to see me go?' Brad trilled.

'Yeah, something like that,' Sam laughed and began to pour the champagne as we all shuffled into place round a bench table. 'A toast for Mr Sampson and all who sail in him. And also,' Sam faltered and smiled at Katie. 'As we are all together I would like to announce that I have asked the beautiful Katie Cook to be my wife.'

'Oh my God, you dark horses!' I exclaimed. 'This is so sudden.'

'Ames, it has to give all singletons hope. We went away and realised that we truly loved each other. I have never ever felt before that I wanted to spend the rest of my life with somebody and there she was, right in front of my nose all of the time.'

'You mingers, I am so bloody excited,' Liv screeched. 'More champagne over here, young man.' She winked at the waiter as he approached.

'Cheers, everyone!' H called out. 'And while we are on the subject of celebrating, Horace and I would like to announce that we are adding to the population.'

'Oh my God, I can't cope with all this excitement in one night, Brad said, flapping. 'It's just so fantastic. I shall even let you bastards off for hijacking my leaving party. All this news is so great.'

I was generally excited for everyone, why wouldn't I be? They were my lovely friends and they deserved every ounce of happiness in the world, so when Liv found me crying in the toilets I felt really guilty.

'Minger, I thought you'd been gone a while. Was worried you were chucking up.'

'Liv, you are so graphic. I'm fine.'

'Oh yeah sure, you're fine, look at your eyes.'

I was frantically trying to rub off the black mascara trails down my cheeks. Liv hugged me tight.

'Amy, you don't have to tell me, I know. You are too lovely to be single for much longer. You will get your fairytale, you know you will.'

'Not looking like this I won't!' I smiled through my watery eyes. 'You go back out there and I'll sort my face out. I don't want anyone to know I've been crying.' I was actually feeling quite drunk. Champagne usually went straight to my head and on this occasion it was no exception.

The doors from the loos into the bar were stable doors. On the way back to our table I pushed them harder than I needed to and one flew back and knocked me flying.

'Oops a daisy,' a voice above me said. 'Too many sherbets, eh? Let me help you.'

The voice sounded familiar but I couldn't place it. Then I realised.

'Amy Anderson, oh my God, how are you?'

'Will, it's you! I can't believe it.' I started jumping up and down on the spot like a madwoman. 'I really can't believe it. You haven't changed one bit.'

'*You* have!' he exclaimed. 'For the better. In fact I may use the word fox if I can be so bold.'

Will (William Wallingford) was one of the funniest men I had ever met. He had been my first love. We had started going out when we were fifteen. We'd had three heady years of young love. Kissing in the back row of the cinema, sharing our first shaky grope and, for me, losing my virginity in a tent in his garden. So many good, good memories. I had actually finished it, way back then. I thought that the grass was greener and ran off with one of his mates who had a Mohican. It turned out that Mr Mohican only loved himself and the Sisters of Mercy. I regretted leaving the lovely Will for the next three years.

And here he was in front of me again. All six foot of him. With the familiar auburn hair, greeny-blue eyes, the full, beautifully shaped mouth, and now a really toned body by the looks of things. He had made me quiver all those years ago and now, taking a real good look at him, he made me quiver again.

'What are you doing here then, oh foxy one?'

'Oh, it's my best friend's leaving do. He's off to America to spend some time with his partner. And you?' I couldn't stop smiling, as this was so surreal.

'Birthday meal for my girlfriend.'

'Oh right.' I felt really disappointed.

'Not a patch on you though, Ames, heh? Never forget your first love and all that.' He grinned. 'Anyway I'd better get back to her, or she'll wonder who this beauty is I'm talking to. Here's my card. Give me a shout next week, then let's meet for a drink and catch up on the last thirteen years.'

And then he was gone, back into the busy throng of the restaurant area. For a moment or two I felt quite shell-shocked. I had been so in love with Will all those years ago. An innocent, almost perfect love. No jobs, nor any ties, still living at home, pleasures were simple and abundant. No expectations or even thoughts of marriage as we were so young. To suddenly see him again out of the blue made my stomach swirl. I tried to pull myself together. He had a girlfriend, it was thirteen years ago and I was clutching at very bendy straws. I collected my thoughts and my ailing legs, then walked over to Brad and threw my arms around his back.

'Brad Sampson, I love you. I'm going to miss you but you should always follow your dreams, so go for your life and enjoy.'

I then couldn't resist telling everyone about Will. Liv, as usual, had the best response. 'I really think you should remember how big his willy was before you try and seduce him.' We all proceeded to get drunker and more debauched and finally got thrown out of the bar at midnight as we had all got on a table to sing a hearty rendition of 'For He's a Jolly Good Fellow!' H crammed us all into her car, as now, with child, she hadn't been drinking. Liv gave a knowing wave and wink from the back of a taxi in front of us and proceeded to snog the young waiter's face off.

'Monogamy,' she had once explained, 'is Latin for get real!'

Chapter Twenty-four

Pisces: *A friend in need is a friend indeed. Your fishy compassion will be required to deal with what life throws at you this week.*

We all gave Brad a tearful farewell at the airport.

'Lucky sod!' Liv exclaimed.

'Come over and see me, Prinny,' he shouted as he disappeared through Passport Control. What a week! My best friend was heading off to pastures new with a new love; I had bumped into my first love and had also arranged a date with the delicious Jon from next door.

Life was going well in general at the moment. I was actually enjoying work and having fun with my friends rather than worrying about men. Christopher hadn't come forward with any contenders lately. I did actually ring him one evening asking if he thought I needed to change my photo to that of a top model.

'Amy, you don't need me to tell you that you look gorgeous in your photo *and* in the flesh. I just haven't had any suitors on the books lately that would be good enough for you,' Christopher said nicely. Actually I *did* need telling as I had the typical Piscean trait of needing constant reassurance. But bless dear, sweet Christopher nonetheless. He was always looking out for me.

Brad had been gone nearly two weeks now and I was already missing him. He had phoned me once, to say that they were getting on really well, and that Sean's apartment was amazing and situated right on the beach.

'You must come over,' he said. 'We can keep out of Kieran's way, and we'd have such a laugh.' He sounded so excited and happy I was pleased for him.

'Do you know what, Brad Sampson? I'll be over sooner than you think. Give me a few weeks to save up and I'll be with you.'

'Have a nice day now, Ames, seeya.'

'Seeya, darling boy, very soon.'

I knocked on Jed's door. 'Fancy coming out to play with the girl next door?'

'I'll just ask my mum, hang on.' He smiled and shut the door behind him.

'I'm starving. Shall we go to JoJo's, I fancy pizza?'

'Sounds good to me.'

I proceeded to drink a whole bottle of Pinot Grigio to myself, while Jon consumed several beers. We got on like a house on fire and I was flirting outrageously from my first bite of garlic dough ball.

'Thanks again, Gloria, for making an old man happy in his last few years. My grandfather did adore you, for some reason.

I laughed. 'I'd rather have been making a young man happy,' I replied seductively, looking over the table at him.

'When's your birthday, by the way?'

'Oh you're into all that rubbish too, are you? I should really make you guess, shouldn't I, but after all that wine it would probably take you hours. I'm an Aquarius.'

'Tell me a bit about yourself then and I shall tell you if you're a typical water bearer.'

'Well, being the eleventh sign of the zodiac, I'm quick-witted, intelligent, and have tons of friends. I can, however, be impatient and fixed in my opinions. I like to travel. Any more?' he asked cockily.

'Jon McDonald, you've sneaked in and stolen an astrology book off my shelf. That is just pure textbook Aquarius!'

Jon laughed and continued, 'Oh, and they have been known to drop the occasional bombshell.'

'You've got me on that one,' I replied quizzically.

'The reason I know all of this stuff because my boyfriend, Andrew, writes the stars for the *Sunday News*.'

I took a large gulp of wine. 'That is absholutely fantastic,' I slurred.

'What, the fact I'm gay?' Jon enquired, worried how I was going to react to his revelation.

'No, the fact that your boyfriend writes horoscopes for a living. How exciting, I must meet him.'

Jon smiled at my excitement and mocked. 'I shall check his crystal ball and see when he's free.' He then went all sensible on me. 'I'm sorry if I gave out the wrong signals to you earlier.'

'Don't be silly. The way my hormones are lately, if the dustman smiles at me I think I'm on to a winner. My best friend Brad is gay. He was at the funeral with me, not sure if you noticed him. He'd like you, I just know it'

'No, I didn't see him, but it's interesting that you

think he'd like me.'

'I'll think we'll stop that thought now, shall we, as by the sound of it you are both happily married.'

'Spoilsport,' Jon teased.

'Friends?' I said, and held my hand out to him.

'Friends.' He smiled. 'Let's have another drink.'

'When are you back up to Scotland?'

'I'm down south for a couple of weeks, as I want to sort out a few estate details of Grandpa's. Talking of Grandpa, what did you spend your money on?'

I bit my lip and looked down. I had been dreading this moment.

'What's the matter, Amy? Look, it doesn't matter if you spent it on a complete luxury. It was your money to do what you wanted with.'

'I so wish it was that. No, something terrible happened. I have been so stupid.'

Jon sensed my apprehension and reached for my hand across the table. I suddenly realised what a mess I'd made of this dating lark and began to wish I'd never ever gone to Starr & Sun.

'I've been such a fool, Jon. I got hoodwinked into lending my so-called boyfriend a lot of the money and basically he stole it and ran off to Australia, taking it all without a word.'

He squeezed my hand as I continued. 'I am so, so sorry. Jed must have worked so hard for that money and on a stupid whim, because I thought I was in love, I threw the whole lot away. God, they say love is blind. Where I'm concerned it's deaf as well.'

I then proceeded to tell Jon the whole sorry story of Declan O'Shea.

'What a complete bastard,' he said angrily. 'It just

makes it so much worse that he used the cancer story to get cash out of you. Are you going to try and find him?'

'What's the point? It's highly unlikely that he'll ever hand the cash over, and to be honest I never want to speak to him, let alone see him again. I do want you to know that I didn't make that decision lightly though.'

'If ever, and I mean this, Amy, if ever you do hear that he is back in the country, you let me know, because I'll make sure he hands over the cash and more.'

'Thanks for being so understanding, and I am truly sorry for being so gullible.'

'Look, it wasn't your fault. Put it down to a bad experience and learn from it. What goes around comes around, and you can be certain that one Mr O'Shea will not always live a life of roses.'

Bless Jon. Everything was guided by the hand of fate and, despite losing my newfound wealth and another potential suitor, I had now gained a very lovely new friend.

We got back to number 21 around midnight.

'Come in for a coffee?' I urged Jon.

'On one condition.'

'Don't worry, I'm not going to jump on you, you're not a dustman!' I laughed.

'On the condition that you don't let me anywhere near that stinking pond of yours!'

My answerphone light was flashing when I got in, plus I had ten missed calls on my mobile as I had amazingly forgotten to take it with me. 'Must be all my admirers.' I felt quite excited to find out who so desperately wanted to get hold of me. My excitement soon turned to anguish when I heard Brad's frantic and tearful voice.

'Prinny, bad, bad accident. Please call me... it doesn't matter what time.'

Jon bit his bottom lip and looked at me tenderly. 'Do you want me to stay here with you while you make the call?' I nodded. I felt sick at the thought of Brad being in such a state and quickly dialled the Florida apartment.

I was surprised to hear Brad's voice and not Sean's on the end of the phone.

'Brad, it's me, babe. What on earth's happened?'

With his reply I fell back on the sofa in complete shock.

'It's Sean. He's dead.'

'Oh, my darling Brad, oh no, I'm so sorry.'

'We were having such a lovely day.' He began to sob again.

'We went water-skiing. We'd only just swapped over and suddenly this other boat appeared out of nowhere. It was going really fast and was out of control and it hit him. It hit my gorgeous, lovely Sean. The paramedics said that he would have died instantly and wouldn't have suffered.'

I knew all about grief, in fact, I was quite an expert on the subject. My mum had died when I was seventeen. She was involved in a hit and run accident. One moment I was waving goodbye to her as I went off to school, the next I was throwing a rose into her grave. I felt the same pain talking to Brad as when the policeman came to the house to tell me, Dad and Anna the terrible news that day. I knew though that for Brad's sake I had to keep control at this precise moment.

'Are you coming straight home?' I asked.

'No, I'm waiting for his parents to come out. They are travelling back to Ireland with his body.' His voice broke. 'Amy, I don't know what to do with myself. I don't want to be alone here tonight. Although I was so close to Sean, it's as if I don't count in his life now this has happened.'

'Of course you count, babe. Why don't you call Kieran?' I felt so desperate that my best friend was a million miles away and I couldn't console him properly.

'I have, he's with the authorities sorting everything out.'

'I shall phone the airport now and see how quickly I can get to you,' I said reassuringly. I could almost hear Brad sigh with relief. 'Amy, I do love you, you know.'

'And I you. Now try to get some rest and I'll call you from the airport.'

I started to cry myself now, big heavy sobs. Short of experiencing the death of a loved one yourself, feeling the grief of somebody close to you is almost as bad. Jon put his arms around me.

'Now, don't worry about Pen, I shall feed him. Let me phone the airport now and see what we can sort out. I've had too much to drink to drive so get packing and I'll phone for a taxi as well. Don't forget your passport. Oh, and I've got some dollars in my wallet from a recent trip to America that you can have to see you through the first day.'

'Thank you so much, Jon. You really are an angel.'

Chapter Twenty-five

Pisces: *Travel plans are on the cards for you fishes today. You'll need to reserve all of your energies for an unwanted encounter.*

How nice to be in a hot country, but how sad to be here under such traumatic circumstances. The taxi ride to Sean's apartment was difficult. I so wanted to see Brad to ease his pain but also dreaded seeing him as I couldn't bear the thought of him hurting so badly. I rested my head back on the seat attempting to relax, and began to take in the Florida scenery. Everything seemed that much bigger than in England. The roads were a lot wider and I was amazed at the amount of garages, drive-in eating haunts, and motels we passed along the way. On the coastal road, nearing Sarasota, I noticed the impressive white-sandy beaches and almost forgot why I was here. It wasn't until we passed several golf courses that reality hit: poor Sean, what a tragic loss.

As soon as I arrived Brad walked slowly out to greet me. His head was slightly bowed. He looked grey, his eyes were swollen from crying, and he was unshaven. I gave him a massive hug.

'No words are enough, I know, just that I'm here and will always be here for you.' I dumped my stuff in the spare room and made him a sandwich, as he hadn't eaten since the accident. I then lay on his bed and held him, stroking his head until he fell into a fitful sleep.

The ground-floor, air-conditioned apartment was spacious and comfortable. Patio doors led straight out to a private beach. I was tired from the flight but couldn't sleep so started flicking through the zillions of TV channels to find something of interest. After nearly buying The Most Serious Ab Cruncher in the Universe and a mechanical flea plucker for Penelope from one of the many shopping channels, I heard a key being turned in the door. I suddenly thought of all those American films I'd seen and wondered if I should dive behind the sofa and look for a cabinet that housed a gun. In fact, I actually should have done both as in walked the delicious Kieran Docherty. Even though his eyes were bloodshot from weeping and he didn't look like he'd washed for weeks, I guiltily thought that if he had asked me to bend over the dishwasher there and then, I would have done so. It was at times like these that I realised that even if I was a religious person I would never be summoned to the suburbs of heaven, let alone to the Pearly Gates.

'Kieran, I'm so sorry.' I moved awkwardly towards him to give him a hug.

'It's shit, Amy, a God awful shitty thing to happen. I loved him so much. He was so young, it's just not fair.'

'I know, I know,' I said soothingly, as if what had happened between us had never taken place.

'How's Brad?' Kieran asked gruffly.

'Not good. He's asleep, totally exhausted with

everything.'

'I feel the same, I want to sleep but every time I try to I just have pictures of us as kids flashing through my mind.'

Half of me so wanted to kiss him. To tell him everything would be all right. To say that I would help him through this terrible time. But it wasn't my place to do so. The other half wanted to shout at him and say did he realise that yes we had only had two sweaty shags, but they were the best sweaty shags I'd had in a long time and he had really hurt me. Initially, I was quite pleased to hear Sinead approaching, as I didn't want to create any disharmony in a situation as tragic as this.

'Kieran, darling, where are you?'

'Just here, my sweet.'

I thought I would vomit. He really was a bastard. But I guessed considering the enormity of the situation, infidelity and the feelings of others were the last thing on his mind.

'Oh hello, Amy isn't it? Brad said you were coming over. What a good friend you are to him. Poor, poor Sean and my poor, poor boy. I don't know how he's going to cope.'

Despite the horrendous circumstances I still wanted to tell her how her poor, poor Kieran was a complete philanderer.

'How's your ankle, by the way?' she went on. 'Hope it didn't affect your enjoyment of our wedding too much.'

I was amazed she could still come out with general chit-chat at a time like this. Maybe she suspected something? I gulped, looked straight at Kieran, who was too grief-stricken to care whether his marriage was about to be blown apart, and replied, 'It's fine now thanks.'

'Thought you might have broken it, the fuss you made.'

I wanted to cry out that the only thing broken that night was my heart, but instead I just weakly smiled. Kieran then went over to a desk in the corner of the room, shuffled with some papers and said, 'Right, we've got more stuff to sort out re the flight home. Goodbye, Amy, and thanks for being here for Brad.'

He squeezed my arm as he went past. He might just as well have wrung my heart out and thrown it to the floor. How could I love this man? *Did* I love this man? Lust, it had to be lust.

Back in Reading, Brad stayed at mine for a couple of nights and then he left and I was all alone again with Penelope. It felt like weeks since I'd had a chance just to be. It was a dreary Sunday and I decided that I would spend the whole day tidying the house, the garden and generally getting my life back into some sort of order again. As I shifted papers off the coffee-table, a business card fell to the floor. I picked it up and smiled at the memory of seeing Will again. With all the recent goings-on, I had completely forgotten about calling him back. I could do with a bit of light relief.

I was amazed that my heart was beating really fast as I dialled his mobile number. Trust him, I thought, just to have his name and mobile number on a card. I wondered what he did for a living now? He had always been a real entrepreneur and so full of energy and ideas when we were younger. I couldn't wait to meet up with him; it seemed like a lifetime ago that we were snogging in the back row of the cinema. My excitement was soon extinguished as the frustrating drone of an unobtainable number greeted my eardrum. I tried again, thinking I might have misdialed but no, he must have changed his number since we had last met. I didn't even know where he lived now.

Pen wandered in to see what was going on. 'Oh well, it's obviously not meant to be,' I told him. 'He's a flirtatious Sagittarius anyway, so it's probably for the best.'

So that was that. If he hadn't had a girlfriend I might have tried harder to track Will down, but to be honest I was trying to steer myself away from the complications of attached men forever more. I could imagine Anna giving me a lecture: 'Ames, if they've got baggage it's far too easy for them to go straight back to Baggage Reclaim when the going gets tough!'

I sat down, duster in hand, and felt suddenly very tired and depressed. It had been a long wait to say a final goodbye to Sean, what with him having to be flown home and then arrangements being made in Ireland. The funeral was due to take place in Dublin next Friday and I was already apprehensive. Firstly, because funerals always evoke my own grief over the loss of my mother, and secondly because I had to face Kieran again. I had acknowledged that he was very much married and there would never be a chance for us. I had also faced the fact that he was a cheating bastard anyway and I was worth more. Then every so often, usually after a glass or two of something, I put on my rose-coloured spectacles and saw us sorting everything out and living happily ever after.

Abandoning my housework duties I switched on the TV and my mood was immediately lifted as I saw that *Casablanca* had just started. Bliss, a dreary Sunday afternoon, snuggled on the sofa watching my favourite film. I was just wiping my tears away at the end of it when the phone rang. It was Christopher. Strange, he never usually called on a Sunday.

'Amy. How are you doing?'

'A bit tired but I'm OK, thanks.'

'Cordelia said you had contacted us to say that you would be away for a few days. I'm so sorry to hear the terrible news about your friend. If there's anything I can do to help?'

'I'm fine, but it's really sweet of you to think of me, thanks.'

'Also, since you've been away I've had a very nice Leo register. Thought a date might take your mind off everything that's been going on. Cordelia emailed his profile and photo to you on Friday, thought you might have looked at them by now?'

'I'll have a look. Thanks a lot, catch up soon, yeah?'

'Yeah. See you, Amy. Take it easy and enjoy the rest of your Sunday.'

I was looking forward to going on a new date, hoping that it would finally get Kieran out of my system. Sad as it was, once the funeral was over there was no reason why I should ever have to see him again. I phoned Brad to see if he was OK and he told me he was packing to go and stay with his mum until Thursday.

'I've booked us on the 8 a.m. flight, Friday. I'll pick you up from home at six. I've also sorted us a hotel in Dublin for the night,' he said.

'Thanks, babe, take good care. Give my love to your mum and I'll see you Friday.'

'Amy.' Brad faltered. 'I just wanted to say that I really do love you, kid.'

I could hear his voice cracking. 'Shit off and I'll see you Friday.' I said trying to keep his spirits up, but when I put the phone down I started to cry my eyes out. Poor Brad, he didn't deserve this. In his usual sympathetic way, Penelope jumped on my lap and began to purr loudly.

'Right,' I said out loud, in the words of my father. 'Drag yourself up, brush yourself down, and get on with it, girl.'

Chapter Twenty-six

Scorpio: *There is a light at the end of the tunnel if you choose the correct path. Consider other people's emotions rather than your own today.*

With bleary eyes Brad and I were checking onto our flight from Heathrow when Liv appeared from nowhere. Despite it being silly o'clock in the morning she had on full warpaint, mini-skirt, tight red T-shirt, and stilettos.

'Morning, darlings, I couldn't let you go through this without me so I'm coming along to make sure that you are both OK throughout your trip. This way I can practise for my dream job of being PA to the stars.'

Despite the tragic situation, you couldn't help but laugh. Liv was really all heart. Brad even managed a smile.

'Looks like you actually fell into the make-up bag this morning, you old tart,' he said gamely.

I started falling about laughing.

'Brad, you're a bitch, Amy, you're a minger, and I quite fancy seducing a nice Irish boy so let's go.'

We checked into our hotel early as arranged. Luckily I had a twin room so Liv had somewhere to lay her auburn locks. I was so glad she was here. She knew how worried I was about Brad and about seeing Kieran again, and I couldn't have asked for a better distraction than her. The funeral was at 2 p.m., so we had plenty of time to get ready and meet for a tactical brandy before we left. Brad looked grey when we met him downstairs in the bar. He also looked extremely handsome in his well-cut black suit, black shirt and tie. He gulped down his first brandy in one and wailed, 'I don't know how I'm going to get through this.'

Liv squeezed his hand. 'We're with you all the way, babe.'

For once, she was actually looking quite reserved in a plain black dress, which was at a length that even her granny would have been proud of. The barman obviously realised from our attire that we were off to a funeral and kept topping up our brandy glasses free of charge. By the time the taxi came we were all quite tipsy.

'I so hope we don't have to sing 'Onward Christian Soldiers',' Liv piped up while we were waiting for the cab.

'Why ever not?' I asked.

Luckily Brad was on his mobile to his mum so he didn't hear the next bit.

'Because I used to go out with a bloke called Christian Solders and every time we were about to shag I used to shout 'Onward Christian Solders' at the top of my voice and I'm scared that I might laugh.'

'Liv, yes that is highly amusing but get a grip now, we've got to hold this together for Brad now.'

'Of course, you know I wouldn't do anything silly really.'

Brad sat at the front of the church with Sean's parents, grandparents, Kieran and Sinead. We had wanted to be next to him so we could hold his hand but he was happy to be up front with the family so that he felt more involved. Despite my religious disbeliefs, whenever I do go into a church, I feel kind of serene and I do always without fail pray that Mum is happy wherever she is.

Liv and I had never been to a Catholic service before, let alone a funeral service, and I found it extremely harrowing. I almost wanted Christian Solders to appear so we could shout out Liv's mating cry. Some strange women had walked in from the street and were mumbling behind us in the pews, it all seemed very bizarre to me. The priest then started wafting around incense over the coffin.

Sean's was the saddest funeral I've ever been to, next to my mother's. There were so many young people there. Mr and Mrs Docherty were completely distraught, as was Kieran. I could see his big shoulders shaking as he sobbed. Sinead just stood motionless, facing front, and made no move to comfort him. I wanted to run up and put my arms around him right there and then. Brad, I was proud to observe, was a credit to Sean. He remained dignified and held his head high until Sean's friend, Jack stood up.

'Sean Docherty!' He looked up to the roof of the beautiful church. 'I know you're looking down at us now. You're probably thinking, cut all the sad stuff and get down that pub. You were a good man. Your family and friends all loved your sense of humour, your kindness, your generosity, and your ability to make people feel good about themselves even when they were really down.' His voice started to crack. 'We're gonna miss you, mate.'

There wasn't a dry eye in the church.

'Before I stand down I also want to mention a particularly important person in Sean's life, Brad Sampson. Although they weren't together very long, I know how much Sean thought of Brad and what happiness he brought to his life over the past few months.' He looked over at Brad and gave him a watery smile.

What a lovely person Jack was, to include Brad. He was obviously aware that Brad was feeling a little lost as he had not known Sean's friends and family long. His kindness would mean a lot to Brad, and to us, his friends.

The wake was even wilder than I had expected it to be. There were about a hundred of us all crammed into a back room of an old pub in Dublin. Everybody's tears seemed to have dried and heavy drinking had commenced all round. I noticed that Grandpa Ferret had hit the Jameson's and was chatting to every female who would talk to him. Liv couldn't believe her luck. Not only was the gorgeous Jack being attentive, there were also several other broad, brooding, dark-haired Irishmen vying for her attention. Maybe, in future, she would realise that she didn't have to wear short skirts to get what she wanted. For myself, I thought this wasn't really the time or the place to be on a manhunt. I was intent on making sure that Brad was comfortable and not too distressed, and that I kept as far away from Kieran as I could.

I then noticed Kieran out of the corner of my eye; he was sitting with his mother and holding her hand. His dad was standing up beside them, looking very tired. I felt so sorry for all of them. Sinead was chatting away excitedly to a handsome, red-faced redhead in the corner. I thought indignantly that if that were me, I would be looking after my bereaved husband.

Brad steered me outside to get some air. 'Ames, I don't think I will ever meet somebody who I loved as much as Sean.'

I put my hand on his shoulder. 'Even if you don't, babe, at least you've felt what real love is, not everyone can say that. At the moment you are so raw with grief that everything will seem a negative. I know it's an old cliché that time's a healer but actually that's true.'

'Do you really think so?' He sounded utterly broken.

'I know so, Brad. I used to wake up every single day after Mum died for at least a year thinking, my mum is dead, how am I going to get through this day?' Then gradually as time goes by you don't wake up every morning and think about it. You get on with your life and you start to remember the good times you had.'

'I don't want to forget him or what we had,' Brad said softly.

'You never will forget him,' I promised. 'I don't think you ever get over losing someone you really love, you just learn how to deal with it. There will always be a special place in your heart reserved just for Sean, and no one will ever be able to touch that place. That doesn't mean to say you won't meet anyone else either, because I know you will. You are a beautiful person, Brad Sampson, and if you don't meet someone, well, we can always get the stirrups and baster out, that'll take your mind off it.'

Brad managed a smile. 'Amy Anderson, what would I do without you?'

'Your life would be a duller place. Now let's go and get a drink, and see if we need to find a shitty stick to beat the men off of Liv!'

As we walked back into the bar, Kieran was coming towards us. 'Amy, have you got a minute?' he said.

Brad gave me one of his concerned looks. I gave a small nod and mouthed, 'I'm fine, babe.' I confidently responded to Kieran, 'Sure, what's up?' although my legs were shaking like jelly.

'Let's go outside. I need to go somewhere and I want you to come with me.'

I followed him outside, wondering what he was up to.

'We need to get a cab.'

I didn't answer, just followed him like a little lap dog to the nearest taxi rank. Minutes later we were back at the church. Kieran led me to a bench in the graveyard.

'Sit down, Amy, I want to talk to you.'

I did as I was told. He took both of my hands in his and looked at me intently. His eyes were full of tears.

'I don't know how I'm going to move forward without my brother. He was my twin; he was half of me. The day of the accident I felt a pain in my chest the time it happened.'

'Oh Kieran, it is so terrible I know, but things will get better.' I felt like shouting, 'Why are you telling me this? Why have you brought me here?'

Then as if he had been reading my mind he said, 'I expect you're wondering why I've brought you here. I just wanted to be near the two people who I really care about, that's all.' A tear trickled down his cheek. He continued hoarsely, 'Amy, I've had a lot of time to think of what's really important to me over the past few days. I've realised that I've done some bad things, and hurting you was one of them. From the little I know of you, you are not only incredibly sexy, you are a kind, funny, and loving soul.'

I bit my lip and held back my own tears. My inner voice was warning me not to listen, but after all Kieran Docherty had put me through I had to hear him out.

'I know when I saw you in Florida I didn't seem to care, but as you can understand I was in a real mess.' He faltered. 'I still am obviously. On the flight home I had a really long think about you. Only a special person would fly all the way out to America for a couple of days.'

'Anyone would do that for a good friend,' I said softly.

'Actually, Amy, they wouldn't. You really are a beautiful person.' He then took my face tenderly in his two big hands and pulled me towards him. I know that I should have resisted. I had vowed before I left England that I would not let this happen again. His mouth was as soft as I had remembered it from all those months ago. His tongue explored me gently and then, as our bodies moved together, the same urgency to have this man inside me went right through me like an electric current.

'Oh Amy,' Kieran gasped. 'I have to have you, here, right now.' He started kissing me with an intensity I had never experienced before.

'Not here, we can't. It wouldn't be right,' I panted through his kiss.

We got up and walked with urgency down a path between the gravestones. At the end of the path was a row of bushes. Kieran took off his black jacket and laid it on the ground. He lifted me up gently, kissed the back of my neck, causing my nipples to shoot out like bullets, then laid me on our makeshift bed. He pulled my dress up and gently entered me with his fingers, stroking and caressing until I was buzzing with desire. He continued to kiss me, tenderly now.

'Kieran Docherty,' I told him huskily. 'I want that amazing cock of yours inside of me right now.'

'Oh, do you now? Let's see what we can do about that, shall we.'

He unzipped his trousers and pulled them down so I could feel him stiff and proud against me. I gasped as he entered me. We moved together slowly at first until passion took over. Our orgasms were so intense that we lay panting for ages just holding each other tightly.

I turned to face Kieran. 'I can't believe I've given into you again.'

'Amy, please don't say that. We just made love. It wasn't just sex. I wanted to be close to the whole of you. It felt real, it felt really right.'

Suddenly I saw red. 'How can you use the words *real* and *right* when this situation is so terrible?

We've just shagged in the graveyard where your brother is buried. You are married. You live in America. If you'd cared one bit about me, you would have contacted me somehow to see if I was OK after your wedding night.'

In true male fashion he replied, 'I did think of doing that.'

'Don't even bother to go on, I don't want to hear.'

'Amy, please don't be like this. I do really care about you, you know.'

'You don't care about me enough to want more than an extra-marital shag, and do you know what, Kieran Docherty? I don't give a damn any more.'

'Maybe, when I've had a chance to recover from losing Sean we should talk about seeing each other more.'

My heart was being pulled towards this man. How could I be so stupid as to want to prolong this? But he had just said that he wanted to maybe start seeing more of me in the future and just hearing these words made me tingle. If I hadn't been so completely in lust with this man, I would have noted that the word *maybe* in the male dictionary means *bullshit*. Instead, I replied using the female dictionary version of *maybe* which means *Of course I will but I'm not telling you that now.*

'Maybe, Kieran, maybe.'

We hurried back to the pub, where the wake was in full swing. The Waterboys were blaring away and Grandpa Ferret was just about to be hit over the head with Grandma Ferret's handbag. Kieran disappeared to talk to a group of Sean's mates in the corner. My main concern was for Brad. How could I have selfishly abandoned him like this? I found him in mid-conversation with Sean's mum and dad. I almost ran over to him. Brad grasped my hand.

'Hi, Ames. Everything OK?'

'Fine thanks, babes. Would any of you like a drink?'

'Three Jameson's please, mi darlin',' piped up Mr Docherty.

Liv appeared at the bar. In her best Irish accent she exclaimed, 'Amy, you look a little flushed. You haven't been doing things a nice Catholic girl shouldn't be doin', have you?'

Being the sex-fiend that she was, I guessed she would know that look. I started to whisper, 'Liv, I have. I've only gone and done it again.'

'Oh, Amy, you know what we all said. It's a shame he's so bloody cute though. I know why you did it. But he's so bloody married too.'

'He did say that maybe when his head was straight about Sean he'd be in touch.'

'Oh God, I really don't think he's worth pinning your hopes on.'

'But, Liv, I actually think he does really care this time. He said he'd had a long think about us and he thought I was a beautiful person. The sex this time, well, it was different.'

'Did he come out with the niceties before or after he shagged you?' Liv said knowingly.

'I know it looks bad but I could so easily fall in love with this man.'

Just as Liv was about to reply the music stopped. Mr Docherty stood up and tapped his glass on the table. Sinead was by his side. He put his arm around her.

'Firstly everybody, I would like to thank you all for coming and giving my boy such a good send-off. I know he's looking down on us now so let's drink to my wonderful son and thank God that we had the pleasure of knowing his beautiful soul, albeit for too few years.' He held up his glass. 'To Sean.'

'To Sean,' everybody chanted.

He continued shakily. 'And also, while I have my daughter-in-law by my side I want to give everybody some good news on this very sad day. My son, my other very special son Kieran, and his lovely wife here, are expecting a baby Docherty.'

A cheer went up and everybody proceeded to the bar to pre-wet the baby's head. In total shock I looked over to where Kieran was standing and caught his eye. He smiled cockily and raised his glass at me. From that moment on I hated him with a passion and knew that for the sake of my own sanity I could never have anything more to do with him. He had totally used me yet again, and it hurt. It hurt really badly.

I don't know how I did it, but for once in my life I managed to keep my pride. I felt like making my own special announcement about precious Kieran Docherty there and then. Luckily, Liv grasped my hand protectively when the announcement was made. Being a true friend she didn't say, 'I told you so'. Instead she got my coat for me and rounded up Brad who was now asleep in a chair in the corner of the room. She then walked us outside as best she could and pushed us into a cab.

'Amy, go back to the hotel, tuck Brad up, then tuck yourself up. I'll be along later. I just need to say goodnight to Jack.'

Despite the trauma I was facing I had to smile to myself. Olivia Irving was never off-duty where men were concerned.

Chapter Twenty-seven

Pisces: *Positivity is the key to happiness this week. Grab life by the gills and start smiling again.*

It was a relief to get home. I was feeling totally drained and exhausted from the past couple of weeks. Still reeling from Kieran and Sinead's baby announcement I felt like just getting into bed and staying there for a week. I really longed for somebody to come round, give me a huge cuddle, make me some scrummy food and tell me that everything would be all right. Brad was usually the man for this but at the moment I was his rock and not the other way round. Jon wasn't around either, as he had flown to see Jackie in Scotland that morning.

I unpacked, put on my sloppiest clothes, got myself a coffee and slumped on the sofa. Even Pen realised how down I was as he just kept popping in, jumping up on me, and putting his paw on my face as if to say that he was here if I needed him. Jon had obviously looked after him well. My mobile rang, startling me out of my doze.

'Amy? Hi it's Christoper. Just wondered if you'd had a chance to look at your Leo yet?'

'Oh hiya,' I replied sleepily, and glanced over at the pile of unopened mail on the coffee-table. 'Chris, sorry but I'll have to call you back. I've got someone here at the moment.'

'Ooh, have you indeed? OK then, call me soon.'

'Will do,' I replied, trying to sound bright and breezy when I wished everyone would just leave me alone. I felt bad lying to Christopher, but going on a new date was the last thing on my mind. In fact, at this precise moment I felt like joining a hippy commune in the Outer Hebrides. The local paper was in the pile of unopened post. I flicked to the horoscopes to see if that would lighten my mood, and read: Pisces: Positivity is the key to happiness this week. Grab life by the gills and start smiling again.

Right, that was it. Tomorrow I would swim to the top again.

'What a beautiful day,' blared out on the clock radio.

'Today, Penelope,' I announced, 'is the first day of a new beginning in the life of Amy Jane Anderson.'

I sang in the shower, put on my favourite red shirt and little black skirt, and headed downstairs. Even the fact that it was a rainy Monday morning was not going to deter me. I went into the kitchen, made myself a coffee, and began to open my post. It consisted

of two bills, a circular trying to sell me yet another credit card and the familiar green Starr & Sun envelope.

Mr Leo, I discovered, was a complete babe. He had a round, smiley face and collar-length blond wavy hair and looked a bit of a surf dude to me. He was also only twenty-nine, which made him even more appealing. His name was Charlie Collins, majoring in fun, pleasure, extreme sports, and drinking. Why not? I could do with a bit of fun. When I arrived at work, Mr Parkinson, for some reason seemed really pleased to see me. He called me into his office.

'Amy, it's good to have you back,' he said sincerely while looking right down my red shirt. 'I've missed them, I mean I've missed you.'

'Thanks, Mr Parkinson, and thanks again for letting me take time off at such short notice.'

Liv, surprisingly, was already in on a Monday morning. I got straight on to email without even acknowledging her.

Dearest Liv,
Did you wet the bed or have you got early personal calls to make?

Dearest minger
I object to your rudeness. As you know I live for my work and not work for a living like some people. Oh and I did have to give Jack a quick call before he went off to work to remind him of my address. He's coming over to stay next weekend!

Dearest Liv
I take it Alec, the world's richest man, has been dunked then?

Dearest minger
I thought I'd told you already that you should have one in rehearsal, one in the wings, and one on the stage. Now please do get on.

PS: Glad to see you've already given Mr Parkinson a hard-on!

I never thought I'd say it but I was actually pleased to be back at work. It took my mind off the past couple of weeks. Brad had also returned to work today. I gave him a quick call to check he was OK and he didn't seem too bad. I was still was having trouble getting my head around the fact that Sam was marrying Katie. It just seemed so surreal. He strolled in at 10 a.m. with the flushed look that I could now recognise myself.

'Sam Clark, you've been shagging on a Monday morning, you lucky bastard.'

'Good to see you back, babe.' he said, and handed me a gift bag. I opened it and my eyes filled with tears. It contained a little book entitled plainly *Friends* and inside it were pictures with anecdotes of what a good friend is.

'Thanks, Sam, you really are so sweet.'

'I just wanted you to know that you are a very special friend and I'm proud of you for looking after Brad the way you did.'

The day carried on in normal Monday fashion. My newfound positivity must have kicked in as I even paid for a car park ticket at lunchtime. The churchyard experience in Dublin had obviously disturbed me as I was now actually worrying if I would go to heaven or not. Thinking about this, as I got back into my car to return to the office, I handed my ticket to a fellow parker as I still had half an hour left on it. Later that afternoon I gave Christopher a quick call. He was delighted to hear from me.

'I was beginning to miss you,' he said, and I could tell he was smiling. 'Nobody else gives me such entertaining feedback after dates. Now, did you approve of Mr Leo?

'I did actually, he looks quite a babe.'

'Shall I get him to call you directly on the mobile?'

'Yes, OK. Ask him to call me tonight if he can.'

I got into bed that night feeling calmer about life than I had done for a long time. In a way, knowing that Kieran was going to be a father made me realise that he was out of my life once and for all. Having a sneaky shag with a married man was bad enough, but a sneaky shag with a married man with a baby on the way was totally out of bounds. If I did want Saint Peter to let me in those Pearly Gates then I would have to stick to my guns on this one.

Chapter Twenty-eight

Pisces: *You'll feel a great surge of energy today. Make sure you channel it down the right track or it could all end in tears.*

Brad looked better than he had for a long time. I gave him a big hug when I arrived at his house.

'I know you're just hugging me because you feel guilty for using my house as a pick-up joint,' he said sulkily.

'Actually, darling boy, I am here an hour early so we can have a little drinkette before I leave.' I produced a bottle of wine from behind my back. 'Now get those glasses and quit being so shitty.'

We sat down at his kitchen table. I leant over it and gave my friend a kiss on the cheek.

'It's going to be OK, you know,' I told him quietly.

'I know it is,' he replied. 'Now let's get this bottle open. Where are you going tonight anyway?'

'Don't know. Mr Leo said that he was going to surprise me. He also said that he was going to take me for the ride of my life and I had to wear jeans.'

'Oh my God, how exciting!' Brad shrieked.

'I know, I love surprises,' I enthused. 'I was thinking he might be taking me to a fairground but I don't know of any local ones around at the moment.'

'Hang on, Ames, he's probably just got a fast car like Gibbon Man.'

'As long as it's not ice-skating I really don't care.'

Just as I was saying this we heard the unmistakable sound of a motorbike pulling into the drive. It was my turn to say, 'Oh my God.'

Brad was in hysterics.

'It's not funny! I panicked. 'How on earth am I going to stay on? I feel a bit pissed after that wine now.'

Mr Leo was very charming. After saying a quick hello and goodbye to Brad, he gestured towards his huge black motorbike and proudly announced, 'Ms Anderson, your chariot awaits. Here's your helmet. Have you ever been on a bike before?'

Not wanting him to think that I had led a sheltered life, I confidently replied, 'Of course I have. Love them, my cousin used to have one, went on it all the time.'

'Good, good. I won't have to teach you how to lean into corners then.'

In a way I was glad that I'd had half a bottle of wine or I might have feigned illness there and then. 'Where are you taking me on this amazing machine then?' I asked jauntily.

'Now that would be telling.' He laughed. 'Right, hop on.'

I could see Brad peering round from behind the front room curtain and knew that he would still be in hysterics. I clambered clumsily onto Mr Leo's mean machine and clung to him like a limpet clinging to a rock. I can honestly say I have never been so scared in my whole life. I was so glad that I had commenced my path to righteousness as on several occasions, as we rounded bends, I obviously leaned the wrong way and thought that my time was up. Finally we pulled into what looked like an industrial estate.

'You OK back there?' Mr Leo asked, his voice muffled by his helmet.

'Fine, fine!' I exclaimed.

I've never been so glad to stand on terra firma in my whole life. When I pulled my helmet off I could feel my hair sticking down to my head. I quickly ruffled it up and hoped I didn't look like a complete minger. In the background I could hear a lot of fast engine noise. As we walked across the car park, I saw a sign: WW Go-Karts – Dare or be Square. If Brad had been laughing when I left he'd have been beside himself now.

'Told you you'd be getting the ride of your life,' Mr Leo said proudly.

'I thought I'd just had it,' I spluttered.

'Reckoned you'd be up for this from the way Christopher described you.'

Christopher Starr, just you wait!

'Let's have a quick drink in the bar first and then we can get you kitted out. We'll have an hour on the track and then I thought we could go to a nice pizza place I know round the corner. Hope that's OK with you?'

Charlie Collins had big brown, honest eyes. His wavy blond hair had been pushed flat to his head, which made him look even younger than his twenty-nine years. He also had the fullest, most succulent lips I had seen in a while. My loins responded to this lion's charm.

'Charlie, that sounds just great,' I smiled.

'CC to you from now on, Amy. Follow me.'

I was slightly concerned that I had already had half a bottle of wine and I was now drinking a large rum and coke for Dutch courage. Could you get done for drink-driving in a go-kart?

I walked over to my assigned kart, number six, looking quite gorgeous – *not* – in a red boiler-suit and matching red helmet. My feet were laced into smelly boots and my hands stuck in dirty leather cut-off gloves. There were four other drivers joining us on the track. Here was I, thinking that it would just be me and the lovely CC pottering around at our own pace. Realistically, how could a gregarious Leo do anything sedately?

'Right, listen up.' A Cockney accent travelled across the track as we were getting into the karts. 'We'll send you round on four laps and time ya. Fastest lap goes first on the grid and so on. We'll then start the race and it's up to you to go for it. No bumping on purpose. Look out for the blue flag, it means someone wants to overtake so move over. Red flag means stop, there's been a bad pile-up ahead. Obviously, for the lady in the pack, the black and white flag means the end of the race. Now enjoy yourselves.'

Cheeky bloody bastard! The smelly helmet was making me feel claustrophobic, not least because by now was actually quite drunk. I had a terrible fear that I might be sick and no one would be able to get my helmet off in time and I would choke on my own vomit. As I put my foot over the throttle pedal, ready to speed off, I could feel the male testosterone all around me. I let them all speed off in front of me so I could get a feel of the kart. Once I actually got going I found I wasn't that bad. Lifting up the visor on my helmet, I felt the exhilarating rush of wind on my face. The alcohol in my system was obviously making me quite reckless. I started cornering really well and at one stage even overtook a disgruntled-looking contender. Then Charlie lapped me, letting out a big whoop as he did so.

I was really pleased that I wasn't at the back of the grid and I could see the pride on the lion's face as we prepared ourselves for the actual race. I got ready to press my foot hard on the throttle as we waited for the flag to go down. I don't know if it was the excitement of being involved in a proper race or the fact that my coordination was waning as the large rum and coke took effect. But all of a sudden I was screeching, at what felt like a 100 mph, towards the other karts on the grid. I crashed into not one, not two, but three of them and ended up hanging almost upside down on a crash barrier. I could see stars. I heard Cockney Man exclaiming, 'Bloody women drivers.' My legs felt like they had been crushed in a vice. I started to cry.

I then heard another voice shouting, 'Bloody hell, Vince, stop your bullshit and get her out of there! She looks hurt.' In a fuzzy haze I then heard running and the new, but strangely familiar, voice again. 'It's OK, love, let's take your helmet off gently.'

I looked up with my mascara-stained face directly in to the beautiful, bluey-green eyes of Will Wallingford. Before I had a chance to say anything, Charlie was by my side.

'Amy, are you OK? That was some driving.'

I was in no mood for this, I just wanted to get out of this blessed kart and I wanted to get out now. 'Will somebody help me out of this bloody thing,' I wailed. My legs were really hurting.

'Careful as you go, Amy.' Will said caringly, as he lifted me free of the damaged kart. He sat me down on the crash barrier. 'Let's just check your legs, shall we.' He moved his hands up and down both legs and suddenly the pain seemed to disappear as the memories of Will's gentle touch came flooding back to me. He looked towards Charlie.

'She's just badly bruised, mate, but I think you should take her to hospital as she may have a bit of concussion.' Will then turned to me. 'Good to see you again, Amy. You know where I am now. That's if this insurance claim doesn't bankrupt me!' He laughed and then wandered back to see how Cockney Man was getting on with clearing up the damage.

'How do you know, Will?' Charlie asked.

'Oh, I used to go to school with him,' I replied nonchalantly.

Leaving the massacre behind us on the track, Charlie rang for a taxi as thankfully he didn't think it would be safe for me to go to casualty on the back of the bike.

'Right, let's get you to the hospital then.'

'Actually I don't feel too bad now,' I told him. 'I would just like to go home, have a hot bath and go to bed.'

'I feel so responsible for this, I'm really sorry. If you feel ill at all in the night, make sure you get checked out, won't you?'

'Yes, of course,' I meekly replied.

'Here's a tenner for the taxi. I'll call you tomorrow.'

As the taxi pulled away I noticed the sign again, W.W. Go-Karts, and smiled to myself. Trust Will to be running this sort of empire.

Chapter Twenty-nine

Pisces*: A dramatic change to your lifestyle could be on the cards.*

I woke up feeling as if I had been run over by a steamroller. My head was thumping and I could barely move my legs. I looked under the covers to check they were still attached to my body and gasped as between my knees were the biggest bruises I had ever seen. There was no way I could go into work. What on earth was I going to say to Mr Parkinson? 'Sorry, Mr P, but I got drunk and threw myself round a go-karting track last night and I cannot walk.' I'd have to consult Anna. She was the world's best liar when it came to sick time.

'Morning, dear sister.'

'You're up early, Ames. How was your date?'

By the time I had finished telling her she was in absolute hysterics.

'Glad I have the support of my sister when I lose the use of my limbs,' I said, laughing.

'Cool seeing Will again though, wasn't it?' She had really liked him when I went out with him all those years ago.

'Yeah, it was good to see him. I still think he's gorgeous but he's got a girlfriend and, after the

Kieran debacle, I'm not ever going to go down that road again.'

'It seems as if he's keen for you to contact him though.'

'Yes, but you know what I'm like. I don't think I could just have a polite chit-chat evening with him. I'd want to jump him!'

'Amy, sometimes I don't think we came out of the same pod, the things you come out with!' Anna exclaimed in mock horror. 'Anyway, back to your skive excuse. Go straight through to Mr P, do the bit that you realise that you have had a lot of time off lately and you are really grateful for his support. Then say that you have woken up with the most horrendous period pain and feel that you need to stay in bed with a hot water bottle and will see him Monday. Men never question period pain.'

'Good one, Anna, I shall do that. How are your bowels, by the way?'

'I forgot to tell you, Sam got me this homeopathic pill and I seem to be cured. Shitted for England the first few days I took it but it seems to have sorted itself now.'

'Lovely, glad I'm not eating my Coco-Pops!' I laughed. 'See you soon.'

'Yeah, seeya and good luck with Mr P!'

Before I rang work, I took a couple of painkillers and ran a hot bath to soothe my aching limbs. When I checked my mobile for messages, the text message sign was flashing: two messages. The first one was from Brad: GOOD RIDE? The second was from Charlie: HOPE YOU'RE NOT TOO SORE. CALL ME xx.

I sank into the bath and let out a sigh of relief as the pressure was taken off my aching limbs. Good old Anna, thinking of the period pain excuse. I couldn't believe I hadn't thought of it myself, must have been that bump on the head. It was then that an awful realisation overtook me. I sat bolt upright in the bath and squealed in pain and also fear. My period had been due three days ago.

'Stupid, stupid cow,' I said out loud.

How could I have let this happen to me again? I felt my boobs to see if they were tender. They felt normal. I pushed my stomach in to see if it felt any different. It seemed the same size. I was never late. I got out of the bath, regained my composure and phoned Mr Parkinson on his direct line, speaking the script my sister had prepared for me. It made me cringe telling the period pain lie, especially as I might not be suffering from the curse for the next nine months.

I got back into bed and for once instead of going in to my usual Piscean emotional state I began to think logically. I was thirty-three years old I had my own house, a good job, and fantastic friends and family. I would be quite capable of bringing up a child on my own. Nobody need ever know it was Kieran's. I could say that it was a one-night stand. On the other hand I was an adult; I could make my own decisions. I could have an abortion and nobody would ever know about it. It was when I thought about this option that I did start to cry. I had lost one baby in traumatic circumstances; there was no way that I was going to lose this one too.

However, I was too terrified to go and get a test.

At least not knowing for a little while would stop me having to make a decision. I didn't feel strong enough to have to face the enormity of this situation just yet. In true Piscean non-confrontational fashion I said to Pen, 'I'll wait a week. I can face it in a week.' Then I put on my smiley mask and put my best fin forward to carry on as normal.

Later that week, Charlie rang and insisted that he took me for Sunday lunch. I couldn't face going on the bike again so said I'd meet him at The Lyndhurst Arms, which was just down the road from my house.

'How are your legs?' was the first thing he said as he greeted me with a kiss on the cheek. I had worn a skirt especially so I could show off my bruises and get the sympathy I thought I deserved.

'Bloody hell!' he exclaimed.

I bruise very easily but even I was surprised at the size and depth in colour of these beauties.

'Let me get you a drink to compensate for leading you into such danger.'

I know that I should have said that I wanted an orange juice; however, the words,

'Large glass of dry white wine, if that's OK?' came falling out of my mouth. My self-destruct key had been pressed and there was no stopping me. Charlie Boy matched me drink for drink.

'Looks like the bike's staying here for the night,' he smirked a couple of hours later. 'You do have a double bed don't you?'

'Of course I do,' I leered back.

Oh God, I was back to my serial shagger status. Where were my morals? I was with child and already contemplating going to bed with another man.

Charlie was certainly good-looking and his boyish charm and excitable ways were adorable. I hadn't had sex on a Sunday afternoon for ages, and just the thought of it was making me feel like grasping my bruised knees to me in anticipation. Alcohol had yet again made me reckless. Again, I blame my alcoholic tendencies on being a fish. I had been reading one of my astrology books in bed the night before as I had worked out that my child was likely to be a Gemini. I skipped to the Pisces chapter and read: "Too many Piseans have a tendency to find relief in alcohol. It's a dangerous vice as it lulls them pleasantly into a false sense of security."

Oh, how true this was this afternoon. As we walked Charlie's bike back to my house and parked it safely in the front garden I felt like I didn't have a care in the world. As soon as the front door was closed he put his arms around me and started kissing me passionately. I drew away.

'Wow, I forgive you for everything after that,' I laughed.

'You'll forgive me for even more once you have a puff of this,' he said pulling a huge joint out of his jacket pocket. I was actually quite shocked. I had led quite a sheltered life in the world of drugs. In fact, my only experience of smoking a joint was at Reading Festival ages and ages ago. Will had been the instigator of this. I remember giggling my head off for about ten minutes, then falling headlong into his lap, snoring, as a group of us sat round a campfire.

'I don't smoke,' I said innocently. 'This might make me want to start again.'

'Oh come on, Amy, the odd puff won't hurt. In

223

fact, it will make you feel really good.'

After choking on the initial drag I began to enjoy myself. It was quite wonderful to feel the rush of nicotine again, and I realised how much I had missed smoking. It was also quite wonderful to suddenly feel so mellow and that life was just so, so good.

'Charles Collins, you have seen me in action on the go-kart track, you are now going to see me in action on the stage.' I stood up, joint in hand. 'Please put your hands together for an Amy Anderson joke.'

Charlie clapped ferociously and I handed back to him the now nearly finished cause of my outlandishness. 'OK, are you ready?'

'Ready,' he replied seriously.

I then started giggling uncontrollably. 'This is just such a funny joke.' More uncontrollable giggling from both parties now. We finally both managed to stop laughing.

'OK, quick, go go, tell it now,' he urged.

'OK, OK. Right, there are two turtles.' I then proceeded to stick out my bottom lip as far as it would go. 'This is the first turtle speaking,' I tried to explain with my lip still sticking out, which made me sound like a dalek. More hysteria. 'When it rains,'

I said in my Turtle No1 voice. 'Do you get water in your mouth?' I then changed into the second turtle and curved my top lip *over* the bottom one as far as it would go. 'OK, this is the second turtle speaking now.' With my lip still curved and my body bent, assuming the look of a turtle, I now sounded like Zippy from *Rainbow* as I delivered the punch line: 'No.'

This was the only joke I ever remembered. H had

told me it years ago and it still made me belly laugh. No one else ever seemed to find it that funny but in our current state Charlie and I did not stop laughing for at least ten minutes. Once we had calmed down I put on some soft music and snuggled up to him on the sofa. He smelt really clean. I put my hand up his shirt and started to stroke his chest. His skin was really smooth. I love smooth-skinned men; hairy chests and backs are an instant turn-off to me.

'I tell you what,' Liv had once confessed on a girly night out, 'this guy I was seeing called Gary Simmons was so hairy everywhere – and I mean *everywhere* – I used to wake up after a night of passion and, no word of a lie, I used to cough up a fur ball!'

There was no chance of this with Charlie. Despite it being broad daylight I shut the curtains. I didn't feel giggly now, just completely mellow.

'Massage time, I reckon CC,' I said to him seductively.

'Yeah, baby,' he mumbled.

I pulled off his shirt and trousers. He was firm in all the right places and I could see just how turned on he was. I felt slightly empowered being fully dressed and pleasuring him with my massage techniques. He moaned softly as I made sure that I didn't miss any areas.

'Now let me see, I think your friend down here wants kissing.' By now I felt completely horny. Drunk, stoned, and with George Michael playing in the background; the atmosphere was just right. I pulled down his Calvin Kleins (full approval on this front) and began to suck him gently at first. Then with a degree of urgency I used my tongue to increase his pleasure.

'Wow!' He exclaimed time and time again. I was enjoying giving this sexy beast pleasure. Then disaster struck. Just as I knew he was about to come, without warning my head started spinning like a waltzer at a fairground.

'Shit, sorry,' I shouted as I ran up the stairs two at a time and promptly threw up in the loo. Afterwards, I put the toilet lid down and sat slumped on it with my head towards the floor. I cannot remember ever feeling this out of control. I was almost incoherent when Charlie, now fully clothed, appeared in the doorway.

'I'm so sorry,' I slurred.

'No worries, Amy. Manyana and all that.'

'I feel so ill,' I wailed. My head was whirling and I felt sick again. As quickly as I could, given my condition, I stumbled off the toilet seat, pulled the lid up, and proceeded to throw up again.

Chapter Thirty

Pisces: *A lucky escape today makes you reassess your whole life.*

The next thing I knew, I was waking up on a cold, bright October Monday morning. I looked over to the other side of the bed, as the awful memory of the night before started coming back to me. Thankfully, it was only Penelope lying there. I had the worst hangover I'd ever experienced. My throat was sore from retching and I felt thoroughly distressed at how badly I had behaved.

I still had my shades on when I sat down at my desk. There was no way I could ring in sick again. Unfortunately, Sam had taken a day's holiday and Liv was nowhere to be seen. I needed the pair of them more than anyone this morning. I got myself a coffee and switched on my computer. I could barely sit upright I felt so terrible. I was supposed to be sourcing a venue today for a dinner for fifty people at a top West End hotel, but there was no way I could talk sense to anyone. I kept my head down, as I couldn't point it any other way anyway and just pretended to be typing away. Good job Mr Parkinson was so short-sighted; even if he had looked over my shoulder he wouldn't have noticed the pages of random keys that I had typed.

Liv strolled in at ten. It was her turn to be flushed. She gave me one of her looks and sat down at her desk. Rules are that if you are late you don't chat, so as not to wind up Mr P further, instead you just get straight on to email.

Dear minger

I don't think I've ever seen you looking so rough. You OK? By the way Jack is an absolute angel and he's certainly not a good Catholic boy!

What with the go-karting accident and being preoccupied with my own selfish problems, I hadn't even wished Liv a good weekend with Jack. I never usually forgot something like that and felt really bad about it. She knew something was badly wrong when I replied.

Dear Liv

I'm in a bad way and it's not just a hangover. Let's meet in the cafe for lunch at 12. Glad you had good w/e.

The Café just down the road from our office was myself and Liv's legendary meeting place. Inhabited by builders and truckers by day and cockroaches by night, it was, despite its seedy appearance, a godsend for hangovers. I have never tasted a better fry-up or cheese baguette and chips anywhere in the world. Mrs Higgins approached our table. She was five-foot-nothing tall and her waist circumference was about the same. She had a constant smile on her face.

'Afternoon, ladies. By the look of you, it's cheese baguette and chips times two.'

'Spot on Mrs. H, thanks,' replied Liv.

'Can I have a fat coke as well please?' I added. 'Oh, Liv.' I put my head into my hands.

'What is it, babe? If you shagged the lion it doesn't matter. You said he was cute and it doesn't make you a bad person.'

'I wish it was that simple.' I took a deep breath and paused. 'Liv, this is serious. I think I'm pregnant.'

For the first time in a long time Liv was speechless. She got her thoughts together, put her arm on mine, and said, 'OK, we can sort this together. Surely not from last night, so I guess it was Dublin?' I nodded. 'Why didn't you tell me before, you stupid cow?'

'You know what I'm like. I thought if I didn't face it then it would go away.'

'How late are you?'

'About a week.'

'Right, as soon as we've eaten we will go and get a test and I will come round yours straight after work.'

After enduring the longest afternoon in the history of Jenkins Software, for the second time in my life I pulled open the foil wrapper of a pregnancy test. Liv waited outside the bathroom. I was terrified.

'Have you done it yet?' she called through the door.

I appeared looking ashen. 'You hold it and look, Liv. I so know it's going to be a blue line and I cannot face it.'

After an hour-long minute, Liv looked down at the test and then looked at me. 'There's no line, nothing, nada. You're OK, Ames.'

'I hope I peed on it properly. These home tests are

evidently extremely accurate but I'm still not convinced.'

An hour later, after getting an emergency appointment at the doctor's I ran out to Liv's car, this time smiling. 'I'm fine,' I told her. 'There's no baby. With all the stress and the travelling to America and then Dublin and back in such a short time it's affected my cycle, that's all.' I let out a huge sigh of relief.

'Halle-bloody-lujah!' Liv exclaimed. 'I think we should go for a drink to celebrate.'

'Actually, Liv, do you mind if we don't? I still feel like shit and I'm worried that I'm drinking too much at the moment.'

'Ames, you're scaring me now. Please don't tell me you've become a vegetarian and will go to church every Sunday as well!'

'Don't be silly. I just think I should take a bit more control over where I want my life to go from now, that's all.'

'All right then, Ames, for starters promise me condoms all the way from now on. I don't think I could go through a day like this again.'

Chapter Thirty-one

Sagittarius: *Being in the wrong place at the wrong time leads to a missed opportunity for happiness today.*

The week flew past. I got my head down at work and limited myself to one glass of wine a night with my dinner. I even stayed in every night, despite constant efforts by Brad and Liv to get me down the pub. Saturday morning arrived, as did my period, hurrah! I had a sumptuous lie-in, followed by my favourite breakfast of carved ham and poached eggs. Life felt better. Christopher hadn't called me yet to check on how my date with Charlie had gone. Strange. Just as I was thinking this, the phone rang and it was him.

'Spooky, I was just thinking about you,' I said.

'Nice things, I hope. Just wondered if you would consider an honest Cancerian as your next contender?'

'I've only just got over Mr Leo and the injuries I sustained from him.'

'Yes, I did hear.'

'Oh, did you indeed?'

'Anyway,' Christopher speedily continued, 'we don't want to talk about him now, we need to find you a new date.'

My Piscean intuition picked up on Christopher's haste to change the subject. 'Spit it out about Mr Leo, come on. I know there's something I should know.' Just saying, 'Spit it out,' brought back embarrassing memories of my mistimed debauchery with Charlie.

'He doesn't want to see you again, Amy Just said he didn't think you were the type of girl for him.'

I thought this might be the case, but just hearing the words were quite hurtful, despite him being a drug taking scallywag! 'Oh well, you win some you lose some, I guess,' I said breezily

'So Mr Cancer?' Christopher reiterated.

I didn't have the heart to tell him yet that one of the life-changing decisions I'd made since my pregnancy scare was that Charlie Collins was the final Starr & Sun contender in my search for a sole-mate. 'I'll call you next week and let you know, bit busy with other things at the moment.'

'Cordelia sends her good wishes, by the way.'

It made me laugh that Christopher and Cordelia had seemed to take me under their wings. I was going to concentrate on just me for the moment. My head still wasn't completely straight after the Kieran incident. I was going to cut down on my drinking, lose the stone I had wanted to lose for years, and basically stop being a certified nymphomaniac. From now on I would wait for Mr Right: someone who cared about me for who I was and who I got to know before I jumped into bed with him.

Thinking about this brought back memories of Will. We had waited a whole year before we had slept together. Granted, we were young but just waiting made the whole event really special. I had been so in love with him. We used to laugh so much together that my sides would be splitting. Will was my rock. He had helped me through the loss of my mother, which had meant a great deal to me. I decided to contact him. Of course I could meet up with him and not sleep with him. He was an outrageous flirt but he had always been faithful to me, so why would he want to sleep with me anyway, as he had a girlfriend? I rang Directory Enquiries and got the phone number for W.W. Go-Karts. The dulcet tones of cockney Vince came down the line.

'Will? Nah, he's not 'ere at the moment, love.'

I didn't want to leave a message. 'Oh, OK. When will he be around and I'll call back?'

'He's on holiday, taken a couple of weeks off with the missus. Thailand, I think he said. I've got a message book here for him, shall I take ya name?'

'No, it's OK, thanks. It's not important. I'll catch up with him when he's back,' I replied despondently. Fate will prevail if we're destined to meet up, I thought. Trust Will to be in Thailand. He really was textbook Sagittarius with his flirtatious ways and love of travel. The phone rang as soon as I put it down. It was Jon.

'Hiya, Amy, how are things?'

'Hello, you,' I replied chirpily. 'Good to hear from you. It's been a bit of a rollercoaster of a few weeks but I'm good at the moment, thanks,' I told him. 'No one bought next door yet then, I see?'

'That's partly why I'm calling. I just wanted to let you know that a handsome, debonair chap will be moving in next weekend.'

'Oh my God, do you know if he's single?'

'Amy, you are such a girl! He is now, unfortunately, but somehow I don't think you're really his type.'

The penny dropped. 'Oh, Jon, sorry you're single but it's bloody fantastic that you're moving in. That has really made my day. Are you OK though? I know how much you cared about Andrew.'

'It's been tough. We're still friends, but leaving Scotland is the best way for me to move forward with my life. OK, Amy, must dash, packing to do. See you next week.'

'Looking forward to it. Bye now.'

Chapter Thirty-two

Pisces: *An attractive proposition leads to you becoming the centre of attention.*

It was ages since the whole of the gang had got together so I arranged an impromptu dinner party at mine the following Saturday night. Jon had now moved in so I thought it was a good opportunity to introduce him to everyone at the same time.

It was to be quite a gathering: H and Horace, Sam and Katie, Liv and Jack, myself, Brad and Jon. Anna and Boyd sadly had other arrangements, although I don't think Anna was that bothered. She had rung the night before to inform me that although her bowels were almost cured, she was sure my cooking could turn even an iron stomach to molten metal. Nice!

Brad arrived early with a bunch of yellow roses and a box of wine in hand. He seemed to be getting stronger by the day now. He kissed me on the cheek.

'Princess, you look wonderful as always. Now what culinary delights are you dishing up tonight? I'm starving.'

'It's an ensemble of dishes taken from my favourite recipes from The Curry Castle Cook Book.'

'What time are they delivering it?' he enquired laughing.

'Hopefully about nine, now let's have a glass of wine while I lay the table.'

Penelope appeared and swiped his paw at Brad's foot.

'I tell you, Amy, that cat is a demon. Mind you, if you'd cut my balls off and called me a girl's name I don't think I'd be too happy either!'

The others started to arrive. H's bump was beginning to show now. Horace was running around her, getting everything she needed. He looked like a mad professor with his mop of curly red hair. When H announced she was marrying Horace four years ago I had said to her, 'You do realise they're going to be gingers, don't you?'

'What are?' she had replied innocently.

'Your kids, silly.'

'Oh, Amy, don't. I had actually thought of that. I'm probably going to be the only mother who hopes the baby is born with no hair. I shall have the hair dye and clippers ready just in case!'

Sam and Katie were so gooey over each other it was quite sickening. They complemented each other fantastically, both with their long flowing locks and good looks. Katie's newfound interest in New Age philosophies meant that there was never a shortage of conversations on yins and yangs, chakras and chis.

'A little gift for you, Ames,' Sam said, thrusting yet another candle into my hand. 'Guessed the old love corner could do with a boost.'

'I'm actually off men at the moment, Mr Clark. I'm looking inward and finding myself before I launch myself at another potential victim.' Just as I was finishing my sentence Liv flew into the dining room, auburn hair flowing, looking completely gorgeous in a green velvet mini-dress.

'This is Jack, everyone,' she announced, and before anyone could say hello, 'Oh, and this is Ryan. Hope you don't mind, Ames, but Ryan is one of Jack's old uni mates and we'd arranged to meet up before your little impromptu soirée.'

'More the merrier, you know me,' I said breezily.

Brad poked me in the back and whispered, 'Sweetie, don't spend *too* long looking inwardly.'

Ryan was a complete babe. He was around six-foot-two, with rugby player build. He had black wavy hair and was dressed immaculately in a crisp white shirt and black jeans. He handed me a flower that he had picked from my front garden.

'Couldn't gatecrash empty handed,' he smiled.

I had expected him to be Irish but he had a West Country accent. 'Oh, so you're not from the Emerald Isle as well then?' I enquired.

'No. I live in London now but I was born and bred in St Ives.'

'How lovely,' I replied. 'I love the coastline of Cornwall. Had many a happy holiday there as a kid.'

'Yeah, it is beautiful. I've still got a holiday place down there but there's not much call for my line of work in a seaside town, unfortunately.'

'What do you do then?'

'I'm a TV producer.'

Liv butted in. 'My dear minger, when you have finished gabbing, any chance of some vino?'

'Surprised you haven't emptied the wine rack already. Help yourself. Dinner will be ready at nine,' I announced.

'I can't smell anything cooking,' said Horace innocently.

With this the doorbell rang.

'Oh, that must be my personal caterers,' I declared in a posh accent. It wasn't actually the caterers, but Jon.

'Come in, come in, babe.' I directed Jon through to the dining room and gave him a quick introduction. I hadn't actually told Brad that he was gay, as I didn't want him to think I was trying to set him up so soon after Sean's death, although quite obviously I was.

When I went to the kitchen to put some plates in the oven to warm and to open some more wine, Brad followed me in.

'Bit of a feast for you tonight, eh Ames? They are both so cute. Ryan's a bit on the tall side for me but Jon is a complete doll.'

'Thought you'd think so, he wouldn't be interested in me though.'

'Oh don't say that, my sweet. You know you're beautiful, there would be no reason why he wouldn't be.'

'The fact that he's just finished with his boyfriend might be one,' I replied, smiling.

'Oh, my God, I don't believe it!' Brad exclaimed. 'And I can't believe you didn't tell me before.'

Everyone was secretly pleased when the takeaway arrived and they didn't have to be subjected to one of my usual disgusting concoctions.

'Dig in!' I invited them.

The wine and conversation flowed. I was really happy to see that Liv had met her match with Jack. What he lacked in the wallet department he made up for with his sense of humour and quick wit. I just knew that she would not get bored with him as she usually did after a couple of dates. She came out with me to the kitchen to clear the dishes.

'Anyone I should know about in the wings or in rehearsal now?' I enquired.

'Actually, my smug minger friend, I expect you can tell that the one on the stage is putting on a fine performance at the moment.' She threw back her head and laughed. 'I love you, Ames, you know me so well.'

Brad and Jon also seemed to be getting on really well. I had heard them talking about Sean and saw Jon put a caring hand on Brad's arm as he was talking. Although Ryan was very good-looking he wasn't really my type. We got on well enough but he wasn't sparky enough for me, plus I'd noticed he had really big ears. He was also very clean-cut and seemed very sensible. He even placed the different Indian foods tidily in piles on his plate, rather than throwing them on like everybody else. Must be a Virgo, I thought to myself. I knew that I couldn't have fancied him or I wouldn't have brought up the subject of the dating agency.

'I want you all to know that I've decided I'm not going to subject myself to any more Horoscope dates,' I announced to the table at large.

'Oh, Amy, why?' H said, quite perturbed by my announcement. 'I was wondering why you hadn't called on me lately for my dresser duties.'

'I thought you wanted to have a date with all twelve star signs?' Katie enquired.

'To be honest I've had a laugh but most of them

were complete disasters. It's only Aquarius, Virgo and Cancer that I've yet to subject myself to. Oh and Sagittarius, but I went out with Will all those years ago and if it was meant to be with him it would have worked out then, wouldn't it?'

Brad, who had been following my every move, pointed out, that although I had lusted after my personal trainer, I hadn't properly dated a Capricorn yet.

'I've taken Capricorn off the list,' I said boldly. 'Christopher is a Capricorn and I've probably had more contact with him than anyone else. He is very sweet, but just doesn't do it for me,' I explained.

Ryan, who had been sitting quietly through my soliloquy, suddenly spoke up. 'I've got a proposition for you.'

Everyone went silent.

'I'm a Virgo and I like attractive brunettes with a good sense of humour.'

I gulped, terrified of what he was going to say next.

'But that's got nothing to do with my proposition.'

Everyone laughed out loud.

'So, what exactly are you proposing?' I enquired.

Ryan then became completely animated. 'I'm working on a show at the moment, it's a dating game show and I'm looking for likely ladies to be contestants to find their dream date.'

'Oh my God, how exciting!' Liv exclaimed. 'Can I come on it?'

Jack looked really hurt.

'Only joking, my sweet,' she said lovingly to him, looked at me and continued, 'Amy, you just have to do it. It's perfect for you. You know you've always secretly wanted to be on TV.'

Brad said camply, 'I shall be your agent. I can see it now. People will be asking who the cute boy is who escorts you everywhere.'

I could tell Ryan was pleased by everybody else's enthusiasm. 'I think you'd be great, too,' he told me. 'What do you say, Amy? We're shooting the first show next Saturday.'

'Ooh, I don't know,' I dithered.

'As her agent I can answer for her,' Brad said. 'And she's doing it.'

Chapter Thirty-three

Pisces: *Shrug off your inhibitions and get involved in something exciting and different today. You never know what it may lead to.*

Brad and I arrived at the Docklands TV studio bright and early on the Saturday morning. I'd never been to a TV studio before and it wasn't even half as glamorous as I had imagined it to be. It was like a big warehouse, with loads of partitioned areas. Lots of stressed looking people were rushing around dodging cabling that was strewn all over the floor.

I was terrified. The new show was entitled *Perfect Date*. Ryan had sent me a brief summary of the format a few days before. Basically, the studio was set-up as a restaurant, there were to be three eligible bachelors, each one sat at a different table, and I had to ask them three simple questions. The one who gave me the answers I liked the most would be chosen by me as my dinner-date for that night. This dinner would then be filmed and shown on the next show. If our date was a success then we, the lucky couple, would get an all-expenses-paid weekend to a destination of our choice. I could choose one question; the other two would be staged. The first I would see of the contestants would be when I sat down opposite them. Brad was beside himself with excitement.

'Prinny, it's going to be a doddle, sweetness. Just ooze sex and confidence. You'll be fine,' he assured me.

'What if I forget the questions?' I panicked.

Ryan appeared in the dressing-room doorway. 'Don't worry, you'll be fine. You'll have an earpiece, which I'll be on the other end of, so I will prompt you. Felix here will do your make-up and hair.'

Felix was six-foot-four, in fact he was the tallest and campest man I had ever met. He was wearing a red shirt with a pink cravat and had cropped white hair, which contrasted dramatically with his ebony skin. 'Ooh just look at you,' he announced on seeing me. 'Biggest bag of nerves I've seen in a while. Don't worry, honey, once I've teased your roots and simmered down that shine you'll be just fine.' He then looked at Brad. 'I could tease *you* later if you fancy it, sweetie.'

Brad looked terrified. 'Just popping to the loo,' he announced, and almost ran out of the room.

The Floor Manager walked me through my positioning for the show. She was a slight Welsh girl called Ffion with a mop of unruly blonde curls. She was extremely friendly but I could sense she would take no nonsense from me, as when I started wailing again that I was worried I might sit at the wrong table, she responded with, 'You can't and you won't.' This made me even more terrified.

The presenter of the show was called Dirk Douglas. He had so much fake tan on he looked orange. He was broad-shouldered, with a really slender waist and long legs, and dressed immaculately in a designer black suit, with an orange shirt and matching orange tie. This made me snort as it just looked like a continuation of his neck. His eyes seemed to dart around his face.

'Amy, darling, I'm Dirk. You can call me Dee but not on air. Now let's have a little run-through, shall we.'

Liv, H, Anna and Sam had arrived and were already sitting in the audience on their own. Ryan had let them in early as he thought they might help to calm my nerves.

'Go, Amy, go,' shrieked Liv from the audience. Dirk turned, gave her a disdainful look, and concentrated back on me. Once I had chatted through what Dirk was going to ask me at the start of the show, Felix appeared.

'Showtime, honey. Let's get you into something shimmery.'

When Felix had finished with me I have to say I felt a million dollars. He had put my hair up and little ringlets fell around my face. I was wearing a fitted black cocktail dress, covered in sequins, and black high-heeled sandals. In this outfit I could have walked down a red carpet to a film premiere and not felt out of place. Brad came in to see me as Felix was spraying my hair into place.

'Whoa, Amy, you look amazing. Now, you go, girl, you will be brilliant. I'm going off to sit with the others.' He kissed me on the cheek and sped off.

The music announcing the start of the show blared out. Ffion waited with me until Dirk said, 'So let's meet the lady who's going to fulfil one of these lucky chaps' fantasies.'

Ffion then pushed me forward with the words, 'Smile for the camera.' I felt like a rabbit that had been caught in the headlights of a car. *Retain composure*, my inner voice said. I could hear the gang clapping and screaming in the audience. Amazingly, I managed to get through the introduction without a hitch. However, I still cringed at the thought of anyone who knew me watching, and regretted Brad ever talking me into this.

Dirk led me to the first table and announced cheesily, 'Amy, meet Colin, Colin meet Amy. Ask a question and test the reaction.'

My mind suddenly went completely blank. I jumped back in my seat as Ryan said in my ear, 'Dog, Amy, dog.'

'Oh yes,' I said, and smiled out at the audience.

Colin was a nerd. He had brown hair, flicked across his right eye, and was wearing a hideous black and white stripy shirt with huge collars.

'Colin, hi. If you were a dog, what sort of dog would you be?'

'I think I would have to be an Alsation, Amy. Rough, tough, and loyal.' He then played up his part by adding. 'You can share *my* kennel any time.'

I thought I was going to be sick. I paused again.

'Second one, Amy, car, car!' Ryan screeched in my ear.

'Now then, Colin.' I was beginning to feel a bit more confident now. I cocked my head to the side and asked, 'What would you say is your favourite type of car and why?'

'Oh, that's easy. I like Ferraris. They're fast, sleek,

and they turn the ladies' heads.'

'OK, thanks for that, and finally,' I could almost hear Ryan quivering at the control desk as he waited for my own final unrehearsed question. 'Finally Colin, what is your star sign?'

'I'm a Scorpio.'

Dirk jumped over to the next table. 'OK, move on Amy and remember...' He looked out at the audience and said even more cheesily than before: 'Ask those questions and test those reactions.'

I waited for Ryan to plant the next question in my ear as I had totally forgotten them all by now. 'Farm animal, Amy, farm animal.'

Andy was sat opposite me. He too was a nerd. Where on earth had they picked these contestants from?

'Andy, nice to meet you.' I was beginning to play up my part now.

'Get on with it, Amy.' Ryan nagged from his post. I made a face as if to tell him to shut up.

'If you were a farm animal, Andy, what animal would you be?'

'Oh, that's easy. I would have to be an elephant, as they never forget anything and I would hate to forget anything as beautiful as you.'

I started to laugh; the audience started to laugh. I thought Andy was going to cry. I then felt sorry for him and whispered, 'I said a farm animal.' But poor Andy was so flustered by then he couldn't think of a single farm animal.

'Just go the last question,' shrieked Ryan in my ear, realising that Andy wasn't the sharpest tack in the box.

'Andy, it's OK. I'm not an animal lover anyway.'

Everyone shrieked with laughter again.

'Brilliant.' Ryan laughed in my ear.

'Finally, what's *your* star sign?'

'An easy one at last,' Andy replied thankfully. 'I'm a Jupiter.'

I was extremely relieved to get to the final contestant. His name was Nick and he was actually the best of a bad lot. He had a shaven head but the most piercing blue eyes and perfect teeth. The sea creature he would be was a dolphin, his favourite colour was blue, and he was a Cancerian. Dirk seemed relieved that it was nearing the end of the show as well. He guided me back to the sofa where he had introduced me.

'So, Amy, you've seen them, you've asked the questions and gauged the reactions. The audience are on the edge of their seats now, so just who is the lucky man who will be dining with you tonight?'

I looked out at the audience, who were calling out different names and caught Liv's eye. She was mouthing Nick to me. I was now beginning to enjoy myself. 'Well, Dirk, they're all pretty sexy, aren't they, but it's just got to be Nick.'

I had picked a Cancerian, when there was a Scorpio on offer. Poor Colin really was that atrocious. Mind you, we fish were also supposed to be compatible with crabs so I would remain open-minded on this one.

Rapturous applause followed. A beaming Nick came and sat next to me on the sofa. Dirk asked him, 'So Nick, you lucky boy, what do you think of your date for this evening?'

'She's OK.'

Bloody OK? I thought. Not gorgeous, attractive, a complete babe but just OK. We were then sent off holding hands, smiling and had, as rehearsed, to wave back at the audience, looking like we really wanted to be together.

As soon as we got out of camera shot Nick looked at me and said, 'Thank God that's over. Cheers for picking me.'

I was actually physically shaking; I didn't realise quite what an ordeal it would be. Nick seemed quite nice but he *so* wasn't someone I would usually go out with. I wasn't really into bald. Suddenly the gang appeared, they all jumped on me, congratulating me and laughing at what an idiot Andy had been. Liv whispered that I'd definitely made the right choice. Ryan also appeared and gave me a pat on the back.

'Well done, Amy, very amusing. No time to relax though. I'll introduce you to the crew going with you to the restaurant and we'll send you on your way.'

'Hiya.' Felix minced over to us. 'I'm coming with you, sweeties.' He then looked at Nick and said, 'I can touch you both up in the toilets.'

Nick and I travelled alone in the taxi to the restaurant.

'Look, Amy, I'm sure you're a really nice girl and everything, but I'm not looking for love, just a break. I'm an actor and hoped this show might be a foot in the door for something else.'

What a prat. I was so pleased that I didn't fancy him.

'Thanks for your honesty. Better to be knocked back before you've jumped the first hurdle rather than fall face first into the water jump.' I replied, putting a brave face on this whole awful situation.

'We'll get some posh nosh anyway,' he added. 'And if we can bear each other after the meal, a free weekend away somewhere cool as well.'

At that precise moment I thought that if Nick were the last man on earth I wouldn't even go to Bognor with him. We were to dine at The Oxo Tower. On arrival, I was impressed at how *cool* this place was. We were seated in a corner, for ease of filming, but still had magnificent views of London, due to the restaurant's trendy, elevated glass structure. Nick, however, was a very *un*cool person. After the starter I'd decided that it was going to be hard to make the best of a bad job. We said and did all the right things for the cameras but both knew that when we said goodbye after the show next Saturday, that would be the last we would ever see of each other.

Chapter Thirty-four

Pisces: *Make an effort to pamper yourself this week. A change is as good as a rest.*

'It was an experience anyway,' Brad said encouragingly over lunch the following Sunday.

'I guess so,' I sighed.

'At least now if anyone recognises you they'll instantly know you're single.'

'Yes, thanks for that Brad,' I said. 'How did your meal go with Jon last night, by the way?' I mentioned it casually, not wanting Brad to think it was any big deal. I knew that he was feeling a bit guilty going out with somebody else so soon after Sean.

'It was really special, Amy. I like him a lot. He respects that I want to take things slowly and that makes me like him even more.'

'Jon is a lovely guy. I'm really pleased for you, babe.'

I breezed into work on Monday, taking no notice of the jibes from colleagues about my disastrous date with Mr Cancer. Even Mr Parkinson had a word to say.

'A crabby crab is not good enough for someone like you, young Amy.'

'Thanks, Mr P.'

I was actually quite touched until he backed it up with, 'Mind you it would be every man's dream to be able to climb back into his shell and get away from a woman's nagging.'

I think that every man must have a rising Cancer sign, as don't they all retreat when the going gets tough? However, I was not going to be on a hate men mission. I was too partial to my entire bra collection to burn any of them, plus I didn't think a pair of DMs would suit me. It was a Piscean's prerogative to change her mind. I would now take control of my own destiny. I had swum right to the bottom of the ocean; I would now swim back up to the surface and the light again. I decided a change of image was required for this new start. I also wanted to be looking good for the pending school reunion disco that Anna had persuaded me to go to. Despite my announcement at the dinner party, I would telephone Christopher and face a new date. The new self-aware, self-confident Amy Jane Anderson would be ready for anyone and anything.

I took an afternoon off, went to the hairdressers and had my hair dyed dark brown and cut into a trendy style. I had a manicure, pedicure and facial. And finally, an hour-long Swedish massage. I was broke by the end of it but I felt good and ready to face anything that the world had to throw at me. It was time to phone Starr & Sun.

'Oh hi, Cordelia, is Chris around?'

'Amy dear, how lovely to hear from you. How are you?'

'I'm fine thanks, Cordelia, I'm really fine.'

'Amy, to what do we owe this pleasure?' Chris's voice was animated.

'I'm ready for another' I said dramatically.

Fate was however to play its trump card and the next date I was ready for was not quite the one that I'd predicted.

It hadn't taken that much persuasion from Anna to get me to attend the school reunion disco. 'It'll get you back into the social swing with your new image,' she had declared the previous Saturday over a cup of coffee at my place.

'I'll come with you, Ames. I would hate to walk in on my own if it was me,' she said caringly. 'I doubt if I'll know many people as it's a reunion for your year, so if you find that you're having a good time and meeting lots of people you remember, then I'll leave you to it. If not we can just get pissed together anyway.'

The reunion was taking place in the local Village Hall. This venue had evidently been chosen due to its proximity to the school, plus the fact it could accommodate comfortably the hundred or so expected ex-students. I felt a flutter of nerves as we walked across to the makeshift bar. A glitter ball was spinning in the middle of the room. Red, blue, and yellow lights were flashing and I was thrown back in time to our old school hall and the many discos that took place there. The familiar sound of the 1980s hit my ears. 'Club Tropicana' was blaring out. I had forgotten how much I had loved Wham. Thank goodness I didn't know way back then that George Michael would never serenade me personally with

'Careless Whisper'; it would have ruined me for life.

'Amy, great to see you. How are you doing?' A short blonde girl came running over to me. She was dressed in a pink mini-skirt and a pink and white spotted cut-off T-shirt. It could have been another one of Cordelia's sisters.

'Hi,' I said casually, not having any recollection of her whatsoever.

'I didn't realise it was fancy dress,' I said biding time for my memory to kick in.

'It's not,' the short girl replied, not offended in any way by this comment. It was

then the penny dropped. The freckles, the turned-up nose: it had to be Angela Addington. She had never been very bright although she compensated for it by being the school gossip. Even way back then she had an appalling dress sense.

'Angie,' I said falsely. 'You look great.'

'So do you, Amy. Amazing what a bit of weight loss can do, isn't it?'

Bitch! Angie continued. 'So what have you been doing over the past decade and a half?'

It was then I realised what a bad move coming to a school reunion was. Did I really want everyone to know that I was still single at thirty-three? Did I really want to tell now complete strangers what I had or hadn't been doing for the past however many years? By the third, 'So what have you been up to? Married? Kids?' I retreated with Anna to a quiet corner with a bottle of wine.

It was at the exact moment when Michael (Music Man) Matthews decided to play 'Joanna' by Kool and the Gang that I looked up and there he was. Will, all six-feet of him, with his trademark bright shirt, auburn hair, those beautiful eyes and now sporting a tan. He was casually leaning against the bar, surrounded by three girls from my old class, laughing, flirting, and gesturing wildly. 'Joanna' always reminded me of him. One of his mates used to go out with a Joanna and the four of us all used to sing it at the top of our voices as we went somewhere or other in Will's battered old Mini. I didn't think he would be back from his travels so I was pleasantly surprised to see him. He must have sensed me looking, or should I say staring, as his eyes moved from the girls he was with and he looked straight at me. He smirked, excused himself and wandered over.

'Just popping to the loo,' Anna shouted over the music.

'Hey, Amy, love of my life, have you recovered yet? I have to say it was a bit of a shocker seeing you at the track. Didn't really think it would be your scene.'

'Full of surprises, me. I have to say I wasn't surprised that you would own such a place. How was your holiday, by the way?' I could have kicked myself then as I'd given away that I had phoned him, hopefully he was too drunk to notice.

'Great, great, anyway I don't want to talk about me, how's Blondie?'

'If you are referring to Charlie, then I don't know how he is.' God, I still fancied him. He had the most amazing smile, and those eyes! Even his freckles were endearing.

Anna returned clutching her stomach. 'Ames, if you don't mind I'm going to head off, not feeling too good. Will you be OK?' She winked discreetly.

Will then interrupted. 'Anna Anderson, you haven't changed a bit either. Come here and give me a snog.' He kissed her on the cheek. 'Of course your dear sister will be OK. How could she not be in the capable hands of one Mr William Wallingford?'

'That's what worries me,' Anna said.

We saw my sister off and then Will jumped into the seat next to me. 'It really is good to see you, you know, Ames. You look great, I like your new hair.'

'Thanks. It's weird seeing you again. It's as if we've never been apart.' I was completely flattered that he'd actually noticed my new hairstyle from the last time we met. But that was Will all over, charming to the core. He then looked at me with those eyes. If I'd been a Funny Face ice-lolly I'd have melted all over the stick.

'It took me six months to get over you running off you know, Ames.'

I didn't dare confess that after leaving him and running off with Mohican Man, I realised what a big mistake I had made. 'I'm sure it didn't take you long to fill my shoes,' I smiled.

'Obviously I made them form an orderly queue.' He still smelt the same. That gorgeous warm, musky smell. Time seemed to fly by and nobody else in the room seemed to matter. It wasn't until 'Oops Upside Your Head' boomed out that Will jumped up.

'Come on, Ames, we've got to do this for old time's sake.'

We hit the floor, Will wrapped his legs around me and I wrapped mine around Phil Jones from 3C. Then we were all swaying from side to side not forgetting one single move. It was just like being at a school disco. In fact, I hadn't had so much fun for ages. The song came to an end and we all jumped up laughing.

'And now, folks, let's see if we can all smooch like we did back in the good old days,' Music Man Michael announced. Smooch? It was a long time since I'd heard that word and even longer since I'd carried out the act itself.

Will looked right into my eyes. 'Fancy a smooch, old bird?'

'Rude not to, ex-lurver,' I smiled.

I blame Randy Crawford for me falling in love all over again with Will Wallingford. As on the first bar of 'One Day I'll Fly Away' he held me gently at first and then kept moving his hands down to my bum and I kept moving them up, just like the old days. I wanted to kiss him there and then but sensing Angie Addington watching our every move and imagining the playground gossip the next day I resisted. We walked outside together.

'Need a lift?' he offered.

'Thought you were drinking?'

'I've only had a couple, got an early start tomorrow.'

'Yes, that would be cool, if you don't mind thanks.' Gone were the days of getting a backie on his bike before he got his Mini.

'Got the van tonight, I'm afraid.'

At that precise moment I wouldn't have cared if the delicious Will Wallingford had still got his Chopper. I hopped in to the W.W. Go-Karts van and felt like a teenager again. We pulled up outside number 21. I wanted to try and be cool but it didn't seem to matter as even after all this time I felt like I knew him so well.

'Coffee?' I enquired.

'There is nothing I'd like more, babe, but I've got an early start tomorrow.'

I'd avoided the girlfriend question up until now but I just had to know. 'Guess you've got to get home to your girlfriend as well?' I said sheepishly. The baggage warning signs were ringing on deaf ears again. All I wanted to do was grab him there and then and kiss him.

'Actually we split up when we got back from holiday. Being together 24/7 made me realise that I fancied the single life again.'

Thank goodness relief didn't express itself as a noise, as the sound of a red arrows' fly-past would have come out of my mouth at that precise moment. Instead I just said, 'Oh, right.'

'Come here, sexy,' Will urged. He leaned over to my side of the van, held my chin up, looked right into my eyes, and gave me the most passionate, toe-curling kiss I had ever had in my life. We came up for air after about ten minutes.

'Wow,' Will gasped. 'I'd forgotten just how sexy you are.' He then looked at his watch. 'Look, Ames, I really must go but give me your number this time. You're not running away from me again.'

I dutifully gave him my mobile number.

'See you later, Alligator.' he shouted out of the window as he pulled off at breakneck speed.

The next morning I called a conference at Sam's flat. Katie had now moved in. There seemed to be more candles alight than ever.

'Thought we needed a good karma as it's obviously ground-breaking relationship news,' Katie laughed. It was so good to see her and Sam so happy.

Anna had even made it. 'Stomach all right now sis?' I asked.

'Yeah, fine thanks. Just popped another one of Sam's wonder pills.'

Brad arrived with Jon. H had terrible morning sickness so had stayed at home. Liv was slumped in the corner wearing dark glasses.

'Yes, yes, I'm here in body, minger, left a lovely warm Jack in my bed so this had better be good.'

'Good is too insignificant a word for this one, chaps,' I announced. 'I've found the man I want to spend the rest of my life with.' I then proceeded to tell them what a wonderful evening I'd had with Will at the reunion and how, just after one kiss, I knew that this felt right. I was so excited. 'I never believed it before when people said they knew as soon as they met the right person as they got the this-is-it feeling, but now I've got it myself. I want to marry him. I love him!'

Sam sounded despairing. 'Oh, Amy, I'm so pleased for you if this *is* it, but do take care. I'm not sure after one kiss you can get us all buying hats.'

I was a bit disgruntled after this comment.

'Please support me on this one. I've never been so sure in my whole life.' My mobile then beeped. Everyone waited in anticipation for me to read the text message: I REALLY ENJOYED LAST NIGHT I CAN'T STOP THINKING ABOUT YOU. 'Told you, told you!' I shrieked.

Another beep: PICK YOU UP FROM YOURS

TOMORROW AT 8.

'That's a bit presumptuous isn't it,' Brad said critically.

'He can be as presumptuous as he likes,' I replied recklessly.

'Just take care, Amy. He has only just split from his girlfriend, you know.'

'Brad, trust me on this one. This is the first time in my life that something feels completely right.'

Chapter Thirty-five

Pisces: *Unexpected developments create a stir in a personal relationship. Make the most of it but take care not to wear your heart on your sleeve.*

Eight o'clock came and went. Nine o'clock came and went. I'd played my new Beyonce album three times over. I didn't want to call to hassle him, but by nine thirty I was beginning to get annoyed. I'd been out and got my hair blow-dried especially. I'd even gone out at lunchtime and bought a new sexy top from an expensive designer boutique. I nervously phoned his mobile and was told that the number I was calling was switched off and to try again later. Must be in a bad signal area, I thought. By the time ten o'clock came I actually hated the bitch on the end of the line constantly getting in the way of my pending marriage. My inner voice was telling me to remain calm. I completely ignored it.

'Liv, it's me.'

'Thought you'd be meeting the vicar by now,' she riposted.

'He hasn't turned up.'

'Oh, babe, his text messages were so positive there must be a genuine reason. Tell you what, get your make-up off and get ready for bed and he's bound to turn up. It's always the way.'

But it didn't work and I hardly slept for worrying that my fairytale was over before it had even begun. I got a phone call at 7 a.m. the next morning, my eyes were barely open.

'Amy, its Will. I am so, so sorry. We had a big group in last night and Vince took it on himself not to turn in. I tried to get away but couldn't. The battery went flat on my mobile and that's the only place I have your number. I'll make it up to you, I promise. I'm not around tonight but I can see you Wednesday.'

'OK,' I replied sleepily. 'Look forward to it.' I looked over at Pen who was lying on the pillow next to me. He opened one eye and then shut it again as if to say, 'Oh no, not again.'

It took an age for Wednesday to come. All day the same butterflies were fluttering in my stomach as I'd felt every time I was due to meet up with Will all those years ago. At eight o'clock on the dot the doorbell rang. I smiled a big smile.

'Hi, babe, I'm here. So sorry again for the other night.' He took a step back, looked me up and down and let out a whistle. 'Wow, Amy, you look amazing. Age certainly does become you!'

I'd put on the same expensive top I'd bought for Monday night that revealed enough cleavage to be sexy without looking like a strumpet. I'd also put on a skirt, which was quite unlike me for a first date. But this was no ordinary date. I was going out with Will Wallingford, the man I was going to marry.

'Thought we could go for a curry,' Will announced.

'That's great. I love curry.'

Even his presumption that I'd want to go for a curry didn't bother me. If he'd said we were going to a supermarket restaurant I would not have cared. I just wanted to be with this gorgeous-smelling, gorgeous-looking, gorgeous kisser of a man. Half an hour later, I thought I'd died and gone to heaven, for not only was I in The Curry Castle, my favourite Indian restaurant, but I was here with Will Wallingford, my first love. The journey to the restaurant had been a bit hairy, mind. His flash Aston Martin went faster in first gear than my old heap went in fourth. He drove like he was on his go-kart track. He had insisted that we sat right at the back of the restaurant; 'I can fondle you under the table then,' he'd laughed. We talked easily throughout the meal. I learned that his family still lived in the same house, his sister had had a baby and his business was very successful.

'Got another little enterprise as well as the karts,' he told me cheerfully. 'I'll surprise you with that later.'

'Sounds cryptic,' I commented.

'Wait and see,' he smiled. 'It's a little surprise for my beautiful Amy.'

After a couple of glasses of wine I felt brave enough to tackle him about his ex.

'How long were you with your girlfriend?' I asked nervously.

'Don't choke on your bhaji, but we were together ten years. I could have done a murder and got out of jail in less time,' he laughed.

'A big decision to leave her then?'

'Like I said the other night, just spending all that

time together on holiday made me realise that I didn't want to be with her for ever.'

'You must be quite sad?' I continued, but got no answer.

Will simply picked up the bottle and said, 'More wine, Ames?'

'So did you live with her then?' I obviously didn't know when to stop, as he then looked me right in the eye.

'Amy, I'm here with you now. I haven't felt the way I'm feeling in ten years. But if it makes you feel better, yes I did live with her, but I've moved out and am now renting a flat. Tania's still in the house but we are in the process of selling it.' He continued, 'I guess meeting up with you again has made me realise what real love is. It is so, so weird but I instantly felt comfortable with you. I also wanted so much to take you inside your house and rip all of your clothes off the other night.'

I could feel my whole body surge towards him. I hadn't had my love feeling since the first heady days of James Crook.

'I just knew if I came in to your house I would never get any sleep and I had a really early start the next day,' Will said. He looked at me through his gorgeous lashes. 'You are a complete fox, Amy Anderson.'

I put my hand on his. 'This is so surreal but I'm loving it.'

'Me too,' he replied. 'Now, bill and home I reckon, don't you?'

'What about your other secret enterprise?'

'That can wait. Come on, let's go.'

We didn't even make it up the stairs. My front door had barely shut behind us before we began to kiss passionately. I felt as if I'd gone into a trance. Who needed drugs when Will Wallingford was flying through my head like a fix? He put his hand up my skirt and felt my stocking tops. I could sense his arousal and he could sense mine.

'Not yet,' he whispered sensing that I couldn't wait. He began to circle my erect nipples through my shirt. 'You are so beautiful,' he said breathlessly.

He helped me out of my clothes, leaving my white lacy underwear on. He undressed, snapped on a condom, and then teased me with his full erection until I could stand it no longer. I grabbed his hips and pulled him into me, pushing my panties to one side. As I felt the rise of my orgasm I could honestly have died at that minute and wouldn't have cared. We lay in each other's arms just kissing and stroking each other in silence until Will said quietly, 'I'm crazy about you, Amy.'

I could feel my eyes welling with tears of happiness.

He continued. 'In fact, Amy Jane Anderson, I love you. In fact I don't think I've ever stopped loving you.'

I so wanted to tell him I loved him too but some instinct prevented me. My love feeling was so evident. It just seemed too early to make this grand statement. There was then no stopping us; we made love on the stairs, on the kitchen table and eventually in bed.

'What are you doing to me?' I laughed breathlessly. 'On a school night as well.'

Will groaned. My comment had obviously brought him back to reality. 'Shit, I've got to be at the track at 7 a.m. and need to get some paperwork from home first. I'd better go.'

I stuck out my bottom lip. 'But I so wanted to wake up with you.'

'Amy, if I stay here now I won't wake up with you as we'll never go to sleep.'

There is nothing quite like the feeling of heady new love. Despite having only had four hours' sleep I felt completely fine. I waltzed into work saying good morning to everybody far too loudly. I sat at my desk humming 'Oh what a beautiful morning'. Amy Jane Anderson was in love and she wanted the whole world to know about it.

Dear minger
Do I sense a night of complete debauchery?

Dear Liv
The only response to that is Yes, yes, yes!

I spent the rest of the day in a complete daze of happiness. I could see Liv and Sam flash a couple of secret smiles at each other. When I received a text that read, 'LOVE YOU LOTS LIKE JELLY TOTS' I felt that my search for a solemate was finally over.

Chapter Thirty-six

Capricorn: *There's something in the wind today. Tell people what you feel and you may be very surprised at the outcome.*

Will was working all weekend and said it would be difficult to see me as he had very early starts. So when Christopher called on Saturday morning I was quite happy to arrange to meet him that night to have an exit interview from Starr & Sun.

'Always good to get feedback to see if we're doing things right,' he had said breezily. I'm sure I also caught a sense of relief in his voice when I agreed to meet him.

'I'll pick you up, at say seven thirty?'

'Yes, that's great. See you later.'

At six thirty I got out of the shower and slung on my comfiest jeans and my favourite powder-blue shirt. I checked myself in the mirror and beamed approvingly. I had lost weight, not even by trying; funny what love does to you. My blue eyes were shining and my skin was glowing.

'This is a bit posh, isn't it?' I exclaimed as we walked into a chic restaurant in the centre of town. I felt underdressed in my jeans.

'Amy, you look beautiful,' he assured me. 'You

shouldn't worry so much what other people think about you.'

I studied Christopher. He was a handsome man. Tonight, he was wearing a grey shirt, which complemented his bluey-grey twinkly eyes nicely. I also noticed his perfect white teeth.

'It must cost you a fortune if you take all your members out like this,' I remarked.

He looked embarrassed. 'It's only for special cases,' he told me.

'So I'm a special case, am I?' I laughed.

Christopher ordered a bottle of Sancerre, then turned to me. 'So, Miss Anderson, what's happening with you now you've left our ranks? You confused me slightly by saying you were ready for another date and then you went quiet on me.'

I felt completely safe with Christopher. His Capricorn nature allowed me to trust and confide in him completely. 'I've found the man I want to marry,' I announced happily.

Christopher's eyes seemed to lose their sparkle for a second. 'That's great news, Amy. Spill the beans then.'

I then gushed out how euphoric I was feeling and how Will and I had kept missing each other but fate had brought us back together at last.

'So where's the lucky man this weekend then?' Christopher wanted to know.

'Oh, working,' I said breezily.

'And he can't find a single moment to spend with his newfound fiancée?' Christopher said sceptically.

I was not going to be deterred by this comment. 'He's really ambitious and work means everything to him. I don't doubt him at all.'

Christopher could sense my agitation. 'Sorry, Amy, I didn't mean to upset you. It's just I would hate to see you hurt, that's all.' He paused. 'If I found somebody as perfect as you I wouldn't leave your side.'

'Oh come on stop mucking about,' I said coyly and jumped up to go to the loo. Then, looking at Christopher's expression I suddenly realised that he wasn't joking, and I didn't know quite how to face the situation. I had to text Will: MISSING YOU ALREADY Ax. I checked myself in the mirror and was horrified, as poking out of my ear was the black spongy earpiece from my mobile phone hands-free kit! I couldn't believe that Christopher hadn't said anything. I returned to the table and held out the offending black article. He laughed out loud.

'Sorry, Amy, I knew you were feeling a bit insecure and I didn't want to make you feel worse.'

'You bastard.' I threw my head back and really laughed. 'Thank goodness this isn't a proper date,' I joked and then realised in the light of the situation what a callous thing to say.

'Yes,' Christopher responded quietly. 'Thank goodness.'

Fortunately, just then the waiter arrived, and said, 'Sir, madam, let me tell you about today's specials.' I don't know what it is but I never listen to the list of specials. I switch off and go into some sort of trance, nod approvingly, and then don't know if there's trout or taglietelle on offer at the end of it.

'Amy?' Christopher enquired.

'You go first, I'm not sure.' I always did this as

well, and feeling completely rushed always ordered something I didn't really want. In this case it was no exception. I eventually settled on avocado vinaigrette to start, followed by quail stuffed with pistachios. We talked easily over dinner. I learned more about Cordelia: that her husband had run off with his secretary and, since their divorce seven years ago, she had been alone as he had hurt her so badly and she had never got over it.

'She's a funny old bird, I know,' Christopher explained. 'But she has a heart of gold and has supported me through thick and thin.'

'So what thins has Christopher Starr had in his life then?' I wanted to know, not thinking for one moment that solid, sensible Christopher would ever screw up.

'Oh, you know, the usual relationship shit that happens.'

'Tell me about it,' I said sympathetically.

'Oh, just that I went out with this girl for three years, she meant everything to me and we got engaged. Then she got cold feet. Decided that she wanted to find herself and went abroad to work for the Red Cross. Said she'd come back when she was ready. Said that true love always finds a way.' He looked really sad. 'Two years later, I'm still waiting.'

'Oh you poor baby!' I exclaimed. He was on a roll now.

'Then a few months ago I suddenly felt the flutter again for somebody new. She's pretty, quirky, fun, and kind.'

'Go on,' I urged.

'She doesn't realise how much I care about her and I've never had the courage to tell her.'

'But you *so* must,' I continued, thankful that I had obviously got the wrong end of the stick about us. 'Or how will she know otherwise?'

Fuelled by the Sancerre trickling through my veins I got on my relationship soapbox. 'That is *so* the problem with men: they go into their caves to protect themselves and forget to come out and announce how they feel.'

He looked straight into my eyes and said quietly, 'I just can't tell her.'

'Why not?' I screwed up my face, not understanding now. Just as Christopher was about to answer I got the most terrible stabbing pain in my lower stomach. I held myself and gasped.

'Amy, are you OK?' he said with real concern.

I was almost doubled over. 'Oh my stomach,' I groaned. 'I'm in agony.'

He put his hand on my shoulder. 'Let me get the bill.'

I was sweating profusely now. 'Toilet,' I gasped. I just had to be alone. I got into the cubicle and phoned Anna. With her nursing experience she'd know what to do.

'What did you eat?' she asked calmly and professionally.

'Quail and pistachios.'

Anna sniggered. Her knowledge of bowels was extensive. 'No bloody wonder you're in pain, you silly cow. Quail and pistachios! Fart, Amy, just fart. You've probably just got trapped wind.'

The pain was now getting worse. What Anna said did make sense. I had had a similar pain before when I had eaten a pound of dried apricots. The only thing for it was for me to get into the yoga position that releases trapped wind. I had been to my first and last yoga class about three years ago, had got into this position and had let out the most resounding fart of my entire life. Everybody had tried not to laugh. I tried not to cry and ran out of the room. And so endeth my search for peace and tranquillity.

Desperate situations called for desperate measures. Manoeuvring myself on all fours in the tight space, almost knocking myself out on the toilet seat, I raised my bum high in the air, assumed the dog pose and rocked slowly. Thank God the cloakroom was posh and the loo floors spotless. I stayed like this for about five minutes but nothing appeared to be happening. I was still in pain. Then I heard a kerfuffle outside.

'You have to let me in; it's my friend you see, she's unwell. Amy?' I could hear Christopher's worried voice.

'In here,' I said in a strangulated voice. In my anxiety to get the wind out I had forgotten to lock the cubicle door. Poor Christopher pulled the door open to be greeted by the sight of me on all fours, my trousers round my ankles, my G-stringed bum in his face, releasing a fart that would have knocked a coke can off a tree from twenty paces. My most embarrassing moment to date had just registered six million on the Richter Embarrassment Scale. Even the disappearance of the agonising pain didn't make me feel one bit better.

All the way home I sat in silent mortification, while Christopher kept breaking into convulsions of laughter. It wasn't until we got to my house that I realised how funny I must have looked, and I started to laugh too. In fact we both laughed until we were crying. When we had calmed down he kissed me on my wet cheek.

'Good luck with Will. I'm always here for you if you need a chat.'

'Thanks for your hospitality, even though it nearly hospitalised me,' I joked as I got out of his car.

Christopher chuckled again. 'Don't ever change, Amy Anderson.'

I waved sheepishly and then nearly fell over with shock as quiet, dependable Christopher leaned out of the window and shouted, 'Nice arse, by the way!'

Chapter Thirty-seven

Pisces: *Be careful not to jump in with both feet today. Enjoy the ride but beware of Cupid's poison arrows.*

I woke up Sunday morning to Penelope licking my ear. I cringed at the memory of last night, and then laughed, remembering Christopher's parting comment. Christopher Starr was a bit of a dark horse, I reckoned. He had also said, 'Don't ever change.' Why was it always the men I didn't want who always said the things I wanted to hear?

My thoughts then turned to Will. Amazingly I had gone to bed without really thinking about him. I checked my mobile. Annoyingly, no reply to my text message. I had to tell him what had happened. He was one person who would find it really funny. I dialled his number, excited at the thought of talking to him, and it just rang and rang. I was surprised that with a business as busy as his he didn't have a message service. Bless him, I thought, he must be busy. I texted him again: MORNING BABE. DON'T WK 2 HARD. CALL ME WHEN YOU GET A MO x.

Beep! I excitedly pressed the message button: LOVE YOU TALK TOM x.

Monday couldn't come quick enough. I wanted to

live and breathe Will Wallingford. I was driving into work and Will's name flashed up on my mobile. I find it so exciting when the name of the person I want to hear from most in the world appears on my phone screen.

'Hey, babe. Just wanted to say I love you, oh and to say try and get a day off tomorrow. It's supposed to be a crispy, sunny autumn day and I want to take you somewhere.'

'I've got so much to tell you,' I said smiling.

'Must go, babe, got another call. Let me know about tomorrow.'

Sometimes Will was so infuriating, but I guess that was part of his appeal. He excited me to the core. When I walked into the office, Liv bounded up to my desk with a bouquet of beautiful yellow roses in her hand.

'You lucky cow!' I exclaimed.

'No, *you* lucky cow. Just picked them up from reception on my way up. They're for you.'

My heart started to pound. Bless Will, he had been so romantic even as a teenager. I ripped open the card.

To the Wind beneath my Wings! Thanks for using Starr & Sun. Cx.

After the initial disappointment that they weren't from Will, I then relayed the whole restaurant debacle to Liv, who ended up laughing so hard a button flew off her tight shirt revealing her pink and white spotty bra. This was a godsend as Mr Parkinson came out of his office to tell us off and had to retreat straight back in as he obviously had got another hard-on.

Will arrived bright and early the next day. He

pulled up in a Jeep this time.

'I hope you don't have as many women as cars?' I laughed.

He smiled. 'Variety is the spice of life and all that, ma cherie. Now let's go.'

'Where are we going anyway?'

'To show you my other venture.'

After a hair-raising ride along the motorway we pulled into a gravel car park. In front of us was a large expanse of water, surrounded by woodland. A timber club-house type of building was to our left.

'A lake!' I exclaimed.

'Not any old lake, darling Amy. It's my baby.'

I remembered back to the good old teenage days and Will's obsession with water-skiing even at that young age.

'I've bought it,' he told me proudly. 'I rent out the land and club-house as a going concern but I can ski any time I like.'

Will never ceased to amaze me.

'Come on, we'll park round the back,' he said. 'I've got my own private car park and jetty.'

It was a glorious autumn day and the water twinkled under the luke-warm sunshine.

'Thought we could go out on the jet-bike today, if you want to, that is?'

'Cool, yeah.' I suddenly felt that same apprehension as when I was about to get on Charlie's motor-bike. If Will's driving was anything to go by, his handling of a jet-bike would be another white-knuckle ride.

'You won't get wet,' he announced as I asked him if I should put on a wet-suit. 'Just keep your feet up,

I'll go steady and you'll be fine. You go on the front and I'll lean over you.'

The jet-bike had a big seat and it actually felt really comfortable. I almost felt safe. Will leaned over me and kissed my neck. 'I really, really love you, you know.'

I had never felt so happy. We surged forward. The wind and spray hit my face. It was exhilarating. It was fun. It was bloody cold!

'You have a go,' Will shouted, moving his hands from the controls.

I nervously grabbed the throttle and twisted it. It was obviously more sensitive than I thought as we started careering towards the bank. Will tried to gain control but in my fear, I panicked and kept hold of the throttle. I then turned the steering as hard as I could to avoid the bank, which threw the whole bike into a spin and caused me to career off the seat headlong into the freezing water. I swam to the jetty. My new jeans clung to me and my jumper revealed my now erect nipples. My hair was like rats' tails hanging down my mascara-smeared face.

'Nice nips.' Will grinned as he brought the jet-bike to a halt. He got me a towel from the jeep. 'I'm sorry, Amy, I should have given you a lesson before we set off. I've got some clean clothes in the car. They'll be a bit big but at least you'll be dry. I'll get the heater on to warm you up.'

I was shivering wildly. Will helped me pull my jumper over my head, revealing my new cream lacy bra from my 'I've got a new boyfriend' collection.

'This will have to come off too,' he smiled, undoing the clasp. 'Wouldn't want you getting a chill now, would we?'

He looked at me with a sparkle in his beautiful eyes and I knew that I wouldn't be able to resist him. My heart was beating faster. I struggled out of my soaking wet jeans and panties and sat naked on the passenger seat. I looked around anxiously.

'It's OK, no one can see us. Now let's warm you up.'

He reached for the towel and gently started to dry me, kissing me tenderly on each part of my body that he dried. I squirmed in my seat as he took his trousers off, revealing the familiar erection that I just knew I had to have inside of me. He pushed my seat back and we awkwardly swapped places.

'Jump on, sexy, and let's see what comes up,' he grinned, and pulled a condom from his wallet. I straddled him on the seat and felt him entering me with ease.

'God, I want you,' I said breathlessly.

The exhilaration of being so cold against his warm body and the excitement of maybe being caught caused me to come within minutes. I urgently moved up and down with his body until the familiar moan of ecstasy growled from his lips. I felt at one with this gorgeous creature. I didn't want to move from this lock of love. I pushed his now sweaty hair back from his forehead and looked at him intently.

'I don't love you, Will Wallingford.'

'Eh?' he answered, completely bewildered.

'Because I am completely 100 per cent *in* love with you.'

He looked at me tenderly. 'And me with you.'

Everything felt so right, so beautiful, and so

meaningful. We sat in silence as we were for what seemed like ages just kissing and stroking each other until Will broke the silence with the words I'd wanted to hear for years.

'Amy? If I asked you to marry me what would you say?'

Without any hesitation I replied, 'I'd say yes.' I felt my eyes well with tears.

He hugged me again. I then became animated. 'But, Will Wallingford, I would actually like an official proposal in somewhere more romantic than a steamed-up jeep in a car park.'

'Obviously! Your life from now on, Amy Jane, is going to be just one big rollercoaster of excitement and surprise!'

We got dressed. I looked hysterical in Will's tracksuit that swamped me. Despite this we headed to the club-house for a drink. I was oblivious to the sceptical glances of the wake-board dudes playing pool in the corner.

'Seriously, I meant what I just said, Amy. I let you go once and I'm not letting you go again. You were my first love and I'm damn sure I'm going to make you my last.'

I looked at him from under my lashes. I couldn't believe this was happening to me.

'Realistically though, I've got to sort out the selling of my house first before I

can make real plans with you.'

'I totally understand that. You've got loads to sort out but I'm not going anywhere, you hear me.' I poked him in the ribs. 'God, you are a bad influence on me.'

'You didn't seem to need much encouragement,' he grinned.

He dropped me back home later that afternoon. 'I've had a great day,' I said fondly. 'Why don't you come back later for dinner?'

'Yum, Amy Anderson on toast, sounds good. Seriously, I'd really love to, babe, but we've got a corporate group in tonight, don't think I'll be able to get away. I'll call you later though, promise.'

I got in and held my knees to my chest on the sofa. I was so happy. Everything I had ever dreamed of was happening to me. My phone beeped: U R 1 RARE BIRD AND I LOVE YOU.

'Bless that boy!' I said out loud.

Chapter Thirty-eight

Pisces: *Big waves in your pond today will disrupt your path to happiness.*

My relationship with Will was certainly the rollercoaster he had predicted. It was a nightmare to pin him down but when I did, the passion and intensity between us was so great it made up for all his misdemeanours. It took just one smile and one look with those eyes of his and I forgave him straight away. Bottom line, his work and lake were very important to him. Being text-book Sagittarius the only thing he wanted to be smothered with was freedom. I tried my best to accommodate this trait but on this particular night I suddenly saw red. How dare he let me down last minute on a Saturday night yet again! As much as I loved him, I couldn't be treated like this any longer. I phoned Liv.

'Hello, it's me. What are you up to?'

'Surprisingly I'm having a night in with a bottle of vino and Robbie Williams. Thought you were with lover boy, anyway?'

'The bastard's let me down again. Some pathetic excuse that a friend of his is having marital problems and he's got to go and see him, as he's worried he might do something stupid. I don't believe him.'

'If he is telling the truth, which I'm sure he is, it's quite sweet that he cares so much about his friends.'

'Liv, I would really like to believe he's telling the truth but I'm suspicious. I think he's seeing someone else. I've actually thought it for a while but I didn't want to shatter my dream of living happily-ever-after and I didn't want all of you to think that I had got myself into yet another stupid mess.'

'Oh Amy, don't be silly. He's so obviously in love with you, he tells you every minute.'

'Call it Piscean intuition, but something doesn't read right here. He doesn't always call when he says he will. He has never stayed over for a whole night, his phone is often switched off, and I've never been invited to his flat. What other explanation is there? He's got to be seeing someone else.'

'I guess when you put it like that, it doesn't sound good. However, when he is so obviously in love with you, why on earth would he be seeing somebody else as well?'

She could, however, tell how distressed I was. There was a pause and I could hear her mind ticking over. 'All right then, minger, a plan of action is required. I could do with a bit of excitement with Jack not being here anyway.'

'Liv,' I said, infuriated, 'this is my life we are discussing here.'

'I know, babe, sorry. Right, what time is he finishing work tonight?'

'He said seven.'

'OK, let me sling some jeans on and I'll be right over. We can't go anywhere in your car.'

'What do you mean, go anywhere?'

'Olivia Irving, sex goddess and private investigator at your service. We are going to follow him is what I mean.'

Half an hour later, a tooting came from the road outside my house. Liv was sitting in her car wearing a baseball cap.

'Get a hat on, Ames, we can't afford to be recognised,' she shouted from the car window. 'Now hurry up and hop in, we don't want to miss him.'

I had both a feeling of fear and excitement as we set off towards WW Go-Karts. The only hat I could find was a cream woolly one with a pink bobble. I looked ridiculous. Will had never seen Liv's dark blue BMW before. In fact he hadn't even met Liv yet, so he wouldn't have a clue who she was even if he spotted the car or her. The plan was to wait down the side road opposite the warehouse that stored the karts and as soon as he pulled out we would follow him. Liv kept the engine running so we would keep warm on this chilly night but turned the lights off.

'I've just had a thought,' I whispered.

'Why are you whispering?' Liv whispered back and we both started hysterically laughing.

'Oh God, I need to pee now.' I was trying to contain my laughter.

'You'll have to have a rural, be quick, it's ten to seven.'

'I can't pee outside,' I said indignantly.

Knowing that I'd have to or I'd wet myself, I crept round the back of the car and crouched down. Thinking that it was a No Through road I was horrified when a car suddenly screeched round the corner. It was a battered old Fiesta full of lads anticipating their Saturday night out. As the headlights picked me out, squatting and in midflow as it were, they beeped the horn and one of them hung out of the window and shouted at the top of his voice, 'Nice beaver!' I was mortified. Not only had I just revealed all to this group of lads, but we were trying to keep a low profile and all this noise might have drawn attention to us. I got back in the car, looked at Liv and straightened my hat.

'Don't ever think of joining the SAS, will you?' she grinned. 'Now what was that thought you had before you so rudely peed all over my back wheel?'

'Oh yeah, I know. He could be in any one of his cars, so keep 'em peeled, Agent Irving.'

'Peeled and ready, Agent Anderson.'

'Oh my God!' I shrieked, my hat bobble hitting the roof. 'There he is, quick.' I knew he'd have the bloody Aston Martin, we'll never keep up.'

'Calm down, Amy, it'll be fine. God, he drives like a madman!'

Somehow we managed to keep up with him.

'My poor tyres!' Liv exclaimed as we screeched around the fifth bend at breakneck speed.

'He's pulling in, Liv. Go round him, we can't follow him in there.'

Will had turned into seedy looking pub car park. There seemed to be loads of vans parked outside. We waited five minutes and then pulled into the car park ourselves.

'The Dog and Duck, nice place,' Liv exclaimed sarcastically. 'If he is with someone else he's not exactly showing her the high life, is he?'

I actually felt quite sick now. I wanted to know

what Will was up to, but I was scared of finding out the truth. 'What now?' I asked subdued.

'I tell you what, Ames, rather than sneak round on all fours to look in the windows, why don't you just call him? We know exactly where he is so, if it's a blatant lie, we know we're on to something.'

Will's mobile, as usual, rang for ages. I was about to hang up when he answered. I could hear the familiar sound of clinking drinks and pub chatter in the background.

'Hi, babes, you all right?'

'Fine, thanks. Just phoned to say I hope that it's not too stressful being an agony aunt this evening.'

He laughed. 'Just arrived at the pub that Jake wanted us to meet at. Never been here before, but it's a real minging place, The Dog and Duck near Gateley. Do you know it?'

'Thankfully not,' I laughed.

'Anyway, sorry again for letting you down. I can see him at the bar so better go. Love you, babe.'

'Right back at you, babe.' I turned to Liv. 'He's only just told me he's here.' I had a huge grin all over my face.

'Told you you were mad,' Liv replied. 'There's no way he'd tell you one of his meeting-places if he was up to something, you know that?'

'Yeah, yeah OK.' I can't believe I doubted him. 'God, I need a drink!' I exclaimed.

'I'm actually starving and that Indian restaurant across the street has our names on the menu. Fancy it, Ames?'

'What if he spots us?'

'Amy, he's a man, drinking with a mate. Even if

they do decide to go for a ruby it won't be 'til closing time and we'll be long gone by then.'

The only free table for two was in the window. I kept gawping over to the pub to see if I could catch a glimpse of Will but it was too dark and dreary to make anybody out. Liv and I spent the entire meal discussing my pending wedding even though he hadn't even officially proposed yet.

'I'm too old to be your bridesmaid,' she told me.

'I don't want your tits upstaging me anyway,' I replied. I finally came to the decision that I would have Brad and Sam as ushers and all of the girls would be at my beck and call for bride-type assistance. Just as we were getting the bill I looked over at the pub car park opposite.

'Liv, that's him!' I put the menu up over my face and started to do a running commentary in my shock of seeing him. 'He's talking to a man, must be his mate. Looks like he's saying goodbye. He is, look, his mate is getting into one of those vans. Liv, it's only 9 p.m. He must be going on somewhere else.'

'Amy, will you stop this.'

'Oh please, let's just see where he goes now.'

'He'll most likely phone you and go round to yours.' She could see the pleading look on my face. 'I think you've gone slightly mad, but OK. I can actually seeing me changing my vocation after this; I'm quite enjoying being a private eye.'

We ran to the car and set off in the same direction as Will. Jake had gone the other way so they obviously weren't meeting up again.

'Shall I call him again?' I asked.

Liv turned to me and gave me one of her special

looks. 'No way. He told you where he was and he said he loved you. He will think you are stalking him if you call again, and that would frighten any man off. He'll probably get in touch in a minute anyway. If he doesn't and he does go home, don't be mad at him as he is probably knackered. He's worked a twelve-hour-day and he's doing it again tomorrow, didn't you say?'

'OK, OK,' I replied. 'But surely if he loved me he'd come straight to me.'

'Ames, will you stop this paranoia. Now shut up and let me concentrate on my hand-brake turns. Where did you say he lived again?' she enquired.

'In theory he should turn right at the next roundabout.'

Will took a left.

'Told you,' Liv said smugly. 'He's heading straight for yours.'

'Shit, shit, what are we going to do now then? I said I was staying in.'

'Amy, you're a free bloody agent. You can say you decided to go out with me as I was at a loose end. Now will you stop being such a minger.'

'Stay back, Liv, he'll have to turn here, when he slows at the junction he'll see us.'

However, instead of turning left towards Reading he carried straight on.

Liv grimaced. 'Oh dear.'

'Stay behind him,' I urged. A feeling of fear went right through me. 'You know where he's heading now, don't you?' I said quietly. 'The village where the house he owns is.'

'Amy, don't be stupid. Why on earth would he be

going there, especially on a Saturday night?'

Just as she said that, Will looked in his mirror. I ducked down, nearly knocking myself out on the dashboard. 'Fuck, he's seen us.'

He hadn't seen us, he had just been checking his face in the mirror.

'Vain bloody bastard!' I exclaimed.

'Do you know the address?' Liv asked.

'No, but I know it's an old converted barn.'

'Wow, what a house,' Liv drooled.

'Shut up, Liv. Go past, go past, quick, now turn round. I want to see if we can see in there.'

We turned the lights off and parked down the road. I pulled my collar up and bobble hat down and sneaked to the end of the dark drive. A security light came on and I quickly jumped back. As Will was approaching the front door, it opened. A tall blonde girl was standing there smiling. I ran back to the car, a tide of anger surging through me.

'The complete fucking bastard. I knew it! How dare he say he loves me? How dare he say he wants to marry me? He's been shagging her all along. He's completely lied to me. What a wanker.' I then started to sob uncontrollably. Liv put her arms round me to try and calm me down but I immediately started ranting again. 'That is it! I'm fucking going in there. I'm going to let that stupid bitch know exactly what her lovely boyfriend has been up to.' I went to open the door but Liv stopped me.

'Don't you dare,' she said forcibly. 'Ames, this is so shit, I know, but please don't make yourself look a fool. We need to think carefully how we are going to deal with this and it really isn't that poor girl's fault.

She doesn't even know what he's been up to.'

'Think fucking carefully?' I repeated disbelievingly. 'He's a lying, cheating shit and he deserves to be hurt the way he's hurt me.'

Liv was quite shocked. She had never seen me this angry before, or heard me swear quite as much. In fact, I was quite shocked myself. James Crook was the only other man in my life who had made me feel like this. I realised then that I must be completely in love with Will Wallingford, as only such a real passion could evoke such a reaction of pure hatred.

'Liv, get me away from here, please.'

'Do you want to come back to mine, babe?' she soothed.

'No, I don't,' I said indignantly. 'If you don't mind, can you take me to his go-kart track? I know exactly what I'm going to do.'

Liv dutifully turned the car around. 'Amy, just calm down, will you? As I've always said revenge is a dish best served cold and all that. You might regret whatever it is you are thinking of doing in the morning.'

I scrabbled about in my handbag, like a woman possessed. 'Perfect, I've got three,' I hissed.

'Three what Amy?' Liv was getting worried now. We pulled up at the go-kart track. It was in complete darkness apart from the sign announcing Will's empire to the world.

'Damn, the gates are locked,' I muttered. 'I'll have to climb over.'

'Amy, whatever are you thinking of? Look, do you think this is a very good idea.'

I didn't wait to hear any more. I leapt out of the car

and, gaining a surge of energy from the anger that was oozing from my every pore, managed to scramble over the gates. I checked that no cars were coming, pulled the three lipsticks I had found earlier out of my pocket and began to write on the sign in large capital letters. When I had finished, I dashed back to the gates and Liv helped to hoist me back over them.

'Quick, run!' I shouted as I could hear a car coming round the corner. We jumped into the car and Liv started to laugh hysterically.

'Oh my God! Oh I'd love to see his face when he arrives tomorrow.'

Glowing in front of us in multi-coloured lipstick were the words:

W W Go-Karts – Dare or be Square

A A
N N
K K
E E
R R

I was now shaking from head to foot with reaction as the adrenaline whooshed around my body. I started to cry again. 'I hate him,' I blurted out between sobs.

'No, you don't,' Liv said softly. 'You love him.'

'What now?' I said miserably.

'You come back to mine, we have a large whisky and I put you to bed. Nothing seems as bad in the morning. We can decide how you tackle Will the Wanker then.'

Even after the large whisky and sleeping tablets

Liv had urged me to take, I hardly slept a wink. When I eventually did drop off, I kept having a repeated dream of Will with the blonde girl. I was so, so hurt. I couldn't understand how he could be so cruel, especially with our history of old. What sense did it make to see both of us? It wasn't as if it was just a sordid affair he was having with me. He saw our future together, he wanted to marry me. He was the love of my life. I couldn't see past him.

I began to cry into my pillow. How on earth would I deal with this? I knew I had to leave him, but at this moment in time I couldn't imagine spending the rest of my life with anyone else.

Chapter Thirty-nine

Pisces: *How right to distrust those whose motives you thought perfectly innocent. Confront the situation, it's the only way.*

When I woke up I didn't initially feel angry, just very sad and hurt.

'What are you going to do, babe?' Liv asked gently, coming in and sitting next to me with a cup of tea.

'Oh, Liv, I'm hurting so badly. I want to be put in a time capsule for a year so I can just sleep and wake up and find that this has all just been a bad dream.'

'Look, there may be a simple explanation.'

I knew she was trying to make me feel better. I wanted to scream and shout at him, but that wouldn't get me anywhere. I would have to go and see him. Remain calm. I would get the facts and walk away with my head held high. I started to cry.

Kissing her goodbye, I went home, made myself look as good as I could under the circumstances and drove to the go-kart track. The sign had been cleaned off. I could hear Liv's voice in my head: 'On no account mention the sign. He could have more enemies than just you now, the way he's been carrying on.' I was shaking as I walked over to the office. I could see Will on the phone smiling and chatting away. His face lit up when he saw me.

'Vince, give us a moment, mate.'

Vince ambled out of the door grumpily.

'Shut it behind you,' I ordered.

'Amy?' Will looked at me quizzically. 'What's the matter?'

I ignored his question and started my prepared conversation. 'What does monogamy mean, my darling?'

He began to shuffle on his chair. 'One woman, one man, isn't it?'

'Correct,' I said. 'And what do you think about monogamous relationships, Will?'

'Amy, I'm not sure where you're going with this?'

'Answer me,' I demanded, anger beginning to rise within me now.

'Well,' he faltered. 'It's the way it has to be, I guess.'

'So why the fuck are you still seeing your ex then?' I had so wanted to be calm but I then completely lost it and with my anger came floods of tears. 'How could you have lied to me so badly? How dare you shag me as well as shagging her? And even worse: all those false promises. What planet are you on, Will?' My tears of anger were being exchanged for tears of complete hurt. 'I can't tell you how stupid you have made me feel. I believed you. I loved you. I loved you with a passion so great I'd have done anything for you. You are my soulmate. My true love. How could you?'

Will put his hands through his hair in despair. 'Amy, I am so sorry.'

His beautiful eyes began to fill with tears and for a brief moment I wanted to draw him to me to comfort him. Even though he had hurt me so badly I still loved him with every inch of my body and soul. In a way I had wanted him to deny it, explain that the blonde woman wasn't his ex but a long-lost sister. As he continued, I could hear Liv's voice again: 'Let him do the talking, Ames. Find out everything. At least if you have the facts it will be easier to get your head round it and get over it without having unanswered questions keep popping up in your head.'

Will began to talk. 'I can't deny it. I do still love Tania. But...' He reached out to hold my hand but I pulled it away. 'But not in a passionate way. I've been with her a long time, Ames. She's my friend more than anything else. We haven't actually had a physical relationship for the past six months, we're more like mates really.'

'Bullshit!' I exclaimed.

'I'm telling you the truth here, Ames. Please believe me.'

'So why stay with her then?' I questioned angrily. I couldn't fathom any reason in this bizarre admission.

'I guess because I'm a weak bastard and I'm scared of hurting her.'

'Surely she knows there is a big problem if you are not sleeping together?'

He faltered again. 'She thinks we can work it out. Thinks it's just a phase we're going through. Thinks it's because I'm tired all the time, because of work. It's not like we don't get on. I've just fallen out of love with her. Please understand, Amy, please.'

I felt better that he hadn't been sleeping with her, but maybe this was just another Will Wallingford lie.

'And the rented flat?'

'OK, I did look to rent a flat, but then thought there was no point as I would be leaving Tania soon anyway.'

'See? You are a fucking liar,' I screamed.

'Please believe me on this though, Amy. I did mean everything I said to you. I love you. I want you. You are everything that has been missing from my relationship with Tania.'

'A good shag you mean,' I replied abrasively.

'No, no. I do want to be with you, I've just got to time things right to avoid causing hurt to another human being who I do care about.'

'Oh, how noble of you,' I said sarcastically. 'I think putting this poor girl's life on hold why you shit on her behind her back is possibly the most hurtful thing you can do to anyone. Let her go, let her get on with life, surely that is the kindest thing to do? But oh no, poor Will, how is he going to cope without Tania in his life? Poor fucking selfish Will. You may say you're just friends with her, but it's obvious from what you are saying that she still wants you.' I took a deep breath. 'If truth is beauty, Will Wallingford, then at this moment I am looking at the ugliest person I have ever met.' I stood up and through gritted teeth told the biggest lie I had ever told in my life. 'I never *ever* want to see you again.'

'Don't do this to me, Amy. Don't walk out on me. I love you so much.'

I turned and ran out of the door with tears streaming down my face. Will ran after me and grabbed me by my shoulders.

'I'll leave her, I'll tell her tonight. I've said it before and I'll say it again now. I let you go once, I'm damn sure I won't do it again.'

I released myself from his grip. 'Don't waste your breath. Just leave me alone, Will. Just leave me alone.'

Chapter Forty

Pisces: *You're always the care; let somebody else look after you for a change.*

In protecting my own self-worth I had caused the biggest self-destruction I had ever experienced in my whole life. I had always thought broken hearts were a myth but the pain I was physically feeling inside made me think that one half of my heart had dropped into my stomach. My whole being was engulfed in the loss of one person. The effect of losing Will was so devastating that I had to take a week off work. I couldn't eat, had no appetite. I could think of nothing else but Will. I missed him with my whole being. I kept breaking down in tears. I spent hours in bed. At least when I was under the safety net of my duvet I could try to sleep and forget about everything. Nobody could console me. The gang would pop round in shifts and just hold me while I sobbed uncontrollably, hearing the same words from me over and over again: 'I still love him.'

Brad was my rock as usual. 'I know you love him, Amy. Look, you've always said to me that we should follow our heart, and if you do decide to forgive him then I won't judge you, you know that.'

Will phoned repeatedly. I rejected his calls. He

knocked on my door many times but I refused to open it. As much as I loved him, I realised that I could never trust him again, and I had to move forward with my life. I asked Brad to contact him for me. 'Just tell him from me that the kindest thing he can do is leave me alone.'

Chapter Forty-one

Pisces: *Your intuition will tell you how best to act today. Honesty is the best policy in affairs of the heart.*

During that terrible week of heartbreak, Christopher had also kept contacting me, assuring me that I was a beautiful person and that I would find someone who really loved me honestly. He urged me to meet him for a drink.

'It'll do you good,' he promised. 'You can't stay locked up at home for the rest of your life. I'll be in your local at one o'clock on Sunday afternoon, so no pressure. If you feel like it then come in and join me.'

It was a relief to see kind, comfortable Christopher sitting at the bar of The Lyndhurst Arms. He gave me a hug when I walked in. 'What are you drinking?'

'Just a Diet Coke please, oh and a packet of crisps.' My appetite was slowly returning. I had lost half a stone in two weeks.

'Quail flavour?' he joked.

'I don't think quail will ever pass my lips again,' I smiled feebly.

'There you go, it's not so hard to smile, is it? You're looking great, by the way.'

I knew I looked a complete minger, but his kind

words did make me feel better. We chatted about nothing in particular for a while. I noticed that Christopher was knocking back the lagers.

'Are you OK?' I enquired.

'Fine, fine,' he said breezily. Then: 'Actually I'm not, Amy. I'm drinking because I'm nervous.'

I frowned uncomprehendingly. 'Nervous? About what?'

'I'm not quite sure how to say what I'm going to say next but I can't keep it in any longer. The timing is shit I know but you have to hear me out. It's time I came out of my cave.'

For some reason I laughed. 'You Tarzan, me Jane and all that?'

'If only,' he replied.

I then realised exactly what he was about to say and I was very scared.

'You know when we had dinner and I told you I had met a special person.'

'Yes,' I said, giving one slow, deliberate nod.

'Well, that special person is...' He paused for breath. 'It's you, Amy.'

My emotions were so mixed up at the moment that I thought I was going to cry.

Christopher went on. 'From the minute you walked into the agency I knew you were special. You've got vibrancy about you, Amy. You are a joy to be with. You are funny, you are caring. You are also extremely sexy.' He paused again. 'It was agony setting you up on dates, and if I'm honest I did actually pick people I didn't think you would get along with.'

'Christopher!'

'I felt so guilty when Declan fleeced you, and although I know that what has happened between you and Will wasn't down to me, I can't bear the way that he has destroyed your self-confidence.'

It all made sense now. His interest in how I got on with my dates. The dinner. The flowers. The constant phone calls.

'I've got a cheque here for you, it's the agency fee back because I feel such a fraud.'

'I don't want your money,' I said, suddenly feeling really sorry for him. 'It's been a fascinating few months and I've had a lot of fun along the way. At least it's proved to me that star sign compatibility doesn't always ring true.' Visions of wicked Kieran 'The Scorpion' Docherty suddenly flashed through my mind. I knew in a minute that I would have to address the matter in hand here but was delaying it as long as I could.

'Another drink?' I asked airily.

Christopher took my hand in his. Oh my God, I thought, and really wished that some wind would get trapped in my colon right now.

'I know you're still getting over Will but he's gone now. You're far too lovely to be treated so badly. How about we give it a go, Ames?' he faltered. 'This is me, plain old Christopher Starr. I know that I may never make your heart rush like Will, but what I can do is always be here for you. I will never cheat on you and my love for you will always be complete.'

I shut my eyes for a second to try and stop the tears that were welling behind them.

As if he gauged my thoughts he continued, 'We can take it slowly, I promise, nothing heavy, just me and you against the world.'

I pulled my hand away from his and brushed my hair back off my face. I wasn't sure how I could turn him down without hurting this lovely human being. Sense and reason said that he would be everything I needed in a man. He was good-looking and, if I was honest with myself, I could fancy him. More importantly he was kind, genuine, and honest, and if I did give it a go, I could maybe grow to love him in time. However, this wasn't enough. I couldn't compromise and it wouldn't be fair on him to do that anyway. He was right; he just didn't have the Will factor. He didn't make my heart rush when I looked at him. He didn't make me laugh just by a single expression. Yes, I fancied him, but I didn't have that urge to jump on him wherever I was and have mad, bad sex. Thoughts of Will brought back the familiar empty ache in my stomach. I was still mind-blowingly in love with him despite everything that had happened.

'Amy? Say something, anything,' Christopher urged.

I took a deep breath and smiled falsely. 'I still can't believe you sabotaged my dates.'

'Amy, stop being funny. You always do this to cover up your real feelings.'

He was right. When faced with a difficult situation I tried to laugh my way out of it. I owed it to Christopher to be honest.

'I'm sorry,' I said quietly. 'It's not that I don't find you attractive, I do. I also like you a great deal. You are a genuine, kind person and you have always treated me with respect. It's just…'

'Just what?' Christopher asked.

'I am still very much in love with Will and I don't want to hurt you.'

'But you'll get over him, Amy, and then what?'

'I don't want you putting your life on hold for me,' I continued. 'I know you could make me very happy but...' I faltered again. 'Christopher I don't know how to continue without hurting you.'

'Just say it, Ames.'

'I just don't feel you would ever be the one.

Christopher gave me a watery smile.

'I'm so, so sorry.'

He composed himself. 'You'll always be special to me, Amy,' he said quietly. 'If you've ever got a problem, I'll be here for you.' He stood up and I grabbed his hand.

'Don't say that as if we're never going to see each other again.' I panicked.

'If you don't mind, Amy, I will take a bit of time out from meeting up with you. Call it cold turkey if you like. We may be mates in time. I just need to sort my head out for now.'

We walked out to the car park. I gave him a huge hug and kissed him on the cheek. 'Don't you be a stranger for long, you. Do you want to wait at mine for a cab?'

'No, I'm going to walk home. Could do with some fresh air.'

'OK,' I said, trying to keep things light.

He hugged me again. It felt lovely to be held so close by somebody who genuinely cared for me. He pulled away and looked into my eyes.

'I love you, Miss Fish.'

I bit my lip and my already broken heart shifted and bled again.

'I know you do.'

Chapter Forty-two

Pisces: *Suddenly you can see things more clearly in your immediate surroundings.*

I walked tearfully back to Layston Gardens, wondering if I had just thrown away my last chance of happiness. Kind, caring men like Christopher were few and far between. Additionally, he had always said, 'Bless you,' on cue, plus he was the only man who had ever said, 'Don't ever change.' When it came to the holding my hand in labour bit, he was in fact so selfless that he would probably have had the baby himself.

It was a chilly November afternoon and I began to shiver. Despite it being only four o'clock, it was dark already. It was when I got back to number 21 that I stopped shivering with the cold, but with pure fear. All the lights were on and I only ever left the hall light on when I went out, so I knew someone else had been in since I had left to meet Christopher. My first terrifying thought was that I'd been burgled. My second was that Penelope might have escaped out on to the road. Bravely I pushed open the door, picked up a large vase for weaponry, and crept through the lounge. I was now more angry than frightened. How dare anyone break into my lovely home? In true

309

Charlie's Angels style I bounded into the dining room which was empty. I then sped through into the kitchen towards the back door. This was ajar too. I kicked it open really hard. Charlie would have been proud of me! I then nearly jumped out of my skin at the sound of a familiar voice.

'Prinny! God alive, you scared the bloody wits out of me!'

And there in my now somewhat overgrown garden was Brad. Brad, my beautiful image-conscious friend, now, gracefully adorned in oversized dark green galoshes, bright pink rubber gloves, and a surgical mask. He was covered from head to foot in what looked like slime. He lowered the mask to reveal his beaming face.

'I didn't think you'd be back so soon. Quick, come and see.' He was acting like an excited child on Christmas morning.

Still feeling bewildered I followed him down to the end of the garden and did one of my open-shut mouth fish impressions. For there in front of me, was a new pond. Not a green, stinking pond but one with water so clear that in the beam of Brad's flashlight you could see right down to the pebbles in the bottom.

'Found two frogs too,' he burbled on. 'Although God knows what they're still doing here in this weather. Look, there's one there. I've made a slide out of some wood for him. Oh, and didn't think you'd mind but thought the sailing boat was quite a nice finishing touch.'

I was completely speechless, just for a second, mind you. Overwhelmed that yet another human being could be so kind to me. Despite his stinking, slimy state, I threw my arms around him, held him tightly, and kissed him full on the lips.

'I love you, Brad Sampson, I really do.'

He grimaced. 'Ergh! Not sure what's worse, dealing with concentrated frogcrap or kissing a girl.'

I smiled through the tears that had begun to fall down my cheeks. 'Thank you so much,' I said with total sincerity.

'Hey, like I said, always here for you, babe.' He then lightened the mood. 'Can we please can we try and keep some sort of order down this end of the garden now? Which means no throwing the poor babies any more raw meat.'

Penelope, who had appeared out of the gloaming, sensing that I might be getting a lecture, brushed against Brad's galoshes, lifted his tail, and farted.

Chapter Forty-three

Pisces: *Unexpected developments will create a stir within a meaningful relationship. Be strong to gain your ultimate reward.*

It was on a frosty December morning that the letter arrived.

My Darling Amy,
I have left Tania for good. I realised straight away what a terrible mistake I had made. Life without you will be like a world without sunshine. But you can't have a rainbow without some rain and all I can do is hope that one day you will forgive me. I will always be here waiting to come and claim my pot of gold. I am so in love with you. Will x

I read the letter over and over again. I hadn't stopped loving or missing Will since the day I walked away from him. In fact, if I was honest, I hadn't stopped loving him for thirteen years. I had to see him. My heart was so drawn to this being. I couldn't forsake a love that was so obviously meant to be, but I had to be sure that I could trust him again. It seemed apt somehow to meet at the lake. He was waiting for me in his van. I climbed up next to him.

'Let's talk here,' I said, trying to stay composed.

Images of the last time I had been here rushed through my mind and I thought I would cry, but managed to hold it together. The banks were glistening with frost and the water was very still. I could have eaten him there and then. I could tell he had made a real effort to look nice. His lovely eyes bore straight into mine. He went to kiss me and I pulled away.

'Hear me out,' I said boldly. 'Your letter was beautiful. I can't deny that I still love you deeply but I've had a long think and I need some space to decide if I want to go down the same road as you now.'

'But, Amy,' he said.

I put my finger to his full lips to shush him. 'Let me have my say,' I continued. 'I don't know if I will ever be able to trust you again, and I have to be sure that I can forgive you fully. I'm not saying it's forever, but at the moment I need to get my mind straight.' I so wanted to just grab him and kiss him there and then but I resisted. I had to be sure that I chose the correct path. My whole future was at stake.

His eyes welled with tears. 'What can I do to make you change your mind?' he asked hoarsely. 'I can't see a future without you in it now. In fact, I don't even want to spend another day without you in it.'

'Hug me,' I said, tears now flowing down my cheeks. He hung on to me tightly. Not allowing myself to weaken I pulled away quickly. 'I'm going now. Goodbye, Will. Get on with your life. Please don't contact me. I'll be thinking of you.'

'Amy, you can't do this to me. I love you!' he shouted after me as I ran to my car and sped away sobbing.

Chapter Forty-four

Pisces: *An important journey lies ahead of you. Head to the water, fishes, and face the truth.*

I needed to redress the balance between my head and my heart as at the moment my heart was getting the gold medals every time. It had been so painful to walk away from Will but I knew it was the only way to deal with my feelings at the moment. He had hurt me so badly that I had to be sure that I was ready to cope with the mistrust that I would so obviously feel if I did make the decision to go back to him. What made it worse was that it was the week before Christmas. The thought of being home alone at this time was too much to bear. Everywhere I went there were happy couples: happy couples shopping; happy couples with their Christmas trees poking out of the back of their cars; happy couples kissing in the street. I just had to spend a few days away from everything familiar, somewhere quiet to make the biggest decision of my life.

I was sitting on the sofa one night watching a travel programme featuring Cornwall when I suddenly remembered a conversation I had had with Ryan way back at my dinner party. St Ives, that was where he came from, and he still owned a holiday place there. I picked up the phone.

Before going upstairs to thrown some clothes in a bag, I left a message on Mr. Parkinson's voice mail. I also sat and wrote a note to Brad, as I feared he would try and stop me if I rang and told him what I was planning. I asked him to look after Pen for me and promised to be back by Christmas Eve.

Ryan's cottage in St Ives was a perfect retreat. It was tiny and cosy, with an open fire in the characterful lounge and a beautiful attic bedroom over looking the sea. The constant crying of the gulls was a comfort as it bought back memories of family holidays in Cornwall when Mum was alive.

With its wild coastline Cornwall was the perfect place for a distressed fish to walk in and think about her future. I replied to Brad's text to let him know I was fine, and phoned Anna to ask her to tell Dad where I was, and told her not to worry. I then amazingly turned my phone off. I had taken Will's letter along with me and every night before I went to sleep I would read it, cry, and put it under my pillow. I was happy that he wanted me back but was still very confused.

One evening after one of my long walks I suddenly felt ravenously hungry. I strolled down to the harbour and peered in the window of one of its pubs. It looked so warm and welcoming inside. The Christmas tree lights were twinkling and the hum of contented people seemed to ooze through the gaps in the old wooden door. I bravely entered alone and ordered a pint of scrumpy, a pasty, and a portion of chips. The food and drink tasted delicious, and for the first time in a long time no longer felt alone. I knew that, in time, I would be one of these smiling people again. However, a couple walking in and announcing their engagement to their waiting family soon turned my way of thinking back to despair. Tears began to trickle down my face. I wanted to marry him, but what if he lied to me again?

I didn't want anyone feeling sorry for me so I gulped back the rest of my drink and walked out to face the cold air and crashing waves. As I looked out to sea, I sensed that somebody was right behind me. Startled, I turned around. Staring at me was an old man with white hair and beard and a face so weathered, you could have made a pair of shoes from it. I felt afraid as he put his hand on my shoulder. However, when he began to talk in his soft Cornish accent, I soon felt completely safe.

'Life is short, young'un, too short to be feeling such pain when there is so much beauty around you.' He pointed up to the sky. 'I've looked up at those stars for the past seventy years. Each one of them is a person that you've loved and lost looking out for you, you know. They've protected me on those seas for the whole of my long life. Look up, my dear, pick one out and make a wish. It will come true, I can promise you.'

Mesmerised, I looked up and did as he said. I picked out the brightest star in the sky. I immediately thought of my mum and made my wish.

The old man smiled knowingly. 'If it's your future you're wishing for, go and see old Mrs Treharne in SeaView Cottage. She'll sort you out.'

Suddenly, there was a big gust of wind and my hair was blown over my face. By the time I had brushed it out of my eyes, I went to thank the old man but there was no sign of him.

The next morning I stood nervously on the white doorstep of SeaView Cottage. The powder-blue front door was only about four feet high and the knocker was that of a beautiful bronze fairy. The gulls overhead cried out as if to say, 'Go on, go on, knock on that door.'

A wizened, white-haired old lady with a stooped back opened the door and greeted me. Her eyes were glassy grey with age. Her whole being seeped wisdom and kindness.

'Hello, Amy. I've been expecting you.'

This was spooky. A cold shiver went right through me. How on earth did she know I was coming?

'Come on in and sit yourself down, my love. Don't take no mind of Pickles.'

Pickles was a huge cat, he must have been in cat years the same age as his owner. He had amazing green eyes. I suddenly thought of Pen and hoped that he was OK. As I settled in to a low chair by the fire, the creature glared at me, then jumped straight onto my lap and started purring loudly. Mrs Treharne sat opposite me on a raggedy chair and covered her knees with a colourful crocheted blanket. Then she reached forward and took both my hands in hers. They were the tiniest, wrinkliest hands I had ever seen.

'Your eyes are the windows to your soul, Amy, so let's see why you are drowning in such sorrow, shall we? Give me your watch now.'

In a slow, deliberate voice she recited The Lord's Prayer. For some reason I felt no fear; I was completely serene and relaxed. Mrs Treharne closed her fading eyes and began to rub my watch.

'You poor little girl, I can feel so much sadness, hurt, and anger.' She then looked upwards and her voice lifted. 'I can see a rainbow and water. The water is good for you. You fish need to be in your own element. The tears are drying. I can hear laughter and see Christmas lights in a row. There is a man, you know him well. He's a wild one, but oh, such beautiful eyes. I can hear the words, 'Face of an angel, mind of a devil'.

She stopped suddenly, opened her eyes, and looked at me. 'Take care, Amy. Old playgrounds are dangerous places.' She shut her eyes again and began nodding. 'The leopard will change his spots if love is true.'

I began to feel scared now, as I didn't want her to say anything that I didn't want to hear. She could obviously see Will, but where were the words happy and ending? I felt like shouting out, 'Just tell me who my future lies with. I need to know!'

And as if she could read my mind she continued, 'There's somebody else. He is a fair-haired man and has kind blue eyes. He cares for you deeply and wants what is best for you. He will lead you to your fairytale.' She nodded and repeated. 'The fair man will lead you to your fairytale, young Amy.' She then fumbled around under the crocheted blanket, pulled out a battered leather hip flask and took a noisy swig. Pickles jumped off my lap and startled me back into reality.

'Anything else?' I asked her urgently.

'Patience, young Amy. If he's worth waiting for, he'll come to you.' She could see how anxious I was and took my hands again. She looked me intently in the eyes. 'He will come to you, my dear.'

There was a knock on the door, which made me jump out of my skin. Oh my God, surely she didn't mean he'd come to me this quickly? I now felt dreadfully confused. She was hinting that Christopher was going to be my destiny. It wasn't what I wanted to hear at all.

'You have a beautiful soul, Amy. He *will* come.'

I looked at the door and she smiled. 'Mrs Tregellis from Sea Spray, tea leaf reading.'

I got up slowly. 'Thanks ever so much, Mrs Treharne. How much do I owe you?'

She pointed to her hip flask. 'Just a winter warmer if you're passing, my dear.'

Chapter Forty-five

I walked back up the steep hill to Sea Gull Cottage. I felt emotionally drained and just wanted to sit in front of the fire and think about what Mrs Treharne had said. I knew that fate would prevail but what if I misinterpreted it and headed in the wrong direction? As I put the key in the lock and pushed open the front door, I heard something clatter to the doorstep. I looked down and saw an arrow; through the arrow was a piece of paper.

Foolish Archer, deeply in love with Beautiful Fish, would like to meet her on the beach as soon as she gets this note. I will wait for you for ever. I love you.

I saw him before he saw me. He was huddled on a rock rubbing his hands together to keep warm. The wind was strong and the waves were crashing on the shoreline. As I walked towards him I saw his face light up. He ran towards me and opened his arms. I could see that his beautiful eyes were full of tears. I hugged him so tightly I thought I would crush him. I then looked up at him, biting my lip. Tears were falling slowly down my face. He wiped them gently one by one as they fell.

I broke the silence. 'How did you find me?' I knew that Brad would never have told him where I was.

'Christopher phoned me this morning.'

Dear, sweet Christopher. He was prepared to sacrifice his love to make me happy.

'I have been so lost without you, Amy. You are my world. I promise that I will never ever hurt you again. There is nobody else in the whole universe that I want to be with more than you. I have never been more certain of anything in my whole life.'

I looked directly at him and felt such intensity of joy, realising there and then that I hadn't really needed time to think at all. Deep down I had known all along that I couldn't live without this crazy creature. Despite the winter sunshine, the wind was bitingly cold. My teeth chattered as plops of rain began to fall. Will suddenly jumped up onto a rock and beat his chest like an ape.

'I love you lots like jelly tots and for my next trick I shall make you smile.' He then jumped down, skidded onto his knees in the sand, and then balanced himself on one knee. He clasped my hands in his and looked right into my eyes again. 'Amy Jane Anderson, what would you say if I asked you to marry me?'

I took a deep breath and looked out at the stormy sea. In the sky there was a beautiful rainbow.

'I'd say yes!' I shouted above the elements. 'Will Wallingford, I'd say yes!'

That evening, we walked arm in arm past Mrs Treharne's cottage and I smiled. A row of coloured fairy lights glowed along the harbour wall.

'A drink to celebrate before bed for the future Mrs Wallingford?' Will suggested.

The Sloop Inn was heaving and noisy but not too noisy for me to hear the familiar shout of, 'minger,' from across the other side of the bar. And there they all were. Sam and Katie, Brad and Jon, Liv and Jack, H and Horace. Even Anna and Boyd.

'Well?' everyone said in unison looking anxiously at Will.

'She said yes!' he shouted raising his arms in the air.

'And this time,' he added. 'I'm grabbing her by both gills and I'm never *ever* letting her go.

Nicola May

For more information go to:

www.nicolamay.com

Printed in Great Britain
by Amazon

33108019R00196